NOTWITHSTANDING

MARY CHOLMONDELEY

NOTWITHSTANDING

NOTWITHSTANDING

By MARY CHOLMONDELEY
AUTHOR OF "RED POTTAGE"

> Und was
> Ist Zufall anders, als der rohe Stein,
> Der Leben annimmt unter Bildners Hand?

LONDON:
JOHN MURRAY, ALBEMARLE STREET, W.
1913

TO

MAY AND JEANNIE

NOTWITHSTANDING

CHAPTER I

" Le vent qui vient a travers la montagne M'a rendu fou ! "
VICTOR HUGO.

ANNETTE leaned against the low parapet and looked steadfastly at the water, so steadfastly that all the brilliant, newly-washed, tree-besprinkled city of Paris, lying spread before her, cleft by the wide river with its many bridges, was invisible to her. She saw nothing but the Seine, so tranquil yesterday, and to-day chafing beneath its bridges and licking ominously round their great stone supports—because there had been rain the day before.

The Seine was the only angry, sinister element in the suave September sunshine, and perhaps that was why Annette's eyes had been first drawn to it. She also was angry, with the deep, still anger which invades once or twice in a lifetime placid, gentle-tempered people.

Her dark eyes under their long curled lashes looked down over the stone bastion of the Pont Neuf at a yellow eddy just below her.

They were beautiful eyes, limpid, deep, with a certain tranquil mystery in them. But there was no mystery in them at this moment. They were fixed, dilated, desperate.

Annette was twenty-one, but she looked much younger, owing to a certain slowness of development, an immaturity of mind and body. She reminded one not of an opening flower, but of a big, loose-limbed colt, ungainly still, but every line promising symmetry and grace to come. She was not quite beautiful yet, but that clearly was also still to come, when life should have had time to erase a certain ruminative stolidity from her fine, still countenance. One felt that in her schoolroom days she must have been often tartly desired not to " moon." She gave the impression of not having wholly emerged from the chrysalis, and her bewildered face, the face of a dreamer, wore a strained expression, as if some cruel hand had mockingly rent asunder the veils behind which her life had been moving and growing so far, and had thrust her, cold and shuddering, with unready wings, into a world for which she was not fully equipped.

And Annette, pale gentle Annette, standing on the threshold of life, unconsciously clutching an umbrella and a little handbag, was actually thinking of throwing herself into the water !

Not here, of course, but lower down, perhaps near St. Germains. No, not St. Ger mains,—there were too many people there,—but Melun,

where the Seine was fringed thick with reeds and rushes, where in the dusk a determined woman might wade out from the bank till the current took her.

The remembrance of a certain expedition to Melun rose suddenly before her. In a kind of anguish she saw again its little red and white houses, sprinkled on the slope of its low hill, and the river below winding between its willows and poplars, amid meadows of buttercups, scattered with great posies of maythorn. She and he had sat together under one of the may trees, and Mariette, poor Mariette, with Antoine at her feet, had sat under another close at hand. And

Mariette had sung in her thin, reedy voice the song with its ever-recurring refrain—

" Le vent qui vient a travers la montagne Me rendra fou, oui, me rendra fou."

Annette shuddered and then was still.

It must have been a very deep wound, inflicted with a jagged instrument, which had brought her to this pass, which had lit this stony defiance in her soft eyes. For though it was evident that she had rebelled against life, it was equally evident that she was not of the egotistic temperament of those who rebel or cavil, or are discontented. She looked equable, feminine, the kind of woman who would take life easily, bend to it naturally,

" As the grass grows on the weirs ";

who might, indeed, become a tigress in defence

of her young, but then what woman would not?

But it is not only in defence of its babes of flesh and blood that the protective fierceness of woman can be aroused. There are spiritual children, ideals, illusions, romantic beliefs in others, the cold-blooded murder of which arouses the tigress in some women. Perhaps it had been so with Annette. For the instinct to rend and tear was upon her, and it had turned savagely against herself.

Strange how in youth our first crushing defeat in the experiment of living brings with it the temptation of suicide! Did we then imagine, in spite of all we saw going on round us, that life was to be easy for MS, painless for us, joyful for us, so that the moment the iron enters our soul we are so affronted that we say, " If this is life, we will have none of it " ?

Several passers-by had cast a backward glance at Annette. Presently some one stopped, with a little joyous exclamation. She was obliged to raise her eyes and return his greeting.

She knew him, the eccentric, rich young Englishman who rode his own horses under a French name which no one believed was his own. He often came to her father's cabaret in the Rue du Bac.

" Good morning, mademoiselle."

" Good morning, M. Le Geyt."

He came and leaned on the parapet beside her.

" Are you not riding to-day ? "

" Riding to-day! Ride on the Flat I Is it likely ? Besides, I had a fall yesterday schooling. My neck is stiff."

He did not add that he had all but broken it. Indeed, it was probable that he had already forgotten the fact.

He looked hard at her with his dancing, irresponsible blue eyes. He had the good looks which he shared with some of his horses, of extreme high breeding. He was even handsome in a way, with a thin, reckless, trivial face, and a slender, wiry figure. He looked as light as a leaf, and as if he were being blown through life by any chance wind, the wind of his own vagaries.

His manner had just the shade of admiring familiarity which to some men seems admissible to the pretty daughter of a disreputable old innkeeper.

He peered down at the river, and then at the houses crowding along its yellow quays, mysterious behind their paint as a Frenchwoman behind her pomade and powder.

Then he looked back at her with mock solemnity.

" I see nothing/' he said.

" What did you expect to see ? "

(< Something that had the honour of engaging your attention completely."

" I was looking at the water."

" Just so. But why ? "

She paused a moment, and then said, without any change of voice—

" I was thinking of throwing myself in."

Their eyes met—his, foolhardy, inquisitive, not unkindly ; hers, sombre, sinister, darkened.

The recklessness in both of them rushed out and joined hands.

He laughed lightly.

" No, no," he said, " sweet Annette—lovely Annette. The Seine is not for you. So you have quarrelled with Falconhurst already. He has managed very badly. Or did you find out that he was going to be married ? I knew it, but I did not say. Never mind. If he is, it doesn't matter. And if he isn't, it doesn't matter. Nothing matters."

" You are right. Nothing matters," said Annette. Her face, always pale, had become livid.

His became suddenly alert, flushed, as hers paled. He sighted a possible adventure. Excitement blazed up in his light eyes.

" One tear," he said, " yes,—you may shed one tear. But the Seine ! No. The Seine is made up of all the tears which women have shed for men—men of no account, worthless wretches like Falconhurst and me. You must not add to that great flood. Leave off looking at the water, Annette. It is not safe for you to look at it. Look at me instead. And listen to what I am saying. You are not listening."

" Yes, I am."

"I'm going down to Fontainebleau for a bit. The doctor says I must get out of Paris and keep quiet, or I shan't be able to ride at Auteuil. I don't believe a word he says, croaking old woman ! But—hang it all, I'm bound to ride Sam Slick at Auteuil. Kirby can look after the string while I'm at Fontainebleau. I'm going there this afternoon. Come with me. I am not much, but I am better than the Seine. My kisses will not choke the life out of you, as the Seine's will. We will spend a week together, and talk matters over, and sit in the sun, and at the end of it we shall both laugh— how we shall laugh—when you remember this." And he pointed to the swirling water.

A thought slid through Annette's mind like a snake through grass.

" He will hear of it. He is sure to hear of it. That will hurt him worse than if I were drowned."

" I don't care what I do," she said, meeting his eyes without flinching. It was he who for a moment winced when he saw the smouldering flame in them.

He laughed again, the old light, inconsequent laugh which came to him so easily, with which he met good and bad fortune alike.

" When you are as old as I am," he said not unkindly, " you will do as I am doing now, take the good the gods provide you, and

trouble your mind about nothing else. For there's nothing in the world or out of it that is worth troubling about. Nothing. Nothing. Nothing."

11 Nothing/ 1 echoed Annette hoarsely.

CHAPTER II

" Et partout le spectre de l'amour, Et nullepart l'amour."

THE train was crawling down to Fontainebleau. Annette sat opposite her companion, looking not at him but at the strange country through which they were gong. How well she knew it 1 How often she had gone down to Fontainebleau. But to-day all the familiar lines were altered. The townlets, up to their eyes in trees, seemed alien, dead. Presently the forest, no longer fretted by the suburbs, came close up on both sides of the rail. What had happened to the oaks that they seemed drawn up in serried lines to watch her pass, like soldiers at a funeral ! A cold horror brooded over everything. She looked at her companion and withdrew her eyes. He had said he was better than the Seine. But now she came to meet his eyes fixed on her, was he better ? She was not sure. She was not sure of anything, except that life was unendurable and that she did not care what happened to her.

There had been sordid details, and there would be more. He had said it would be better if she had a wedding ring, and he had bought

her one. The shopman had smiled offensively as he had found one to fit her. She set her teeth at the remembrance. But she would go through with it. She did not care. There was nothing left in the world to care about. It was Dick Le Geyt who, thoughtless as he was, had shown some little thought for her, had taken her to a restaurant and obliged her to eat, had put her into the train, and then had waylaid and dismissed his valet, who brought his luggage to the station, and who seemed at first determined not to let his master go without him, indeed was hardly to be shaken off, until Dick whispered something to him, when the man shrugged his shoulders and turned away.

Annette looked again at her companion. He had fallen suddenly asleep, his mouth ajar. How old and shrunk and battered he looked, and how strangely pinched ! There was something unnatural about his appearance. A horrible suspicion passed through her mind that he had been drinking. She suddenly remembered that she had once heard a rumour of that kind about him, and that he had lost a race by it. She had to waken him when they reached Fontaine-bleau, and then, after a moment's bewilderment, he resumed all his alertness and feather-headed promptitude.

Presently she was in a bedroom in an old-fashioned inn, and was looking out of the window at a little garden, with tiny pebbled

walks, and a fountain, and four stunted, clipped acacia trees.

The hotel was quite full. She had been asked some question as to whether the room would do, and she had said it would. She had hardly glanced at it. It was the only room to be had. And Dick's luggage was carried up to it. The hotel-people took for granted his baggage was hers as well as his. She remembered that she had none, and smoothed her hair mechanically with her hands, while an admiring little chambermaid whisked in with hot water.

And presently, in the hot, tawdry salle a manger, there was a meal, and she was sitting at a little table with Dick, and all the food was pretence, like the tiny wooden joints and puddings in her doll's house which she used to try to eat as a child. These were larger, and she tried to eat them, but she could not swallow anything. She wondered how the others could. And the electric light flickered, and once it went out, and Dick laughed. And he ordered champagne for her and made her drink some. And then, though he said he must not touch it, he drank some himself, and became excited, and she was conscious that a spectacled youth with projecting teeth turned to look at them. There was a grey-haired Englishwoman sitting alone at the nearest table. Annette saw her eyes rest on her for a moment with veiled compassion.

All her life afterwards, she remembered that evening as a nightmare. But it was not a nightmare at the time. She was only an onlooker : a dazed, callous spectator of something grotesque which did not affect her—a mirthless, sordid farce which for some obscure forgotten reason it was necessary for her to watch. That she was herself the principal actor in the farce, and that the farce had the makings of a tragedy, did not occur to her. She was incapable of action and of thought.

Later in the evening she was in her bedroom again, sitting with her hands in her lap, vacantly staring at the wall with its mustard-coloured roses on a buff ground, when two grinning waiters half carried, half hustled in Dick, gesticulating and talking incoherently. They helped him into bed : the elder one waited a moment, arms a-kimbo, till Dick fell suddenly asleep, and then said cheerfully and reassuringly—

" C'est ça, madame," and withdrew.

Annette got up instinctively to go too, but she remembered that she had nowhere to go, that it was close on midnight, that she was in her own room with which she had expressed herself satisfied, that she and her companion were passing at the hotel as husband and wife. She felt no horror, no sense of the irremediable folly she had committed. She stood a moment, and then drew the curtain and sat down by the window, looking out, as she had sat all the previous night in her little bedroom in her father's cabaret, out of which she had slunk like a thief as soon as it was light. Her spellbound faculties

were absorbed in one mental picture, which was to her the only reality, as the cobra is the only reality to the dove. She forgot where she was. She forgot the heavy breathing of her companion, stirring uneasily in his sleep. She saw only, as she had seen all day, the smoking, hideous ruin of that wonderful castle of dreams which she had built stone by stone during the last year, into the secret chamber of which she had walled up that shy, romantic recluse her heart : that castle of dreams in which she paced on a rainbow mosaic, which she had tapestried with ideals and prayers and aspirations, in the midst of which there was a shrine.

There was nothing left of it now, worse than nothing, only a smoking, evil-smelling hump of debris, with here and there a flapping rag of what had once been stately arras or cloth of gold. It had reeled and crashed down into the slime in a moment's space. The thunder of its fall had deafened her to all other noises ; its smoke had blinded her to all other sights. Oh ! why had she let herself be dissuaded from her only refuge against this unendurable vision seared in upon her brain ? It had been agony. It would be agony again. If Dick had let her alone, she would be at rest now, quite away from it all, her body floating down to the sea in the keeping of the kind, cool river, and her outraged soul escaped—escaped.

But she would do it still. She would creep away a second time at dawn, as soon as the

house was stirring. There must be a river somewhere—if not a big river, a little one with deep pools. She would find it. And this time she would not let herself be dissuaded. This time she would drown herself, if the water were only knee-deep. And her mind being made up, she gave a little sigh, and leaned her aching forehead against the glass.

The man in the bed stirred, and feebly stammered out the word " Annette " once and again. But Annette did not hear him, and after a time he muttered and moved no more.

And when the dawn came up at last, it found Annette, who had watched for it wide-eyed all night, sunk down asleep, with her head upon the sill.

" Vous e"tes bien pale, ma belle, Comment vous appelez-vous ? Je suis l'amante, dit-elle. Cueillez la branche de houx."

ANNETTE stirred at last when a shaft of sunlight fell upon her head. She sat up stiffly, and stared round the unfamiliar chamber, with the low sun slanting across the floor and creeping up the bottom of the door. Nothing stirred. A chill silence made itself felt. The room seemed to be aware of something, to be beforehand with her. Some nameless instinct made her get up suddenly and go to the bed.

Dick Le Geyt was lying on his back, with his eyes wide open. There was a mute appeal in his sharp-featured face, sharper featured than ever before, and in his thin outstretched hands, with the delicate nervous fingers crooked. He had needed help, and he had not found it. He had perhaps called to her, and she had not listened. She had been deaf to everything except herself. A sword seemed to pierce Annette's brain. It was as if some tight bandage were cleft and violently riven from it. She came shuddering to herself from out of the

waking swoon of the last two days. Hardly knowing what she did, she ran out of the room and into the passage. But it must be very early yet. No one was afoot. What to do next? She must rouse some one, and at once. But whom? She was about to knock at the nearest door, when she heard a hurried movement within, and the door opened.

A grey-haired woman in a dressing-gown looked out, the same whom she had seen the night before at dinner.

"I thought I heard some one call," she said. "Is anything wrong?" Then, as Annette leaned trembling against the wall, "Can I be of any use?"

Annette pointed to her own open door, and the woman went in with her at once.

She hastened instantly to the bed and bent over it. She touched the forehead, the wrist, with rapid, business-like movements. She put her hand upon Dick's heart.

"Is he dead?" asked Annette.

"No," she said, "but he is unconscious, and he is very ill. It is some kind of seizure. When did your husband become like this?"

"I—don't know," said Annette.

The woman turned indignantly upon her.

"You don't know! Yet surely you sat up with him? You look as if you had been up all night."

"I sat up, but I did not look at him," said Annette. "I never thought he was ill."

The elder woman's cheek reddened at the callousness of Annette's words, as at a blow. She was silent for a moment, and then said coldly—

"We have only one thing to think of now, and that is how to save his life, if it can be saved."

And in a moment, as it seemed to Annette, the house was awakened, and a doctor and a Sister of Mercy appeared and were installed at Dick's bedside. After a few hours, consciousness came back intermittently; but Dick, so excitable the day before, took but little heed of what went on around him. When, at the doctor's wish, Annette spoke to him, he looked at her without recognition.

The doctor was puzzled, and asked her many questions as to his condition on the previous day. She remembered that he had had a fall from his horse a day or two before, and had hurt his neck; and the doctor established some mysterious link between the accident and the illness, which he said had been terribly aggravated by drink. Had Monsieur taken much stimulant the night before? Yes, Monsieur had appeared to be intoxicated.

Mrs. Stoddart's steel eyes softened somewhat as she looked at Annette. She and the doctor noticed the extreme exhaustion from which she was suffering, and exchanged glances. Presently Mrs. Stoddart took the girl to her own room, and helped her to undress, and made her lie down on her bed.

"I will bring you your dressing-gown, if you will tell me where it is."

"I don't know," said Annette; and then she recollected, and said, "I haven't any things with me."

"Not even a handkerchief?"

"I think not a handkerchief."

"How long is it since you have slept?"

" I don't know." These words seemed her whole stock-in-trade.

Mrs. Stoddart frowned.

" I can't have you ill on my hands too," she said briskly; "one is enough." And she left the room, and presently came back with a glass with a few drops in it. She made Annette swallow them, and put a warm rug over her, and darkened the room.

And presently Annette's eyes closed, and the anguish of the last two days was lifted from her, as a deft hand lifts a burden. She sighed and leaned her cheek against a pillow which was made of rest ; and presently she was wandering in a great peace in a wide meadow beside a little stream whispering among its forget-me-nots. And across the white clover, and the daisies, and the little purple orchids, came the feet of one who loved her. And they walked together beside the stream, the kind, understanding stream, he and she—he and she together. And all was well, all was well.

Many hours later, Mrs. Stoddart and the doctor came and looked at her, and he thrust out his under lip.

" I can't bear to wake her," she said.

" One little half-hour, then," he said, and went back to the next room.

Mrs. Stoddart sat down by the bed, and presently Annette, as if conscious of her presence, opened her eyes.

" I see now," she said slowly, looking at Mrs. Stoddart with the fixed gravity of a child, " I was wrong."

" How wrong, my dear ? "

" Rivers are not meant for that, nor the little streams either. They are not meant to drown oneself in. They are meant to run and run, and for us to walk beside, and pick forget-me-nots."

Mrs. Stoddart's scrutinizing eyes filled with sudden tears. What tragedy was this into which she had thrust herself? She drew back the curtain, and let the afternoon light fall on Annette's face. Her eyelids trembled, and into her peaceful, rapt face distress crept slowly back. Mrs. Stoddart felt as if she had committed a crime. But there was another to think of besides Annette.

" You have slept ? "

1 Yes. I ought not to have gone to sleep while Dick was ill."

" You needed sleep."

11 Is—is he better ?"

" He is somewhat better."

11 I will go to him."

" He does not need you just now."

" Has the doctor found out what is the matter with him ? "

" He thinks he has." Mrs. Stoddart spoke very slowly. " As far as I understand, there is a cerebral lesion, and it is possible that it may not be as serious as he thought at first. It may have been aggravated for the moment by drink, the effects of which are passing off. But there is always the risk—in this case a great risk—that the injury to the brain may increase. In any case, his condition is very grave. His family ought to be communicated with at once."

Annette stared at her in silence.

" They must be summoned," said Mrs. Stoddart.

" But I don't know who they are," said Annette. " I don't even know his real name. He is called Mr. Le Geyt. It is the name he rides under."

Mrs. Stoddart reddened. She had had her doubts.

"A wife should know her husband's name," she said.

"But, you see, I'm not his wife."

There was a moment's silence. Mrs. Stoddart's eyes fell on Annette's wedding ring.

"That is nothing," said Annette. "Dick said I had better have one, and he bought it in a shop before we started. I think I'll take it off. I hate wearing it."

"No, no. Keep it on."

There was another silence.

"But you must know his address."

"No. I know he is often in Paris. But I have only met him at—at a cabaret."

"Could you trust me?" said Mrs. Stoddart humbly.

Annette trembled, and her face became convulsed.

"You are very kind," she said, "very kind,— getting the nurse, and helping, and this nice warm rug, and everything,—but I'm afraid I can't trust anyone any more. I've left off trusting people."

CHAPTER IV

"Et je m'en vais Au vent mauvais Qui m'emporte De?a, dela, Pareille a la Feuille morte."
VERLAINE.

IT was the second day of Dick's illness. Annette's life had revived somewhat, though the long sleep had not taken the strained look from her eyes. But Mrs. Stoddart's fears for her were momentarily allayed. Tears were what she needed, and tears were evidently a long way off.

And Annette fought for the life of poor Dick as if he were indeed her bridegroom, and Mrs. Stoddart abetted her as if he were her only son. The illness was incalculable, abnormal. There were intervals of lucidity followed by long lapses into unconsciousness. There were hours in which he seemed to know them, but could neither speak nor move. There were times when it appeared as if the faint flame of life had flickered quite out, only to waver feebly up again.

Together the two women had searched every article of Dick's effects, but they could find no

clue to his address or identity. Annette remembered that he had had a pocket-book, and seeing him take a note out of it to pay for the tickets. But the pocket-book could not be found, or any money. It was evident that he had been robbed that first evening when he was drinking. Some of his handkerchiefs were marked with four initials, R. L. G. M.

"Richard Le Geyt M. Then he had another name as well," said Mrs. Stoddart. "You can't recall having ever heard it?"

Annette shook her head.

"He is supposed to be an English lord," she said, "and very rich. And he rides his own horses, and makes and loses a great deal of money on the turf. And he is peculiar—very depressed one year, and very wild the next. That is all that people like us who are not his social equals know of him."

"I do not even know what your name is," said Mrs. Stoddart tentatively, as she rearranged Dick's clothes in the drawers, and took up a bottle of lotion which had evidently been intended for his strained neck.

"My name is Annette."

"Well, Annette, I think the best thing you can do is to write to your home and say that you are coming back to it immediately."

"I have no home."

Mrs. Stoddart was silent. Any information which Annette vouchsafed about herself always seemed to entail silence.

"I have made up my mind," Annette went on, "to stay with Dick till he is better. He is the only person I care a little bit about."

"No, Annette, you do not care for him. It is remorse for your neglect of him that makes you nurse him with such devotion."

"I do not love him," said Annette. "But then, how could I? I hardly know him. But he meant to be kind to me. He was the only person who was kind. He tried to save me, though not in the right way. Poor Dick, he does not know much. But I must stay and nurse him till he is better. I can't desert him."

"My dear," said Mrs. Stoddart impatiently, "that is all very well, but you cannot remain here without a scandal. It is different for an old woman like myself. And though we have not yet got into touch with his family, we shall directly. If I can't get a clue otherwise, I shall apply to the police. You must think of your own character."

"I do not care about my character," said Annette in the same tone in which she might have said she did not care for black coffee.

"But I do," said Mrs. Stoddart to herself.

"And I have a little money," Annette continued,—"at least, not much money, only a few louis,—but I have these." And she drew out from her neck a row of pearls. They were not large pearls, but they were even and beautifully matched.

"They were mother's," she said. "They will be enough for the doctor and the nurse and the hotel bill, won't they?"

Mrs. Stoddart put down the bottle of lotion and took the pearls in her hand, and bent over them, trying to hide her amazement.

"They are very good," she said slowly,—"beautiful colour and shape." Then she raised her eyes, and they fell once more on the bottle.

"But what am I thinking of?" she said sharply. "There is the clue I need staring me in the face. How incredibly stupid I am! There is the Paris chemist's name on it, and the number of the prescription. I can wire to him for the address to which he sent the bottle."

"Dick has a valet at his address," said Annette, "and of course he would know all about his people."

"How do you know he has a valet?"

"He met Dick at the station with the luggage. He was to have come to Fontainebleau with him, but Dick sent him back at the last moment, I suppose because of—me."

"Would you know him again if you saw him?"

"Yes. I watched Dick talking to him for several minutes. He would not go away at first. Perhaps he knew Dick was ill and needed care."

"Most likely. Did he see you?"

"No."

"Are you certain?"

"Quite certain."

"There is then one microscopic mercy to be thankful for. Then no one knows that you are here with Mr. Le Geyt?"

"No one, but I dare say it will be known presently," said Annette apathetically.

"Not if I can prevent it," said Mrs. Stoddart to herself as she put on her pince-nez and went out to telegraph to the chemist.

Annette went back to the bedside, and the Sister withdrew to the window and got out her breviary.

Annette sat down and leaned her tired head against the pillow with something like envy of Dick's unconsciousness. Would a certain hideous picture ever be blotted out from her aching brain? Her only respite from it was when she could minister to Dick. He was her sole link with life, the one fixed point in a shifting quicksand. She came very near to loving him in these days.

Presently he stirred and sighed, and opened his eyes. They wandered to the ceiling, and then fell idly on her without knowing her, as they had done a hundred times. Then recognition slowly dawned in them, clear and grave.

She raised her head, and they looked long at each other.

"Annette," he said in a whisper," I am sorry."

She tried to speak, but no words came.

" Often, often, when I have been lying here/ 1 he said feebly, " I have been sorry, but I could never say so. Just when I saw your face clear I always went away again, a long way off. Would you mind holding my hand, so that I may not be blown away again ? "

She took it in both of hers and held it. There was a long silence. A faint colour fluttered in his leaden cheek.

" I never knew such a wind/' he said. " It's stronger than anything in the world, and it blows and blows, and I go hopping before it like a leaf. I have to go. I really can't stay."

" You are much better. You will soon be able to get up."

11 I don't know where I'm going, but I don't care. I don't want to get up. I'm tired—tired."
" You must not talk any more." " Yes, I must. I have things to say. You are holding my hand tight, Annette ? " " Yes. Look, I have it safe in mine." " I ought not to have brought you here. You were in despair, and I took advantage of it. Can you forgive me, Annette ? "

" Dear Dick, there is nothing to forgive. I was more to blame than you."

" It was instead of the Seine. That was the excuse I made to myself. But the wind blows it away. It blows everything away—everything, everything. . . . Don't be angry again like that, Annette. Promise me you won't. You were too angry, and I took a mean advantage of it. ... I once took advantage of a man's anger with a horse, but it brought me no luck. 3 I thought I wouldn't do it again, but I did. And I haven't got much out of it this time either. I'm dying, or something like it. I'm going away for good and all. I'm so tired I don't know how I shall ever get there."

" Rest a little, Dick. Don't talk any more now. 11

" I want to give you a tip before I go. An old trainer put me up to it, and he made me promise not to tell anyone, and I haven't till now. But I want to do you a good turn to make up for the bad one. He said he'd never known it fail, and I haven't either. I've tried it scores of times. When you're angry, Annette, look at a cloud." Dick's blue eyes were fixed with a great earnestness on hers. " Not just for a minute. Choose a good big one, like a lot of cotton wool, and go on looking at it while it moves. And the anger goes away. Sounds rot, doesn't it? But you simply can't stay angry. Seems as if everything were too small and footling to matter. Try it, Annette. Don't look at water any more. That's no use. But a cloud—the bigger the better. . . , You won't drown yourself now, will you ? "

" No."

" Annette rolling down to the sea over and over, knocking against the bridges. I can't bear to think of it. Promise me."

" I promise."

He sighed, and his hand fell out of hers. She laid it down. The great wind of which he spoke had taken him once more, whither he knew not. She leaned her face against the pillow and longed that she too might be swept away whither she knew not.

The doctor came in and looked at them.

" Are his family coming soon ? " he asked Mrs. Stoddart afterwards. " And Madame Le Geyt ! Can Madame's mother be summoned ? There has been some great shock. Her eyes show it. It is not only Monsieur who is on the verge of the precipice."

CHAPTER V

" And he the wind-whipped, any whither wave Crazily tumbled on a shingle-grave To waste in foam."

GEORGE MEREDITH.

TOWARDS evening Dick regained consciousness. " Annette. " That was always the first word 11 Here." That was always the second. " I lost the way back," he said breathlessly.

" I thought I should never find it, but I had to
come."

He made a little motion with his hand, and she took it.

" You must help me. I have no one but you."

His eyes dwelt on her. His helpless soul clung to hers, as hers did to his. They were like two shipwrecked people — were they not indeed shipwrecked ? — cowering on a raft together, alone, in the great ring of the sea.

" What can I do ? " she said. " Tell me, and I will do it."

11 I have made no provision for Mary or — the little one. I promised her I would when it was born. But I haven't done it. I thought of it when I fell on my head. But when I was better
next day I put it off. I always put things
off. . . . And it's not only Mary. There's Hulver, and the Scotch property, and all the rest. If I die without making a will it will all go to poor Harry." He was speaking rapidly, more to himself than to her. " And when father was dying he said,' Roger ought to have it.' Father was a just man. And I like Roger, and he's done his duty by the place, which I haven't. He ought to have it. Annette, help me to make my will. I was on my way to the lawyer's to make it when I met you on the bridge."

Half an hour later, in the waning day, the notary arrived, and Dick made his will in the doctor's presence. His mind was amazingly clear.

" Is he better ? " asked Mrs. Stoddart of the doctor, as she and the nurse left the room.

" Better ! It is the last flare up of the lamp," said the doctor. "He is right when he says he shan't get back here again. He is riding his last race, but he is riding to win."

Dick rode for all he was worth, and urged the doctor to help him, to keep his mind from drifting away into the unknown.

The old doctor thrust out his under lip and did what he could.

By Dick's wish, Annette remained in the room, but he did not need her. His French was good enough. He knew exactly what he wanted. The notary was intelligent, and brought with him a draft for Dick's signature. Dick dictated and whispered earnestly to him.

" Oui, oui," said the notary at intervals. 11 Parfaitement. Monsieur peut se fier a moi."

At last it was done, and Dick, panting, had made a kind of signature, his writing dwindling down to a faint scrawl after the words " Richard Le Geyt," which were fairly legible.

The doctor attested it.

" She must witness it too/' said Dick insistently, pointing to Annette.

The notary glanced at the will, realized that she was not a legatee, and put the pen in her hand, showing her where to sign.

" Madame will write here.' 1

He indicated the place under his own crabbed signature.

She wrote mechanically her full name : Annette Georges.

" But, madame, said the notary, bewildered, " is not then Madame's name the same as Monsieur's ? "

" Madame is so lately married that she sometimes signs her old name by mistake," said the doctor, smiling sadly. He took a pained interest in the young couple, especially in Annette.

" I am not Monsieur's wife," said Annette.

The notary stared, bowed, and gathered up his papers. The doctor busied himself with the sick man, spent and livid on his pillow.

" Approach then, madame," he said, with a great respect. "It is you Monsieur needs." And he withdrew with the notary.

Annette groped her way to the bed. The room had become very dark. The floor rose in long waves beneath her feet, but she managed to reach the bed and sink down beside it.

What matter now if she were tired. She had done what he asked of her. She had not failed him. What matter if she sank deeper still, down and down, as she was sinking now.

" Annette." Dick's voice was almost extinct.

11 Here."

" The wind is coming again. Across the sea, across the mountains, over the plains. It is the wind of the desert. Can't you hear it ? "

She shook her head. She could hear nothing but his thin thread of voice.

" I am going with it, and this time I shan't come back. Good-bye, Annette."

" Good-bye, Dick."

His eyes dwelt on hers, with a mute appeal in them. The forebreath of the abyss was upon him, the shadow of " the outer dark."

She understood, and kissed him on the forehead with a great tenderness, and leaned her cold cheek against his.

And as she stooped she heard the mighty wind of which he spoke. Its rushing filled her ears, it filled the little chamber where those two poor things had suffered together, and had in a way ministered to each other.

And the sick-room with its gilt mirror and its tawdry wall-paper, and the evil picture never absent from Annette's brain, stooped

and blended into one, and wavered together as a flame wavers in a draught, and then together vanished away.

1 The wind is taking us both," Annette thought, as her eyes closed.

CHAPTER VI

" I was as children be
Who have no care ; I did not think or sigh,
I did not sicken ; But lo, Love beckoned me,
And I was bare, And poor and starved and dry, And fever-stricken."

THOMAS HARDY.

IT was five months later, the middle of February. Annette was lying in a deck-chair by the tank in the shade of the orange trees. All was still, with the afternoon stillness of Teneriffe, which will not wake up till sunset. Even the black goats had ceased to bleat and ring their bells.

The hoopoe which had been saying Cuk—Cuk— Cuk all the morning in the pepper tree was silent. The light air from the sea, bringing with it a whiff as from a bride's bouquet, hardly stirred the leaves. The sunlight trembled on the yellow stone steps, and on the trailing, climbing bougainvillea which had flung its mantle of purple over the balustrade. Through an opening in a network of almond blossom Annette could look down across the white water-courses and green terraces to the little town of Santa

Cruz, lying glittering in the sunshine, with its yellow and white and mauve walls and flat roofs and quaint cupolas, outlined as if cut out in white paper, sharp white against the vivid blue of the sea.

A grey lizard came slowly out of a clump of pink verbena near the tank, and spread itself in a patch of sunlight on a little round stone. Annette, as she lay motionless with thin folded hands, could see the pulse in its throat rise and fall as it turned its jewelled eyes now to this side, now to that, considering her as gravely as she was considering it.

A footfall came upon the stone steps. The lizard did not move. It was gone.

Mrs. Stoddart, an erect lilac figure under a white umbrella, came down the steps, with a cup of milk in her hand. Her forcible, incongruous countenance, with its peaked, indomitable nose and small, steady, tawny eyes under tawny eyebrows, gave the impression of having been knocked to pieces at some remote period and carelessly put together again. No feature seemed to fit with any other. If her face had not been held together by a certain shrewd benevolence which was spread all over it, she would have been a singularly forbidding-looking woman.

Annette took the cup and began dutifully to sip it, while Mrs. Stoddart sat down near her.

" Do you see the big gold-fish ? " Annette said.

Her companion put up her pince-nez and watched him for a moment, swimming lazily near the surface.

' He seems much as usual/' she said.

" It is not my fault if he is. I threw a tiny bit of stick at him a few minutes ago, and he bolted it at once ; and then, just when I was beginning to feel anxious, he spat it out again to quite a considerable distance. He must have a very strong pop-gun in his inside."

Mrs. Stoddart took the empty cup from her and put'it down on the edge of the tank.

11 You have one great quality, Annette," she said : " you are never bored."

" How could I be, with so much going on round me? I have just had my first interview with a lizard. And before that a mantis called upon me. Look, there he is again, on that twig. Doesn't he look exactly like a child's drawing of a dragon ? "

A hideous grey mantis, about three inches long, walked slowly down an almond-blossomed branch.

" He really walks with considerable dignity, considering his legs bend the wrong way," said Mrs. Stoddart. " But I don't wish for his society."

" Oh, don't you ? Look 1 Now he is going to pray."

And the mantis suddenly sat up and appeared to engage in prayer.

Annette watched him, fascinated, until his

orisons were over, and he slowly went down again on all fours and withdrew himself into the bougainvillea.

Mrs. Stoddart looked searchingly at her, not without a certain pride. She had still the bruised, sunken eyes of severe illness, and she rolled them slowly at Mrs. Stoddart, at the mantis, at the sky, at everything in turn, in a manner which exasperated the other occupants of the pension—two ladies from Hampstead who considered her a mass of affectation. The only thing about Annette which was beautiful was her hands, which were transparent, blue-veined, ethereal. But her movements with them also were so languid, so " studied/' that it was impossible for spectators as impartial as the Hampstead ladies not to deplore her extreme vanity about them. To Mrs. Stoddart, who knew the signs of illness, it was evident that she was still weak, but it was equally evident that the current of health was surely flowing back.

" I remember," said Mrs. Stoddart, " being once nearly bored to extinction, not by an illness, but by my convalescence after it."

" I have no time to be bored," said Annette, u even if there is no mantis and no lizard. Since I have been better so many things come crowding into my mind, that though I lie still all day I hardly have time to think of them all. The day is never long enough for me."

There was a short silence.

" I often wonder/' said Annette slowly, " about you"

" About me ? "

' Yes. Why you do everything for me as if I were your own child, and most of all why you never ask me any questions — why you never even hint to me that it is my duty to tell you about myself."

Mrs. Stoddart's eyes dropped. Her heart began to beat violently.

' When you took charge of me you knew nothing of me except evil."

" I knew the one thing needful."

11 What do you mean ? "

" That you were in trouble."

" For a long time," said Annette, " I have been wanting to tell you about myself, but I couldn't."

" Don't tell me, if it distresses you." ' Nothing distresses me now. The reason I could not was because for a long time I did not rightly know how things were, or who I was. And I saw everything distorted—horrible. It was as if I were too near, like being in a cage of hot iron, and beating against the bars first on one side and then on the other, till it seemed as if one went mad. You once read me, long ago, that poem of Verlaine's ending ' Et l'oubli d'ici-bas.' And I thought that was better than any of the promises in the Bible which you read sometimes. I used to say it over to myself like a kind of prayer : ' Et l'oubli d'ici-bas. 1 That would be heaven—at least, it would have been

to me. But since I have got better everything has gone a long way off—like that island." And she pointed to the Grand Canary, lying like a cloud on the horizon. " I can bear to think about it and to look at it."

" I understand that feeling. I have known it. 11

" It does not burn me now. I thought it would always burn while I lived. 1 '

" That is the worst of pain—that one thinks it will never lessen. But it does."

" Yes, it lessens. And then one can^attend to other things a little."

And Annette told Mrs. Stoddart the long story of her life. For at twenty-two we have all long, long histories to unfold of our past, if we can find a sympathetic listener. It is only in middle age that we seem to have nothing of interest to communicate. Or is it only that we realize that when once the talisman of youth has slipped out of our hand, our part is to listen ?

Mrs. Stoddart certainly listened. She had been ready to do so for a long time.

And Annette told her of her childhood spent in London under the charge of her three spinster aunts. Her mother, an Englishwoman, had been the only good-looking one of four sisters. In the thirties, after some disappointment, she had made a calamitous run-away marriage with a French courier.

' I always thought I could understand mother running away from that home," said Annette. " I would have run away too, if I

could. I did once as a small child, but I only got as far as Bethnal Green."

' Then your mother died when you were quite small ? "

11 Yes ; I can just remember being with her in lodgings after she left father—for she had to leave him. But he got all her money from her first—at least, all she had it in her power to give up. I can remember how she used to sob at night when she thought I was asleep. And then, my next remembrance is the aunts and the house in London. They meant to be kind. They were kind. I was their niece, after all. But they were Nevills. It seems it is a very noble, mysterious thing to be a Nevill. Now, I was only half a Nevill, and only half English, and dark like father. I take after father. And of course I am not quite a lady. They felt that."

" You look like one," said Mrs. Stoddart.

" Do I ? I think that is only because I hold myself well and know how to put on my clothes."

" My dear Annette ! As if those two facts could deceive me for a moment!"

" But I am not one, all the same," said Annette. " Gentle-people, I don't mean only the aunts but— others, don't regard me as their equal, or—or treat me so."

She was silent for a moment, and her lip quivered. Then she went on quietly—

' The minute I was twenty-one and independent I came into a hundred a year, and

I left the aunts. I made them a sort of little speech on my birthday. I can see them now, all three staring at me. And I thanked them for their kindness, especially Aunt Cathie, and told them my mind was quite made up to go and live with father and become a professional singer. I had meant to do it since I was twelve."

" Did they mind much ? "

" I did not think so at the time. But I see now they were so astonished that, for the moment, it overcame all other feelings. They were so amazed at my wish to make any movement, go anywhere, do anything. Aunt Harriet the invalid wrung her hands, and said that if only she had not been tied to a sofa my upbringing would have been so different, that I should not have wished to leave them. And Aunt Maria said that she, of all people, would be the last to interfere with a vocation, but she did not consider the stage was a suitable profession for a young girl. Aunt Cathie did not say anything. She only cried. I felt leaving Aunt Cathie. She had been kind. She had taken me to plays and concerts. She hated music, but she sat through long concerts for my sake. Aunt Maria never had time, and Aunt Harriet never was well enough to do anything she did not like. Aunt Cathie used to slave for them both, and when she had time —for me. I used to think that if the other two died I could have lived with Aunt Cathie.

But existing in that house was like just not suffocating under a kind of moral bindweed. When you were vexed with me the other day for tiring myself by tearing the convolvulus off that little orange tree, it was because I could not bear to see it choked. I had been choked myself. But I broke away at last. And I found father. He had married again, a woman in his own rank of life, and was keeping a cabaret in the Rue du Bac. I lived with them for nearly six months, till—last September. I liked the life at first. It was so new and so unaccustomed, and even the slipshodness of it was pleasant after the dry primness of my upbringing. And after all I am my father's daughter. I never could bear her, but he was kind to me in a way, while I had money. He had been the same to mother. And like mother, I did not find him out at first. I was easily taken in. And he thought it was a capital idea that I should become a singer. He was quite enthusiastic about it. I had a pretty voice. I don't know whether I have it still. But the difficulty was the training, and the money for it. And he found a man, a well-known musician, who was willing to train me for nothing when he had heard me sing. And I was to pay him back later on. And father was very keen about it, and so was I, and so was the musician. He was rather a dreadful man somehow, but I did not mind that. He was a real artist. But after a little bit I found

4

he expected me to pay him another way, and I had to give up going to him. I told father, and he laughed at me for a fool, and told me to go back to him. And when I wouldn't he became very angry, and asked me what I had expected, and said all English were hypocrites. I ought to have known from that that I could not trust father. And then, when I was very miserable about losing my training, an English gentleman began to be very kind to me."

Annette's voice faltered and stopped. Mrs. Stoddart's thin cheek flushed a little.

Across the shadow of the orange trees a large yellow butterfly came floating. Annette's eyes followed it. It settled on a crimson hibiscus, hanging like a flame against the pale stem of a coral tree. The two ardent colours quivered together in the vivid sunshine.

Annette's grave eyes watched the yellow wings close and expand, close and expand, and then rise and float away again.

" He seemed to fall in love with me," she said. " Of course now I know he didn't really ; but he seemed to. And he was a real gentleman—not like father, nor that other one, the man who offered to teach me. He seemed honourable. He looked upright and honest and refined. And he was young — not much older than myself, and very charming-looking. He was unlike any of the people in the Quartier Latin. I fell in love with him after a little bit. At first I hung back, because I

thought it was too good to be true, too like a fairy story. I had never been in love before. I fell in—very deep. And I was grateful to him for loving me, for he was much above me, the heir to something large and a title—I forget exactly what—when his old uncle died. I thought it was so kind of him not to mind the difference of rank. ... I am sure you know what is coming. I suppose I ought to have known. But I didn't. I never thought of it. The day came when he asked me very gravely if I loved him, and I said I did, and he told me he loved me. I remember when I was in my room again alone, thinking that whatever life took from me, it could never take that wonderful hour. I should have that as a possession always, when I was old and white-headed. I am afraid now I shall have it always."

Annette passed her blue-veined hand over her eyes in a manner that would have outraged the other residents, and then went on:—

" We sat a long time together that evening, with his arm round me, and he talked and I listened, but I was not listening to him. I was listening to love. I knew then that I had never lived before, never known anything before. I seemed to have waked up suddenly in Paradise, and I was dazed. Perhaps he did not realize that. It was like walking in a long, long field of lilies under a new moon. I told him it was like that, and he said it was the same to him. Perhaps he thought he had said things to show

me his meaning. Perhaps he thought father had told me. But I did not understand. And then—a few hours later—I had to understand suddenly, without any warning. I thought he had gone mad, but it was I who went mad. And I locked myself into my room, and crept out of the house at dawn, when all was quiet. I realized father had sold me. That was why I told you I had no home to go to. . . . And I walked and walked in the early morning in the river mist, not knowing what I was doing. At last, when I was worn out, I went and sat where there was a lot of wood stacked on a great wharf. No one saw me because of the mist. And I sat still and tried to think. But I could not think. It was as if I had fallen from the top of the house. Part of me was quite inert, like a stupid wounded animal, staring at the open wound. And the other part of me was angry with a cold anger that seemed to mount and mount : that jeered at everything, and told me I had made a fuss about nothing, and I might just as well go back and be his mistress—anybody's mistress : that there was nothing true or beautiful or pure or clean in the world. Everything was a seething mass of immorality and putrefaction, and he was only the same as all the rest. . . . And all the time I could hear the river speaking through the mist, hinting at something it would not quite say. At last, when the sun was up, the mist cleared, and workmen came, and I had to go.

And I wandered away again near the water. I clung to the river, it seemed to know something. And I went and stood on the Pont Neuf and made up my mind. I would go down to Melun and drown myself there. . . . And then Mr. Le Geyt came past, whom I knew a little— a very little. And he asked me why I was looking at the water. And I said I was going to drown myself. And he saw I meant it, and made light of it, and advised me to go down to Fontainebleau with him instead, for a week. And I did not care what I did. I went with him. I was glad in a way. I thought— he —would hear of it. I wanted to hurt him."

" You did not know what you were doing."

" Oh yes, I did. I didn't misunderstand again—I was not so silly as that. It was only the accident of Dick's illness which prevented my going wrong with him."

Mrs. Stoddart started.

" Then you never " she said diffidently,

but with controlled agitation.

" No," said Annette, " but it's the same as if I had. I meant to."

There was a moment's silence.

" No one," thought Mrs. Stoddart, " but Annette would have left me all these months believing the worst had happened—not because she was concealing the truth purposely, but because it did not strike her that I could regard her as innocent when she did not consider herself so."

1 It is not the same as if you had," said Mrs. Stoddart sternly. " If you mean to do a good and merciful action, and something prevents you, is it the same as if you had done it ? Is anyone the better for it ? "

" No."

11 Well, then, remember, Annette, that it is the same with evil actions. You were not actually guilty of it. Be thankful you were not."

" I am."

" When I saw you that first night at Fontaine-bleau, I thought you were on the verge of brain fever. I never slept for thinking of you."

" Well, you were right," said Annette tranquilly. " I suppose that is what you nursed me through. But that night I had no idea I was ill."

" You were absolutely desperate."

" Was I ? I was angry. I must never be angry like that again. Dick said that, and he was right. Do you know what I was thinking of when you came out to me with the milk ? Once, long ago, when I was a child, I was sent to a country farm after an illness, and I saw one of the farm hands moving some faggots. And behind it on the ground was a nest with a hen, a common hen, sitting on it, and a little baby-chicken looking out from under her wing. She was just hatching them out. I was quite delighted. I had never seen anything so pretty before. And the stupid men frightened her, and she thought they were coming for her young ones. And first she spread out her wings over them, and then she became angry. A kind of dreadful rage took her. And she trod down the eggs with her great feet, the eggs she had sat patiently on so long ; and then she killed the little chickens with her strong beak. I can see her now, standing at bay in her broken nest with her bill streaming, making a horrible low sound. Don't laugh at me when I say that I felt just like that old hen. I was ready to rend everything to pieces, myself included, that night. When I was a child I thought it so strange of the hen to behave like that. I laughed at her at the time—just as Dick laughed at me. But I understand her now—poor thing."

CHAPTER VII

" The larger the nature the less susceptible to persona injury."

IT was a few days later. Annette, leaning on Mrs. Stoddart's arm, had made a pilgrimage as far as the low garden wall to look at the little golden-brown calf on the other side tethered to a twisted shrub of plumbago, the blue flowers of which spread themselves into a miniature canopy over him. Now she was lying back, exhausted but triumphant, in her long chair, with Mrs. Stoddart knitting beside her.

" I shall be walking up there to-morrow," she said audaciously, pointing to the fantastic cactus-sprinkled volcanic hills rising steeply behind the house on the northern side.

Mrs. Stoddart vouchsafed no reply. Annette, more tired than she would allow, leaned back. Her eyes fell on the same view, which might have been painted on a drop scene so fixed was it, so identical in colour and light day after day. But to-day it proved itself genuine by the fact that a large German steamer, not there yesterday, was moored in the bay, so placed that it seemed to be impaled on the spike of the tallest tower, and keeping up the illusion by making irom time to time a rumbling and unseemly noise as if in pain.

" You must own now that I am well," said Annette.

" Very nearly. You shall come up to the tomato-gardens to-morrow, and see the Spanish women working in their white trousers."

" My head never aches now."

" That is a good thing."

" Has the time come when I may ask a few questions ? "

Mrs. Stoddart hardly looked up from her knitting as she said tranquilly—

" Yes, my child, if there is anything on your mind."

" I suppose Dick Le Geyt is—dead. I felt sure he was dying that last day at Fontainebleau. It won't be any shock to me to know that he is dead."

11 He is not dead."

A swift glance showed Mrs. Stoddart that Annette was greatly surprised.

" How is he ? " she asked after a moment. " Did he really get well again? I thought it was not possible."

" It was not."

" Then he is not riding again yet ? "

"No. I am afraid he will never ride again."

" Then his back was really injured, after all ? "

" Yes. It was spinal paralysis."

" He did enjoy life so," said Annette. " Poor Dick!"

" I made inquiries about him again a short time ago. He is not unhappy. He knows nothing and nobody, and takes no notice. The brain was affected, and it is only a question of time—a few months, a few years. He does not suffer. 1 '

" For a long time I thought he and I had died together."

" You both all but died, Annette."

" Where is he now ?'"

" In his aunt's house in Paris. She came down before I left."

11 I hope she seemed a kind woman."

" She seemed a silly one. She brought her own doctor and Mr. Le Geyt's valet with her. She evidently distrusted the Fontainebleau doctor and me. She paid him up and dismissed him at once, and she as good as dismissed me."

11 Perhaps," said Annette, " she thought you and the doctor were in collusion with me. I suppose some lurid story, with me in the middle of it, reached her at once."

" No doubt. The valet had evidently told her that his master had not gone down to Fontainebleau alone. She arrived prepared for battle."

" And where was I all the time ? "

" You were in the country, a few miles out of Fontainebleau, at a house the doctor knew of. He helped me to move you there directly you became unconscious. Until you fell ill you would not leave Mr. Le Geyt. It was fortunate you were not there when his aunt arrived."

' I should not have cared."

" No. You were past caring about anything. You were not in your right mind. But surely, Annette,"—Mrs. Stoddart spoke very slowly,— " you care now?"

Annette evidently turned the question over in her mind, and then looked doubtfully at her friend.

' I am grateful to you that I escaped the outside shame," she said. " But that seems such a little thing beside the inside shame, that I could have done as I did. I had been carefully brought up. I was what was called good. And it was easy to me. I had never felt any temptation to be otherwise, even in the irresponsible milieu at father's, where there was no morality to speak of. And yet—all in a minute—I could do as—as I did, throw everything away which only just before I had guarded with such passion. He was bad, and father was bad. I see now that he had sold me. But since I have been lying here I have come to see that I was bad too. It was six of one and half a dozen of the other. There was nothing to choose between the three of us. Poor Dick with his unpremeditated escapade was snow-white compared to us, the one kindly person in the sordid drama of lust and revenge."

" Where do I come in ? " asked Mrs. Stoddart.

"As an unwise angel, I think, who snatched a brand from the burning."

1 You are the first person who has had the advantage of my acquaintance who has called me unwise," said Mrs. Stoddart, with the grim, benevolent smile which Annette had learnt to love. " And now you have talked enough. The whole island is taking its siesta. It is time you took yours."

Mrs. Stoddart thought long over Annette and her future that night. She had made every effort, left no stone unturned at Fontaine-bleau, to save the good name which the girl had so recklessly flung away. When Annette succumbed, Mrs. Stoddart, quick to see whom she could trust, confided to the doctor that Annette was not Mr. Le Geyt's wife and appealed to him for help. He gravely replied that he already knew that fact, but did not mention how during the making of the will it had come to his knowledge. He helped her to remove Annette instantly to a private lodging kept by an old servant of his. There was no luggage to remove. When Mr. Le Geyt's aunt and her own doctor arrived late that night, together with Mr. Le Geyt's valet, Annette had vanished into thin air. Only Mrs. Stoddart was there, and the nurse to hand over the patient, and to receive the cautious, suspicious thanks of Lady Jane Cranbrook, who con-

tinually repeated that she could not understand the delay in sending for her. It was, of course, instantly known in the hotel that the pretty lady who had nursed Monsieur so devotedly was not his wife, and that she had fled at the approach of his family. Mrs. Stoddart herself left very early next morning, before Lady Jane was up, after paying Annette's hotel-bill as well as her own. She had heard since through the nurse that Mr. Le Geyt, after asking plaintively for Annette once or twice, had relapsed into a state of semi-unconsciousness, in which he lay day after day, week after week. It seemed as if his mind had made one last effort, and then had finally given up a losing battle. The stars in their courses had fought for Annette, and Mrs. Stoddart had given them all the aid she could, with systematic perseverance and forethought.

She had obliged Annette to write to a friend in Paris as soon as she was well enough, rather before she was well enough to hold a pen, telling her she had been taken ill suddenly at Fontaine-bleau but was with a friend, and asking her to pack her clothes for her and send them to her at Melun. Later on, before embarking at Marseilles, she had made her write a line to her father saying she was travelling with her friend Mrs. Stoddart, and should not be returning to Paris for the present. After a time, she made her resume communications with her aunts, and inform them who she was travelling with

and where she was. The aunts wrote rather frigidly in return at first, but after a time became more cordial, expressed themselves pleased that she was enjoying herself, and opined that they had had the pleasure of meeting Mrs. Stoddart's sister, Lady Brandon. They were evidently delighted that she had left her father, and even graciously vouchsafed fragments of information about themselves. Aunt Maria had just brought out another book, Crooks and Coronets, a copy of which found its way to Teneriffe. Aunt Harriet, the invalid, had become a Christian Scientist. Aunt Catherine, the only practical one of the family, had developed a weak heart. And they had all decided to leave London, and were settling in a country farm in Lowshire, where they had once spent a summer years before.

Mrs. Stoddart with infinite care had reestablished all the links between Annette's past life and her present one. The hiatus, which after all had only occupied six days, was invisible. Her success had apparently been complete.

"Only apparently," she said to herself. "Something may happen which I cannot foresee. Mr. Le Geyt may get better, though they say he never will; or at any rate he may get well enough to give her away, which he would never do if he were in full possession of his faculties. Or that French chamber-maid who was so endlessly kind may take service in England, and run up against

Annette ; or the valet who, she says, did not see her at the station, may have seen her after all, and may prove a source of danger. Or, most likely of all, Annette may tell against herself. She is quite capable of it."

Next day she said to Annette—

" Remember your reputation is my property. You threw it away, and I picked it up off the dunghill. It belongs to me absolutely. Now promise me on your oath that you will never say anything about this episode in your past to anyone, to any living creature except one— the man you marry."

"I would rather not promise that," said Annette. "I feel as if some time or other I might have to say something. One never can tell."

Mrs. Stoddart cast at her a lightning glance in which love and perplexity were about evenly mixed. This strange creature amused and angered her, and constantly aroused in her opposite feelings at the same moment. The careful Scotchwoman felt a certain kindly scorn for Annette's want of self-protective prudence and her very slight realization of the dangers Mrs. Stoddart had worked so hard to avert. But mixed in with the scorn was a pinch of respect for something unworldly in Annette, uncalculating of her own advantage. She was apparently one of that tiny band who are not engrossed by the duty of "looking after Number One."

Mrs. Stoddart, who was not easily nonplussed, decided to be wounded.

"You are hard to help, Annette," she said. 11 I do what I can for you, and you often say how much it is, and yet you can tranquilly talk of all my work being thrown away by some chance word of yours which you won't even promise not to say."

Annette was startled.

"I had not meant that," she said humbly. "I will promise anything you wish I"

"No, my dear, no," said Mrs. Stoddart, ashamed of her subterfuge and its instant success "I was unreasonable. Promise me instead that, except to the man you are engaged to, you will never mention this subject to anyone without my permission."

"I promise," said Annette.

And Mrs. Stoddart, who never kissed anyone if she could help it, kissed her on the forehead.

"Thou hast led me astray, my youth, till there is nowhere I can turn my steps."—KOLTSOV.

IT was the middle of April. The ginger tree had at last unsheathed the immense buds which it had been guarding among its long swordlike leaves, and had hung out its great pink and white blossoms at all their length. The coffee trees had mingled with their red berries the dearest little white wax flowers. The paradise tree which Annette had been watching day by day had come out in the night. And this morning, among its innumerable hanging golden balls, were cascades of five-leaved white stars with violet centres.

Annette was well again, if so dull and tame a word can be used to describe the radiance which health had shed upon her, and upon the unfolding, petal by petal, of her beauty. The long rest, the slow recovery, the immense peace which had enfolded her life for the first time, the grim, tender "mothering" of Mrs. Stoddart, had all together fostered and sustained her. Her life, cut back to its very root by a sharp frost, had put out a superb new shoot. Her coltishness 5 and a certain heavy, naive immaturity had fallen from her. Her beauty had shaken them off and stood clear of them, and Mrs. Stoddart recognized, not without anxiety, that the beauty which was now revealed was great. But in the process of her unduly delayed and then unduly forced development it was plain that she had lost one thing which would have made her mother's heart ache if she had been alive. Annette had lost her youth. She was barely twenty-two, but she had the dignity and the bearing of a woman of thirty. Mrs. Stoddart watched her standing, a gracious slender figure in her white gown under the paradise tree, with a wild baby-canary in the hollow of her hands, coaxing it to fly back to its parents, calling shrilly to it from a neighbouring thicket of lemon-coloured honeysuckle. She realized the pitfalls that lie in wait for persons as simple and as inapprehensive as Annette, especially when they are beautiful as well, and she sighed.

Presently the baby-canary fluttered into the honeysuckle, and Annette walked down the steep garden path to meet Victor the butler, who could be seen in the distance coming slowly on the donkey up the white high road from Santa Cruz, with the letters.

Mrs. Stoddart sighed again. She had safeguarded Annette's past, but how about her future? She had pondered long over it, which Annette did not seem to do at all. TenerifTe was becoming too hot. The two ladies from

Hampstead had already gone, much mollified towards Annette, and even anxious to meet her again, and attributing her more alert movements and now quite unrolling eyes to the fact that they had made it clear they would not stand any nonsense, or take " airs " from anyone. Mrs. Stoddart was anxious to get home to London to her son, her one son Mark. But what would happen to Annette when they left Teneriffe ? She would gladly have kept her as her companion till she married,—for, of course, she would marry some day, — but there was Mark to be considered. She could not introduce Annette into her household without a vehement protest from Mark to start with, who would probably end by falling in love with her. It was hopeless to expect that Annette would take an interest in any man for some time to come. Would she be glad or sorry if Annette eventually married Mark ? She came to the conclusion that in spite of all the drawbacks of Annette's parentage and the Le Geyt episode, she would rather have her as her daughter-in-law than anyone. But there was Mark to be reckoned with, a very uncertain quantity. She did not know how he would regard that miserable episode, and she decided that she would not take the responsibility of throwing him and Annette together.

Then what was to be done ? Mrs. Stoddart had got through her own troubles with such assiduous determination earlier in life that she

was now quite at liberty to attend to those of others, and she gave a close attention to Annette's.

She need not have troubled her mind, for Annette was coming towards her up the steep path between the high hedges of flowering geraniums with a sheaf of letters in her hand, and her future neatly mapped out in one of them.

She sat down at Mrs. Stoddart's feet in the dappled shade under the scarlet-flowering pomegranate tree, and they both opened their letters. Annette had time to read her two several times while Mrs. Stoddart selected one after another from her bundle. Presently she gave an exclamation of surprise.

" Mark is on his way here. He will be here directly. Let me see, the Fiirstin is due tomorrow or next day. He sends this by the English mail to warn me. He has not been well, overworked, and he is coming out for the sake of the sea-journey and to take me home."

Mrs. Stoddart's shrewd eyes shone. A faint colour came to her thin cheeks.

11 Then I shall see him," said Annette. " When he did not come out for Christmas I was afraid I should miss him altogether."

" Does that mean you are thinking of leaving me, Annette ? "

" Yes," said Annette, and she took her friend's hand and kissed it. " I have been considering it some time. I am thinking of staying here and setting up as a dressmaker."

" As a dressmaker I " almost gasped Mrs. Stoddart.

" Yes. Why not? My aunt is a very good dressmaker in Paris, and she would help me— at least, she would if it was worth her while. And there is no one here to do anything, and all that exquisite work the peasant women make is wasted on coarse or inferior material. I should get them to do it for me on soft fine nainsook, and make a speciality of summer morning gowns and children's frocks. Every one who comes here would buy a gown of Teneriffe-work from me, and I can fit people quite well. I have a natural turn for it. Look how I can fit myself. You said yesterday that this white gown I have on was perfect."

Mrs. Stoddart could only gaze at her in amazement.

" My dear Annette," she said at last, " you cannot seriously think I would allow you to leave me to become a dressmaker 1 What have I done that you should treat me like that ? "

" You have done everything," said Annette,— "more than anyone in the world since I was born,—and I have accepted everything—haven't I ?—as it was given—freely. But I felt the time was coming when I must find a little hole of my own to creep into, and I thought this dressmaking might do. I would rather not try to live by my voice. It would throw me into the

kind of society I knew before. I would rather make a fresh start on different lines. At least, I thought all these things as I came up the path ten minutes ago. But these two letters have shown me that I have a place of my own in the world after all."

She put two black-edged letters into Mrs. Stoddart's hand.

" Aunt Catherine is dead," she said. " You know she has been failing. That was why they went to live in the country,"

Mrs. Stoddart took up the letters and gave them her whole attention. Each of the bereaved aunts had written.

" MY DEAR ANNETTE (wrote Aunt Maria, the eldest),—I grieve to tell you that our beloved sister, your Aunt Catherine, died suddenly yesterday, from heart failure. We had hoped that the move to the country undertaken entirely on her account would have been beneficial to her, entailing as it did a great sacrifice on my part who need the inspiration of a congenial literary milieu so much. She had always fancied that she was not well in London, in which belief her doctor encouraged her—very unwisely, as the event has proved. The move, with all the inevitable paraphernalia of such an event, did her harm, as I had feared it would. She insisted on organizing the whole affair, and though she carried it through fairly successfully, except that several of my MSS have been mislaid, the strain had a bad effect on her heart. The doctor said that she ought to have gone away to the seaside while the

move was done in her absence. This she declared was quite impossible, and though I wrote to her daily from Felixstowe begging her not to over-fatigue herself, and to superintend the work of others rather than to work herself, there is no doubt that in my absence she did more than she ought to have done. The heart attacks have been more frequent and more severe ever since, culminating in a fatal one on Saturday last. The funeral is to-morrow. Your Aunt Harriet is entirely prostrated by grief, and I may say that unless I summoned all my fortitude I should be in the same condition myself, for of course my beloved sister Catherine and I were united by a very special and uncommon affection, rare even between affectionate sisters.

" I do not hear any more of your becoming a professional singer, and I hope I never shall. I gather that you have not found living with your father quite as congenial as you anticipated. Should you be in need of a home when your tour with Mrs. Stoddart is over, we shall be quite willing that you should return to us ; for though the manner of your departure left something to be desired, I have since realized that there was not sufficient scope for yourself and Aunt Catherine in the same house. And now that we are bereaved of her, you would have plenty to occupy you in endeavouring, if such is your wish, to fill her place.—Your affectionate aunt, MARIA NEVILL."

Mrs. Stoddart took up the second letter.

" MY DEAR ANNETTE, —How can I tell you—how can I begin to tell you—of the shattering blow that has fallen upon us ? Life can never be the

same again. Death has entered pur dwelling. Dearest Cathie—your Aunt Catherine—has been taken from us. She was quite well yesterday—at least well for her —at quarter-past seven when she was rubbing my feet, and by seven-thirty she was in a precarious condition. Maria insisted on sending for a doctor, which of course I greatly regretted, realizing as I do full well that the ability to save life is not with them, and that all drugs have only the power in them which we by wrong thought have given to them. However, Maria had her way as always, but our dear sister succumbed before he arrived, so I do not in any way attribute her death to him. We were both with her, each holding one of her dear hands, and the end was quite peaceful. I could have wished for one last word of love, but I do not rebel. Maria feels it terribly, though she always has great self-control. But of course the loss cannot be to her, immersed in her writing, what it is to me, my darling Cathie's constant companion and adviser. We were all in all to each other. What I shall do without her I cannot even imagine. Maria will naturally expect— she always has expected—to find all household matters arranged without any participation on her part. And I am, alas ! so feeble that for many years past I have had to confine my aid to that of consolation and encouragement. My sofa has indeed, I am thankful to think, been a centre from which sympathy and love have flowed freely forth. This is as it should be. We invalids live in the lives of others. Their joys are our joys. Their sorrows are our sorrows. How I have rejoiced over your delightful experiences at Teneriffe —the islands of the blest! When it has snowed here, how often I have said to myself, ' Annette is in the sunshine.' And

now, dear Annette, I am wondering whether, when you leave Teneriffe, you could make your home with us again for a time. You would find one very loving heart here to welcome you, ever ready with counsel and support for a young girl's troubles and perplexities. / never blamed you for leaving us. I know too well that spirit of adventure, though my lot bids me sternly silence its voice. And, darling child, does it not seem pointed out for you to relinquish this strange idea of being a professional singer for a life to which the call of duty is so plain ? I know from experience what a great blessing attends those who give up their own will to live for others. The surrender of the will I That is where true peace and happiness lie, if the young could only believe it.

I will say no more.—-With fondest love, your affectionate AUNT HARRIET."

II H'm ! " said Mrs. Stoddart, " and so the only one of the trio whom you could tolerate is the one who has died. They have killed her between them. That is sufficiently obvious. And what do you think, Annette, of this extremely cold-blooded suggestion that you should live for others ?"

" I think it is worth a trial," said Annette, looking gravely at her. " It will have the charm of novelty, at any rate. And I haven't made such a great success of living for myself so far."

Mrs. Stoddart did not answer.

Even she, accustomed as she was to them by now, always felt a tremor when those soft veiled violet eyes were fixed upon her. " Sweetest

eyes were ever seen," she often said to herself.

Annette went on : "I see that I have been like the man in the parable. When I was bidden to the feast of life I wanted the highest seat, I took it as my right. I was to have everything—love, honour, happiness, rank, wealth. But I was turned out, as he was. And I was so angry that I flung out of the house in a rage. If Dick had not stopped me at the door I should have gone away altogether. The man in the parable behaved better than that. He took with shame the lowest seat. I must do like him—try and find the place intended for me, where I shan't be cast out."

" Well, this is the lowest seat with a vengeance."

" Yes, that is why I think it may be just what I can manage."

" You are sure you are not doing this from a false idea of making an act of penance ? "

11 No, directly I read the letters I thought I should like it. I wish now I had never left them. And I believe now that I have been away I could make a success of it."

" I have no doubt you could, but "

" I should like to make a success of something, after being such a failure. And—and "

" And what, my child ? "

" I had begun to think there was no corner in the world for me, as if the Giver of the Feast had forgotten me altogether. And this looks

as if He hadn't. I have often thought lately that I should like—if I could—to creep into some little place where I should not be thrust out, where there wouldn't be any more angels with flaming swords to drive me away."

CHAPTER IX

" Oh, is the water sweet and cool, Gentle and brown, above the pool ? And laughs the immortal river still Under the mill, under the mill ? "

RUPERT BROOKE.

I DO not think you have ever heard of the little village of Riff in Lowshire, Reader, unless you were born and bred in it as I was. If you were, you believe of course that it is the centre of the world. But if you were not, it is possible you may have overlooked it in your scheme of life, or hurried past it in the train reading a novel, not even looking out as I have done a hundred times to catch a glimpse of it lying among its water meadows behind the willows.

But unless you know exactly where to look you can only catch a momentary glimpse, because the Rieben with its fringe of willows makes a half-circle round Riff and guards it from inquisitive eyes.

Parallel with the Rieben, but half a mile away from it on higher ground, runs the great white high road from London to Yarmouth.

And between the road and the river lies the

village of Riff. But you cannot see it or even the top of its church tower from the road, because the park of Hulver Manor comes in between, stretching in long leafy glades of oak and elm and open sward, and hiding the house in its midst, the old Tudor house which has stood closed and shuttered so long, ever since Mr. Manvers died.

When at last the park comes to an end, a deep lane breaks off from the main road, and pretending that it is going nowhere in particular and that time would be lost in following it, edges along like a homing cat beside the park wall in the direction of Riff, skirting a gate and a cluster of buildings, laiterie, barn and dovecot, which are all you can see of Red Riff Farm from the lane. I point it out to you as we pass, for we shall come back there later on. Riff is much nearer than you think, for the ground is always falling a little towards the Rieben, which is close at hand though invisible also.

And between the park and the river lies the hidden village of Riff.

You come upon it quite suddenly at the turn of the lane, with its shallow ford, and its pink-plastered cottages sprinkled among its high trees, and its thatched Vicarage, and " The Hermitage " with" the honeysuckle over the porch, and the almshouses near the great Italian gates of Hulver Manor, and somewhat apart in its walled garden among its twisted

pines the Dower House where Lady Louisa Manvers was living, poor soul, at the time this story was written.

I have only to close my eyes and I can see it all—can imagine myself sitting with the Miss Blinketts in their little parlour at The Hermitage, with a daguerreotype of the defunct P£re

Blinkett over the mantelpiece, and Miss Amy's soft voice saying, " They do say Lady Louisa's cook is leaving to be married. But they will say anything at RifF. I never believe more than half I hear."

The Hermitage stood on a little slice of ground which fell away from the lane. So close was The Hermitage to the lane, and the parlour windows were so low, and the lane beyond the palings so high, that the inmates could only guess at the identity of the passers-by by their legs. And rare guests and rarer callers, arriving in the wagonnette from the Manvers Arms, could actually look into the bedroom windows, while the Miss Blinketts' eyes, peering over the parlour muslins, were fixed upon their lower limbs.

And if I keep my eyes tightly shut and the eyes of memory open, I can see as I sit stroking Miss Blinkett's cat the legs of the new Vicar pass up the lane outlined against a lilac skirt. And Miss Amy, who is not a close observer of life, opines that the skirt belongs to Miss Janey Manvers, but Miss Blinkett senior instantly identifies it as Annette's new spotted muslin, which she had seen Mrs. Nicholls " getting up " last week.

But that was twenty years ago. I can only tell you what Riff was like then, for it is twenty years since I was there, and I am not going there any more, for I don't want to see any of the changes which time must have wrought there, and if I walked down the village street now I should feel like a ghost, for only a few of the old people would remember me. And the bright-eyed, tow-headed little lads whom I taught in Sunday school are scattered to the four winds of heaven. The Boer War took some of them, and London has engulfed more, only a few remaining at Riff as sad-looking middle-aged men, farm hands, and hedgers and ditchers, and cowmen.

And I hear that now the motors go banging along the Yarmouth high road day and night, and that Riff actually has a telegraph office of its own and that the wires go in front of The Hermitage, only the Miss Blinketts are not there to see it. A literary lady lives there now, and I hear she has changed the name to " Quill Cottage," and has made a garden in the orchard where old Nan's cottage was by the twisted pear tree : old Nan the witch, who grew mistletoe in all the trees in her domain, and cured St. Vitus' dance with it. No, I will not go to Riff any more, for I do not want to see any of these things, and least of all the literary lady who is writing her novels in the quiet rooms where my two old friends knitted and read Thomas a Kemp is.

Twenty years ago, in the days when my father was doctor at Riff and when Annette came to live there, we could not help noticing— indeed, Mrs. Nicholls often mentioned it—what a go-ahead place Riff was, far more up to date than Sweet Apple Tree, and even than Meverly Mill. We measured everything in those days by Sweet Apple Tree, and the measurement was always in our favour. We did not talk much about Riebenbridge, where the " 'Sizes" were held, and the new " 'Sylum" had just been built. We were somewhat awed by Riebenbridge, but poor lag-behind Sweet Apple Tree, lost amid its reeds together with the Rieben, was the subject of sincere pity to the Riff folk. The Sweet Appiers, according to Mrs. Nicholls, were " that clunch they might have been brought up in a wood." At Riff everything was cast in a superior and more modern mould. Riff had a postman on a bicycle with an enormous front wheel, and if he brought a letter in the morning you could if necessary post an answer to it the same day in the red slit in the churchyard wall. Now at Sweet Apple Tree the old man in a donkey-cart blowing on a little horn who brought the Sweet Apple letters, took away directly the donkey was rested those which the inhabitants had just composed. And even he did not call if " the water was out. 1 '

Before I was born, when the Miss Blinketts were young and crinolined and their father was Vicar of Riff, Sweet Apple Tree, as they have often told me, had no choir, and the old

Rector held a service once or twice a year in his Bath chair. After he took to his bed there was no service at all for twenty years. No wonder the Sweet Apple folk were " clunch " ! How different from Riff, with its trombone and fiddle inviting the attention of its Creator every Sunday, and Mr. Blinkett, whose watchword was "No popery," preaching in his black gown two sermons a week to the favoured people of Riff.

It was Mr. Jones, Mr. Blinkett's successor, that lamentable person, meaning well, but according to the Miss Blinketts quite unable to perceive when a parish was worked on the right lines, it was young Mr. Jones from Oxford, who did not marry either of the Miss Blinketts, but who did put a stop to the trombone and fiddle, and actually brought the choir out of the gallery, and took away the hour-glass from the south window below the pulpit, and preached in his surplice, and made himself very unpopular by forbidding the congregation to rise to its feet when the Manvers family came into church, almost as unpopular as by stopping the fiddle. You can see the old fiddle still in the cottage of Hesketh the carrier, next the village stocks. His father had played on it, and turned "chapel" when his services were no longer required. And 6

it was young Mr. Jones who actually had the bad taste openly to deplore the saintly Blinkett's action in demolishing all the upper part of the ancient carved and gilded screen because at eighty he could no longer make his voice heard through it.

It was, of course, Mr. Jones who started the mixed choir sitting in the chancel behind the remains of the screen.

In the last days of the mixed choir, when first Mr. Black came to Riff (after Mr. Jones was made a bishop), Annette sang in it, with a voice that seemed to me, and not to me only, like the voice of an angel.

With the exception of Annette and the under-housemaid from the Dower House, it was mainly composed of admirable domestic characters of portly age—the 6lite of Riff—supplemented by a small gleaning of deeply virtuous, non-fruit-stealing little boys. We are told nowadays that heredity is nothing. But when I remember how those starched and white-collared juvenile singers were nearly all the offspring of the tenors and basses, and of Mrs. Nicholls and Mrs. Cocks who were trebles, I feel the last word still remains to be said about heredity.

Annette did not sing in it long—not more than a year, I think. It was soon after she left it that Mr. Black—so I am told—started a surpliced choir. And here am I talking about her leaving the choir when I have not yet told you of her arrival in Lowshire, or anything about Red Riff

Farm where her two aunts lived, and where Aunt Maria wrote her famous novel, The Silver Cross, of which you have of course often heard, and which if you are of a serious turn of mind you have doubtless read and laid to heart.

CHAPTER X

" Nothing is so incapacitating as self-love."

RED RIFF FARM stands near the lane, between the village and the high road, presenting its back to all comers with British sang-froid. To approach it you must go up the wide path between the barn and the dovecote on one side, and on the other the long, low laiterie standing above its wall, just able to look at itself in the pool, where the ducks are breaking up its reflection. When you pass through the narrow iron gateway in the high wall which protects the garden on the north side, the old Jacobean house rises up above you> all built of dim rose-red and dim blue brick, looking benignly out across the meadows over its small enclosed garden which had once been the orchard, in which some of the ancient bent apple trees are still like old pensioners permitted to remain.

When Annette first passed through that gateway, the beautiful dim old building with its latticed windows peered at her through a network of apple blossom. But now the apple trees have long since dropped their petals, and

you can see the house clearly, with its wavering

tiled string courses, and its three rounded gables, and the vine flung half across it.

The low, square oak door studded with nails stands wide open, showing a glimpse of a small panelled hall with a carved black staircase coming down into it.

We need not peer in through the window at the Shakespeare Calendar on Aunt Maria's study table to see what time of year it is, for everything tells us : the masses of white pinks crowding up to the threshold and laying their sweet heads against the stone edging of their domain, the yellow lichen in flower on the roof, the serried ranks of Sweet William full out. It is certainly early June. And the black-faced sheep moving sedately in the long meadows in front of the house confirm us in our opinion, for they have shed their becoming woollen overalls and are straddling about, hideous to behold, in their summer tights. Only the lambs, now large and sedate, keep their pretty February coats, though by some unaccountable fatality they have all, poor dears, lost their tails.

Lowshire is a sedate place. I have never seen those solemn Lowshire lambs jump about as they do in Hampshire. A Hampshire lamb among his contemporaries with the juice of the young grass in him ! Hi ! Friskings and caperings ! That is a sight to make an old ram young. But the Lowshire lambs seem ever to see the shadow of the blue-coated butcher in the sunshine. They move in decorous bands as if

they were going to church, hastening suddenly all together as if they were late.

Lowshire is a sedate place. The farm lads still in their teens move as slowly as the creeping rivers, much slower than the barges. The boys early leave off scurrying in shouting bands down the lanes in the dusk. The little girls peep demurely over the garden gates, and walk slowly indoors, if spoken to.

We have ascertained that it is early June, and we need no watch to tell us what o'clock it is. It is milking-time, the hour when good little boys " whom mother can trust " are to be seen hurrying in an important manner with milk-cans. Half-past four it must be, for the red cows, sweet-breathed and soft-paced, have passed up the lane half an hour ago, looking gently to right and left with lustrous, nunlike eyes, now and then putting out a large red tongue to lick at the hedgerow. Sometimes, as to-day, the bull precedes them, hustling along, surly, affairé, making a low, continuous grunting which is not anger, for he is kind as bulls go, so much as " orkardness," the desire of the egotist to make his discontentment public, and his disillusionment with his pasture and all his gentle-tempered wives.

Annette came down the carved staircase, and stood a moment in the doorway in a pale lilac gown (the same that you will remember the Miss Blinketts saw half an hour later).

Her ear caught the sound of a manly voice mingled with Aunt Maria's dignified tones, and the somewhat agitated accompaniment of the clink of tea-things. Aunt Harriet was evidently more acutely undecided than usual which cup to fill first, and was rattling them in the way that always irritated Aunt Maria, though she made heroic efforts to dissimulate it.

Annette came to the conclusion that she should probably be late for choir practice if she went into the drawing-room. So she walked noiselessly across the hall and slipped through the garden. A dogcart was standing horseless in the courtyard, and the delighted female laughter which proceeded from the servants' hall showed that a male element in the shape of a groom had been added to the little band of women-servants.

What a fortunate occurrence that there should be a caller !—for on this particular afternoon Aunt Maria had reached a difficult place in her new book, the hero having thrown over his lady-love because she, foolish modernist that she was, toying with her life's happiness, would not promise to leave off smoking. The depressed authoress needed a change of thought. And it would be pleasant for the whole household if Aunt Harriet's mind could be diverted from the fact that her new air-cushion leaked ; not the old black one, that would not have mattered so much, but the new round red society one which she used when there were visitors in

the house. Aunt Harriet's mind had brooded all day over the air-cushion as mournfully as a hart's tongue over a well.

Annette hoped it was a cheerful caller. Perhaps it was Canon Wetherby from Rieben-bridge, an amiable widower, and almost as great an admirer of Aunt Maria's works as of his own stock of anecdotes.

In the meanwhile if she, Annette, missed her own lawful tea at home, to which of the little colony of neighbours in the village should she go for a cup, on her way to the church, where choir practice was held ?

To the Dower House? Old Lady Louisa Manvers had ceased to come downstairs at all, and her daughter Janey, a few years older than herself, poor downtrodden Janey, would be only too glad to see her. But then her imbecile brother Harry, with his endless copy-book remarks, would be certain to be having tea with her, and Lady Louisa's trained nurse, whom Annette particularly disliked. No, she would not go to the Dower House this afternoon. She might go to tea with the Miss Blinketts, who were always kind to her, and whose cottage lay between her and the church.

The two Miss Blinketts were about the same age as the Miss Nevills, and regarded them with deep admiration, not unmixed with awe, coupled with an evident hope that a pleasant intercourse might presently be established between The Hermitage and Red Riff Farm.

They were indeed quite excited at the advent among them of one so gifted as the author of Crooks and Coronets, who they perceived from her books took a very high view of the responsibility created by genius.

Annette liked the Miss Blinketts, and her knowledge of Aunt Maria's character had led her to hope that this enthusiastic deference might prove acceptable to a wearied authoress in her hours of relaxation. But she soon found that the Miss Nevills with all the prestige of London and a literary milieu resting upon them were indignant at the idea that they could care to associate with " a couple of provincial old maids/'

Their almost ferocious attitude towards the amiable Miss Blinketts had been a great shock to Annette, who neither at that nor at any later time learned to make the social distinctions which occupied so much of her two aunts' time. The Miss Nevills' acceptance of a certain offering of ferns peeping through the meshes of a string bag brought by the Miss Blinketts, had been so frigid, so patrician, that it had made Annette more friendly than she would naturally have been. She had welcomed the ferns with enthusiasm, and before she had realized it, had become the object of a sentimental love and argus-eyed interest on the part of the inmates of The Hermitage which threatened to have its embarrassing moments.

No, now she came to think of it, she would
not go to tea with the Miss Blinketts this afternoon.

Of course, she might go to the Vicarage. Miss Black, the Vicar's sister who kept house for him, had often asked her to do so before choir practice. But Annette had vaguely felt of late that Miss Black, who had been very cordial to her on her arrival and was still extremely polite, did not regard her with as much favour as at first : in fact, that as Mr. Black formed a high and ever higher opinion of her, that of his sister was steadily lowered to keep the balance even.

Annette knew what was the matter with Mr. Black, though that gentleman had not yet discovered what it was that was affecting his usually placid temper and causing him on his parochial rounds so frequently to take the short cut past Red Riff Farm.

She had just decided, without emotion but with distinct regret, that she must do without tea this afternoon, when a firm step came along the lane behind -her, and Mr. Black overtook her. For once he had taken that short cut to some purpose, though his face, fixed in a dignified preoccupation, gave no hint that he felt Fortune had favoured him at last.

The Miss Blinketts had heard it affirmed " by one who knew a wide sweep of clergy and was therefore competent to form an opinion," that Mr. Black was the handsomest vicar in the diocese. But possibly that was not high

praise, for the clergy had evidently deteriorated in appearance since the ancient Blinkett, that type of aristocratic beauty, had been laid to rest under the twisted yew in the Riff churchyard.

But, anyhow, Mr. Black was sufficiently good-looking to be called handsome in a countryside where young unmarried men were rare as water ousels. He was tall and erect, and being rather clumsily built, showed to great advantage in a surplice. In a procession of clergy you would probably have picked out Mr. Black at once as its most impressive figure. He was what the Miss Blinketts called " stately." When you looked closely at him you saw that his nose was a size too large, that his head and ears and hands and feet were all a size too large for him. But the general impression was pleasant, partly because he always looked as if he had that moment emerged as speckless as his surplices from Mrs. NichohV washtub.

It was an open secret that Mrs. Nicholls thought but little of Miss Black, " who wasn't so to call a lady, and washed her flannels at home." But she had a profound admiration for the Vicar, though I fear if the truth were known it was partly because he " set off a surplice so as never was."

Mr. Black allowed his thoughtful expression to lighten to a grave smile as he walked on beside Annette, determined that on this occasion he would not be commonplace or didactic, as he feared he had been after the boot and shoe club.

He was under the illusion, because he had so often said so, that he seldom took the trouble to do himself justice socially. It might be as well to begin now.

" Are you on your way to choir practice ? "

11 What a question 1 Of course I am."

11 Have you had tea ? "

" No." "

" Neither have I. Do come to the Vicarage first, and Angela will give us some." " Angela " was Miss Black.

Annette could not find any reason for refusing.

" Thank you. I will come with pleasure."

" I would rather go without any meal than tea."

Mr. Black felt as he said it that this sentiment was for him inadequate, but he was relieved that Annette did not appear to find it so. She smiled and said—

" It certainly is the pleasantest meal in the day."

At this moment, the Miss Blinketts and I saw, as I have already told you, the legs of the Vicar pass up the lane outlined against a lilac skirt. We watched them pass in silence, and then Miss Blinkett said solemnly—

" If anything should come of that, if he should eventually make up his mind to marry, I consider Annette would be in every way a worthy choice."

" Papa was always against a celibate clergy," said Miss Amy, as if that settled the question.

Annette and her possible future had nearly reached the Vicarage when a dogcart passed them which she recognized as the one she had seen at Red Riff. The man in it waved his hand to Mr. Black.

" That was Mr. Reginald Stirling, the novelist," Mr. Black volunteered.

" The man who wrote The Magnet ? "

" Yes. He has rented Noyes Court from Lady Louisa. I hear he never attends divine service at Noyes, but I am glad to say he has been to Riff several times lately. I am afraid Bartlett's sermons are not calculated to attract an educated man."

Mr. Black was human, and he was aware that he was a good preacher.

11 I have often heard of him from Mrs. Stoddart," said Annette, with evident interest. " I supposed he lived in Lowshire because some of the scenes in The Magnet are laid in this country."

" Are they ? I had not noticed it," said Mr. Black frigidly.

He had often wished he could interest Annette in conversation, often wondered why he seemed unable to do so. Was it really because he did not take enough trouble, as he sometimes accused himself ? But now that she was momentarily interested he stopped short at once, as at the entrance of a blind alley. What he really wanted was to talk, not about Mr. Stirling but about himself, to tell her how he found good in every one, how attracted he was to the ignorant

and the simple. No. He did not exactly desire to tell her these things, but to coerce the conversation into channels which would show indubitably that he was the kind of man who could discover the good latent in every one, the kind of man who fostered the feeble aspirations of the young and the ignorant, who entered with wide-minded sympathy into the difficulties of stupid people, who was better read and more humorous than any of his clerical brethren in Lowshire, to whom little children and dogs turned intuitively as to a friend.

Now, it is not an easy thing to enter lightly into conversation if you bring with you into it so many impedimenta. There was obviously no place for all this heavy baggage in the discussion of Mr. Stirling's novels. So that eminent writer was dismissed at once, and the subject was hitched, not without a jolt, on to the effect of the Lowshire scenery on Mr. Black. It transpired that Mr. Black was the kind of man who went for inspiration to the heathery moor, and who found that the problems of life are apt to unravel themselves under a wide expanse of sky.

Annette listened dutifully and politely till the Vicarage door was reached.

It seemed doubtful afterwards, when he reviewed what he had said, whether he had attained to any really prominent conversational peaks during that circumscribed parley.

He felt with sudden exasperation that he

needed time, scope, opportunity, lots of opportunity, so that if he missed one there would be plenty more, and above all absence of interruption. He never got a chance of really talking to her.

CHAPTER XI

" It ain't the pews and free seats as knows what music is, nor it ain't the organist. It is the choir. There's more in music than just ketching a tune and singing it fort here and pianner there. But Lot ! Miss, what do the pews and the free seats know of the dangers ? When the Vicar gives them a verse to sing by themselves it do make me swaller with embarrassment to hear 'em beller.

They knows nothing, and they fears nothing." — MRS. NICHOLLS.

ON this particular evening Annette was the first to take her seat in the chancel beyond the screen, where the choir practices always took place. Mrs. Nicholls presently joined her there with her battered part-book, and she and Annette went over the opening bars of the new anthem, which like the Riff bull was " orkard " in places.

Mr. Black was lighting the candles on long iron sticks, while Miss Black adjusted herself to the harmonium, which did the organ's drudgery for it, and then settled herself, notebook in hand, to watch which of the choir made an attendance.

Miss Black was constantly urging her brother to do away with the mixed choir and have a surpliced one. She became even more urgent on that head after Annette had joined it. Mr.

Black was nothing loth, but his bishop, who had but recently instituted him, had implored him not to make a clean sweep of every arrangement of his predecessor, Mr. Jones, that ardent reformer, whose principal reforms now needed reforming. So, with laudable obedience and zeal, Mr. Black possessed his soul in patience and sought to instil new life into the mixed choir. Annette was part of that new life, and her presence helped to reconcile him to its continued existence, and to increase Miss Black's desire for its extinction.

Miss Black was older than her brother, and had already acquired that acerb precision which lies in wait with such frequent success for middle-aged spinsters and bachelors.

She somehow gave the comfortless impression of being u ready-made " and " greatly reduced," as if there were quantities more exactly like her put away somewhere, the supply having hopelessly exceeded the demand. She looked as if she herself, as well as her fatigued elaborate clothes, had been picked up half-price but somewhat crumpled in the sales.

She glanced with disapproval at Annette whispering amicably with Mrs. Nicholls, and Annette desisted instantly.

The five little boys shuffled in in a bunch, as if roped together, and slipped into their seats under Mr. Black's eye. Mr. Chipps the grocer and principal bass followed, bringing with him an aroma of cheese. The two altoes f 7

Miss Pontifex and Miss Spriggs, from the Infants' School, were already in position. A few latecomers seemed to have dropped noiselessly into their seats from the roof, and to become visible by clearings of throats.

Mr. Black, who was chagrined by the very frigid reception and the stale tea which his sister had accorded to Annette, said with his customary benignity, " Are we all here ? I think we may as well begin."

Miss Black remarked that the choirmaster, Mr. Spillcock, was " late again," just as that gentleman was seen advancing like a ramrod up the aisle.

A certain mystery enveloped Mr. Spillcock. He was not a Riff man, nor did he hail from Noyes, or Heyke, or Swale, or even Rieben-bridge. What had brought him to live at Riebenbridge no one rightly knew, not even Mrs. Nicholls. It was whispered that he had " bugled " before Royalty in outlandish parts, and when Foreign Missions were being practised he had been understood to aver that the lines,

" Where Afric's sunny fountains Roll down their golden sand,"

put him forcibly in mind of the scenes of his earlier life. Whether he had really served in the army or not never transpired, but his grey moustache was twirled with military ferocity, and he affected the bearing and manner of a retired army man. It was also whispered that

Mrs. Spillcock, a somewhat colourless, depressed mate for so vivid a personality, " was preyed upon in her mind " because another lady had a prior or church claim to the title of Mrs.

Spillcock. As a child I always expected the real Mrs. Spillcock to appear, but she never did.

" Good evening all," said Mr. Spillcock urbanely, and without waiting for any remarks on the lateness of the hour, he seized out of his waistcoat pocket a tuning-fork. "We begin, I presume, with the anthem ' Now hunto 'Im.' Trebles, take your do. Do, me, sol, do. Do." Mr. Spillcock turned towards the trebles with open mouth, uttering a prolonged falsetto do, and showing all his molars on the left side, where apparently he held do in reserve.

Annette guided Mrs. Nicholls and Mrs. Cocks and the timid under-housemaid from the Dower House from circling round the note to the note itself.

" Do," sang out all the trebles with sweetness and decision.

"Now, then, boys, why don't you fall in?" said Mr. Spillcock, looking with unconcealed animosity at the line of little boys whom he ought not to have disliked, as they never made any sound in the church, reserving their voices for shouting on their homeward way in the dark.

" Now, then, boys, look alive. Take up your do from the ladies."

A faint buzzing echo like the sound in an

unmusical shell could be detected by the optimists nearest to the boys. It would have been possible to know they were in tune only by holding their bodies to your ear.

" They have got it," said Mr. Black valiantly.

Mr. Spillcock looked at them with cold contempt.

" Altoes, me," he said more gently. He was gallant to the fair sex, and especially to Miss Pontifex and Miss Spriggs, one dark and one fair, and both in the dew of their cultured youth.

" Altoes, take your me."

The two altoes, their lips ready licked, burst into a plaintive bleat, which if it was not me was certainly nothing else.

The miller, the principal tenor, took his sol, supported at once by " the young chap " from the Manvers Arms, who echoed it manfully directly it had been unearthed, and by his nephew from Lowestoft, who did not belong to the choir and could not sing, but who was on a holiday and who always came to choir practices with his uncle, because he was courting either Miss Pontifex or Miss Spriggs, possibly both. I have a hazy recollection of hearing years later that he had married them both, not at the same time, but one shortly after the other, and that Miss Spriggs made a wonderful mother to Miss Pontifex's baby, or vice versa. Anyhow, they were both in love with him, and I know it ended happily for every one, and was con-

sidered in Riff to be a great example to Mr. Chipps of portly years, who had been engaged for about twenty years " as you might say off and on " to Mrs. Cocks' sister (who was cook at the Dower House), but who, whenever the question of marriage was introduced, opined that " he felt no call to change his state/'

Mr. Black made several ineffectual attempts to induce the basses to take their lower do. But Mr. Chipps, though he generally succumbed into singing an octave below the trebles, had conscientious scruples about starting on the downward path even if his part demanded it, and could not be persuaded to make any sound except a dignified neutral rumbling. The other basses naturally were not to be drawn on to dangerous ground while their leader held aloof.

" We shall drop into it later on," said Mr. Black hopefully, who sat with them. " We had better start."

" Pom, pom, pom, pom," said Mr. Spillcock, going slowly down the chord, and waving a little stick at trebles, altoes, tenors, and basses in turn at each pom.

Every one made a note of sorts, with such pleasing results, something so far superior to anything that Sweet Apple Tree could produce, that it was felt to be unchivalrous on the part of

Mr. Spillcock to beat his stick on the form and say sternly—

" Altoes, it's Hay. Not Hay flat."

" Pommmm ! " in piercing falsetto.

The altoes took up their note again, caught it as it were with a pincers from Mr. Spillcock's back molars.

"Righto," said Mr. Spillcock. "Altoes, if you find yourselves going down, keep yourselves hup. Now hunto 'Im."

And the serious business of the practice began.

CHAPTER XII

" Not even in a dream hast thou known compassion . . . thou knowest not even the phantom of pity; but the silver hair will remind thee of all this by and by."— CALLIMACHUS.

THE Dower House stands so near to the church that Janey Manvers sitting by her bedroom window in the dusk could hear fragments of the choir practice over the low ivied wall which separates the churchyard from the garden. She could detect Annette's voice taking the same passage over and over again, trying to lead the trebles stumbling after her. Presently there was a silence, and then her voice rose sweet and clear by itself—

" They shall hunger no more, neither thirst any more, neither shall the sun light on them, nor any heat:'

The other voices surged up, and Janey heard no more.

Was it possible there really was a place somewhere where there was no more hunger and thirst, and beating, blinding heat ? Or were they only pretty words to comfort where no comfort was ? Janey looked out where one soft star hung low in the dusk over the winding river and its poplars. It seemed to her that night as if she had reached the end of her strength.

For years, since her father died, she had nursed and sustained her mother, the invalid in the next room, through what endless terrible days and nights, through what scenes of anger and bitterness and despair. Janey had been loyal to one who had never been loyal to her, considerate to one who had ridden rough-shod over her, tender to one who was harsh to her, who had always been harsh. And now her mother, not content with eating up the best years of her daughter's life, had laid her cold hand upon the future, and had urged Janey to promise that after her death she would always keep Harry, her half-witted younger brother, in the same house with her, and protect him from the world on one side and a lunatic asylum on the other. Something desperate had surged up in Janey's heart, and she had refused to give the promise. She could see still her mother's look of impotent anger as she turned her face to the wall, could hear still her hysterical sobbing. She had not dared to remain with her, and Anne the old housemaid was sitting with her till the trained nurse returned from Ipswich, a clever, resourceful woman, who had made herself indispensable to Lady Louisa, and had taken Harry to the dentist—always heretofore a matter difficult of accomplishment.

Janey realized with sickening shame this evening that she had unconsciously looked forward to her mother's death as a time when release would come from this intolerable burden which she had endured for the last seven years. Her poor mother would die some day, and a home would be found for Harry, who never missed anyone if he was a day away from them. And she would marry Roger, dear kind Roger, whom she had loved since she was a small child and he was a big boy. That had been her life, in a prison whose one window looked on a green tree : and poor manacled Janey had strained towards it as a plant strains to the light. Something fierce had stirred within her when she saw her mother's hand trying to block the window. That at any rate must not be touched. She could not endure it. She knew that if she married Roger he would never consent that Harry and his attendants should live in the house with them. What man would ? She felt sure that her mother had realized that contingency and the certainty of Roger's refusal, and hence her determination to wrest a promise from Janey.

She was waiting for her cousin Roger now. He had not said whether he would dine or come in after dinner,—it depended on whether he caught the five o'clock express from Liverpool Street,—but in any case he would come in some time this evening to tell her the result of his mission to Paris. Roger lived within a hundred yards, in the pink cottage with the twirly barge boarding almost facing the church, close by the village stocks.

Janey had put on what she believed to be a pretty gown on his account, it was at any rate a much-trimmed one, and had re-coiled her soft brown hair. The solitude and the darkness had relieved somewhat the strain upon her nerves. Perhaps Roger might after all have accomplished his mission, and her mother might be pacified. Sometimes there had been quiet intervals after these violent outbreaks, which nearly always followed opposition of any kind. Perhaps to-morrow life might seem more possible, not such a nightmare. To-morrow she would walk up to Red Riff and see Annette—lovely, kind Annette—the wonderful new friend who had come into her life. Roger ought to be here, if he were coming to dinner. The choir was leaving the church. Choir practice was never over till after eight. The steps and voices subsided. She lit a match and held it to the clock on the dressing-table. Quarter-past eight. Then Roger was certainly not coming. She went downstairs and ordered dinner to be served.

It was a relief that for once Harry was not present, that she could eat her dinner without answering the futile questions which were his staple of conversation, without hearing the vacant laugh which heralded every remark. She heard the carriage rumble out of the courtyard to meet him. His teeth must have taken longer than usual. Perhaps even Nurse, who had him so entirely under her thumb as a rule, had found him recalcitrant.

As she was peeling her peach the door opened, and Roger came in. If there had been anyone to notice it—but no one ever noticed anything about Janey—they might have seen that as she perceived him she became a pretty woman. A soft red mounted to her cheek, her tired eyes shone, her small, erect figure became alert. He had not dined, after all. She sent for the earlier dishes, and while he ate, refrained from asking him any questions.

" You do not look as tired as I expected," she said.

Roger replied that he was not the least tired There was in his bearing some of the alertness of hers, and she noticed it with a sudden secret uprush of joy in her heart. Surely it was the same for both of them ? To be together was all they needed. But oh ! how she needed that 1 How far greater her need was than his !

They might have been taken for brother and sister as they sat together in the dining-room in the light of the four wax candles.

They were what the village people called " real Manverses," both of them, sturdy, well knit, erect, with short, straight noses, and grey, direct, wide-open eyes, and brown complexions, and crisp brown hair. Each was good-looking in a way. Janey had the advantage of youth, but her life had been more burdened than Roger's, and at five-and-thirty he did not look much older than she did at five-and-twenty, except that he showed a tendency to be square-set, and his hair was thinning a little at the top of his honest, well-shaped head. He was, as Mrs. Nicholls often remarked, " the very statue of the old squire," his uncle and Janey's father.

"Pray don't hurry, Roger. There is plenty of time."

"I'm not hurrying, old girl," with another gulp.

It was a secret infinitesimal grief to Janey that Roger called her " old girl." A hundred little traits showed that she had seen almost nothing of the world, but he, in spite of public school and college, gave the impression of having seen even less. There were a few small tiresomenesses about Roger to which even Janey's faithful adoration could not quite shut its eyes. But they were, after all, only external foibles, such as calling her " old girl," tricks of manner, small gaucheries and gruntings and lapses into inattention, the result of living too much alone, which wise Janey knew were of no real account. The things that really mattered about Roger were his kind heart and his good business-head and his uprightness.

" Never seen Paris before, and don't care if I never see it again," he vouchsafed between enormous mouthfuls. He never listened—at least not to Janey—and his conversation consisted largely of disjointed remarks, thrown out at intervals, very much as unprofitable or waste material is chucked over a wall, without reference to the person whom it may strike on the other side.

" I should like to see Paris myself.'

Roger informed her of the reprehensible and entirely un-British manner in which luggage was arranged for at that metropolis, and of the price of the cabs and the system of pourboires, and how the housemaid at the hotel had been a man. Some of these details of intimate Parisian life had already reached even Janey, but she listened to them with unflagging interest. Do not antiquaries tell us that the extra rib out of which Eve was fashioned was in shape not unlike an ear trumpet ? Janey was a daughter of Eve. She listened.

Presently the servants withdrew, and he leaned back in his chair and looked at her.

" It was no go," he said.

" You mean Dick was worse? "

" Yes. No. I don't know how he was. He looked to me just the same, staring straight in front of him with goggling eyes. Lady Jane said he knew me, but I didn't see that he did. I said, * Holloa, Dick,' and he just gaped. She said he knew quite well all about the business, and that she had explained it to him. And the doctor was there, willing to witness anything : awful dapper little chap, called me Chair Mussieur and held me by the arm, and tried to persuade me, but " Roger shook his head and thrust out his under lip.

" You were right, Roger," said Janey sadly; " but poor mother will be dreadfully angry. And how are you to go on without the power of attorney, if he's not in a fit state to grant it ? "

But Roger was not listening.

" I often used to wonder how Aunt Louisa got Dick to sign before about the sale of the salt marshes—that time when she went to Paris herself—on purpose. But,"—he became darkly red,—" hang it all, Janey, I see now how it was done."

" She shouldn't have sent me," he said, getting up abruptly. " Not the kind for the job. I suppose I had better go up and see her. Expect I shall catch it."

" This man smells not of books."—J. S. BLACKIE.

LADY LOUISA MANVERS was waiting for her nephew, propped up in bed, clutching the bedclothes with leaden, corpse-pale hands. She was evidently at the last stage of some long and terrific illness, and her hold on life seemed as powerless and as convulsive as that of her hands upon the quilt. She felt that she was slipping into the grave, she the one energetic and far-seeing member of the family, and that on her exhausted shoulders lay the burden of arranging everything for the good of her children, for they were totally incapable of doing anything for themselves. In the long nights of unrest and weariness unspeakable, her mind, accustomed to undisputed dominion, revolved perpetually round the future of her children, and the means by which in her handicapped condition she could still bring about what would be best for them, what was essential for their well-being, especially Harry's. And all the while her authority was slipping from her, in spite of her desperate grasp upon it. The whole world and her stubborn children themselves

were in league against her, and the least

opposition on their part aroused in her a paroxysm of anger and despair. Why did every one make her heavy task heavier ? Why was she tacitly disobeyed when a swift and absolute obedience was imperative ? Why did they try to soothe her, and speak smooth things to her, when they were virtually opposing her all the time ? She, a paralysed old woman, only longing for rest, was forced to fight them all single-handed for their sakes.

To-night, as she lay waiting for her nephew, she touched a lower level of despair than even she had yet reached. She suspected that Roger would fail her. Janey had for the first time turned against her. Even Janey, who had always yielded to her, always, always, even she had opposed her—had actually refused to make the promise which was essential to the welfare of poor Harry after she herself was gone. And she felt that she was going, that she was being pushed daily and hourly nearer to the negation of all things, the silence, the impotence of the grave. She determined to act with strength while power to act still remained.

Roger's reluctant step came up the oak staircase, and his tap on the door.

" May I come in ? "

11 Come in."

He came in, and stood as if he were stuffed in the middle of the room, his eyes fixed on the cornice.

" I hope you are feeling better, Aunt Louisa ? "

" I am still alive, as you see."

Deep-rooted jealousy of Roger dwelt in her, had dwelt in her ever since the early days when her husband had adopted him against her wish when he had been left an orphan. She had not wanted him in her nursery. Her husband had always been fond of him, and later in life had leaned upon him. In the depths of her bitter heart Lady Louisa believed he had preferred his nephew to the two sons she had given him, Dick the ne'er-do-well, and Harry the latecomer—the fool.

Roger moved his eyes slowly round the room, looking always away from the bed, till they fell upon the cat curled up in the arm-chair.

" Holloa, puss ! " he said. " Caught a mouse lately ? "

" Did you get the power of attorney? " came the voice from the bed.

" No, Aunt Louisa."

The bed-clothes trembled.

' I told you not to come back without it."

Roger was silent.

" Had not Jane arranged everything ? "

" Everything."

" And the doctor ! Wasn't he there ready to witness it ? "

" Oh Lord ! Yes. He was there." ' Then I fail to understand why you came back without it."

' Dick wasn't fit to sign," said Roger doggedly.

[< Didn't I warn you before you went that he 8 had repeatedly told Jane that he could not attend to business, and that was why it was so important you should be empowered to act for him ?—and the power of attorney was his particular wish."

" Yes, you did. But I didn't know he'd be like that. He didn't know a thing. It didn't seem as if he could have had a particular wish one way or the other. Aunt Louisa, he wasn't fit."

" And so you set up your judgment against mine, and his own doctor's? I told you before you went, what you knew already, that he was not capable of transacting business, and that you must have the power; and you said you understood. And then you come back here and inform me that he was not fit, which you knew before you started."

" No, no. You're wrong there."

How like he was to her dead husband as he said that, and how she hated him for the likeness !

" Don't contradict me. You were asked to act in Dick's own interest and in the interests of the property, and you promised to do it. And you haven't done it."

" But, Aunt Louisa, he wasn't in a state to sign anything. He's not alive. He's just breathing, that's all. Doesn't know anybody, or take any notice. If you'd seen him you'd have known you couldn't get his signature."

" I did get it about the marsh-lands. I went to Paris on purpose last November, when I was too ill to travel. I only sent you this time because I could not leave my bed."

Roger paused, and then his honest face became plum colour, and he blurted out—

" They were actually going to guide his hand."

Lady Louisa's cold eyes met his.

" Well 1 And if they were ? "

Roger lost his embarrassment. His face became as pale as it had been red. He came up to the bed and looked the sick woman straight in the eyes.

" I was not the right man for the job," he said. " You should have sent somebody else. I—stopped it."

" I hope when you are dying, Roger, that your son will carry out your last wishes more effectively than my nephew has carried out mine."

11 But, Aunt Louisa, upon my honour he wasn't "

" Good-night. Ask Janey to send up Nurse to me as soon as she returns."

Roger left the room clumsily, but yet with a certain dignity. His upright soul was shocked to the very core. He marched heavily downstairs to the library, where Janey was keeping his coffee hot for him over a little spirit-lamp. There was indignation in his clear grey eyes. And over his coffee and his cigarette he recounted to her exactly how everything had been, and how Dick wasn't fit, he really wasn't. And

Janey thought that when he had quite finished she would tell him of the pressure her mother was bringing to bear on her to promise to make a home for Harry after her death. But when at last Roger got off the subject, and his cigarette had soothed him, he went on to tell Janey about a man he had met on the boat, who oddly enough turned out to be a cousin of a land agent he knew in Kent. This surprising incident took so long, the approaches having been both gradual and circuitous, and primarily connected with the proffer of a paper, that when it also had been adequately dealt with and disposed of, it was getting late.

" I must be off," he said, rising. " Goodnight, Janey. Keep a brave heart, old girl." He nodded slightly to the room above, which was his aunt's. " Rough on you sometimes, I'm afraid."

11 You always cheer me up," she said, with perfect truthfulness. He had cheered her. It would be a sad world for most of us if it were by our conversational talents that we could comfort those we loved. But Roger believed it was so in his case, and complacently felt that he had broached a number of interesting Parisian subjects, and had refreshed Janey, whom Lady Louisa led a dog's life and no mistake. He was fond of her, and sorry for her beyond measure, and his voice and eyes were very kindly as he bade her good-night. She went to the door with him, and they stood a moment together

in the moonlight under the clustering stars of the clematis. He took his hat and stick and repeated his words : " Keep a brave heart."

She said in a voice which she tried, and failed, to make as tranquil as usual—

" I had been so afraid you weren't coming, that you had missed your train/'

11 Oh no ! I didn't miss it. But just as I got to the gate at eight o'clock I met Miss Georges coming out of the churchyard, and it was pretty dark—moon wasn't up—and I thought I ought to see her home first. That was why I was late."

Janey bade him good-night again, and slipped indoors. The moonlight and the clematis which a moment before had been so full of mysterious meaning were suddenly emptied of all significance.

CHAPTER XIV

" O Life, how naked and how hard when known ! Life said, As thou hast carved me, such am I."

GEORGE MEREDITH.

JANEY lit her bedroom candle with a hand that trembled a little, and in her turn went slowly upstairs.

She could hear the clatter of knives and forks in the dining-room, and Harry's vacant laugh, and Nurse's sharp voice. They had come back, then. She went with an effort into her mother's room, and sat down in her accustomed chair by the bed.

" It is ten o'clock. Shall I read, mother ? "

11 Certainly."

It was the first time they had spoken since she had been ordered out of the room earlier in the day.

Janey opened the Prayer Book on the table by the bedside, and read a psalm and a chapter from the Gospel:—

" Come unto Me, all ye that labour and are heavy laden, and I will give you rest. Take My yoke upon you, and learn of Me; for I am meek and lowly in heart : and ye shall find rest for your souls. For My yoke is easy, and My burden is light."

Janey closed the book, and said timidly, " May I stay until Nurse comes up? "

" Pray do exactly what you like."

She did not move.

" I am heavy laden," said her mother. " I don't suppose you have ever given it one moment's thought what it must be like to lie like a log as I do."

Her daughter dared not answer.

"How many months have I lain in this room?"

"Eight months."

"Ever since I went to Paris last October. I was too ill to go, but I went."

Silence.

"I am heavy laden, but it seems I must not look to you for help, Janey."

Janey's heart sickened within her. When had her mother ever relinquished anything if once her indomitable will were set upon it? She felt within herself no force to withstand a second attack.

The nurse came in at that moment, a tall, shrewd, capable woman of five-and-thirty, with a certain remnant of haggard good looks.

"May Mr. Harry come in to say good-night, milady?"

"Yes."

She went to the door and admitted a young man. Harry came and stood beside the bed, looking sheepishly at his mother. If his face had not been slightly vacant, the mouth ajar, he would have been beautiful. As it was, people turned in the street to see him pass. He was tall, fair, well grown, with a delightful smile. He smiled now at his mother, and she tried hard to smile back at him, her rigid face twitching a little.

"Well, my son! Had you a nice day in Ipswich?"

'Yes, mamma."

"And I hope you were brave at the dentist's, and that he did not hurt you much?"

"Oh no, mamma. He did not hurt me at all."

"Not at all?" said his mother, surprised.

The nurse stepped forward at once.

"Mr. Harry did not have his tooth out, milady."

"No," said Harry slowly, looking at the nurse as if he were repeating a lesson, "the tooth was not taken out. It was not."

"Mr. Milson had been called away," continued the nurse glibly.

"Called away," echoed Harry.

"Then the expedition was all for nothing?" said Lady Louisa wearily.

"Oh no, mamma."

The nurse intervened once more, and recounted how she had taken Harry to have his hair cut, and to buy some gloves, and to an entertainment of performing dogs, and to tea at Frobisher's. They could have been home earlier, but she knew the carriage was ordered to meet the later train.

Harry began to imitate the tricks which the dogs had done, but the nurse peremptorily interrupted him.

"Her ladyship's tired, and it's past ten o'clock. You must tell her about the dogs to-morrow."

"Yes, to-morrow," echoed Harry, and he kissed his mother, and shuffled towards the door. Janey slipped out with him.

Lady Louisa did not speak again while the nurse made the arrangements for the night. She was incensed with her. She had been too peremptory with Harry. It was not for her to order him about in that way. Lady Louisa was beginning to distrust this capable, indefatigable woman, on whom she had become absolutely dependent; and when the nurse had left her for the night, and was asleep in the next room with the door open between, she began to turn over in her mind, not for the first time, the idea of parting with her, and letting Janey nurse her entirely once more,

as she had done at first. Janey with Anne the housemaid to help her could manage perfectly well, whatever the doctor might say. It was not as if she wanted anything doing for her, lying still as she did day after day. She should never have had a trained nurse if her own wishes had been consulted. But when were they ever consulted ? The doctor, who understood
nothing about her illness, had insisted, and Janey had not resisted the idea as she ought to have done. But the whole household could not be run to suit Janey's convenience. She had told her so already more than once. She should tell her so again. Even worms will turn. There were others to be considered besides Janey, who only considered herself.

Lady Louisa's mind left her daughter and went back, as if it had received some subtle warning, to the subject of the nurse. She was convinced by the woman's manner of intervening when she had been questioning Harry, that something had been concealed from her about the expedition to Ipswich. She constantly suspected that there was a cabal against her. She was determined to find out what it was, which she could easily do from Harry. And if Nurse had really disobeyed her, and had taken him on the water, which always excited him, or to a theatre, which was strictly forbidden, then she would make use of that act of disobedience as a pretext for dismissing her, and she would certainly not consent to have anyone else in her place. Having settled this point, she closed her eyes and tried to settle herself to sleep.

But sleep would not come. The diligent little clock, with its face turned to the strip of light shed by the shaded nightlight, recorded in a soft chime half-hour after half-hour. With forlorn anger, she reflected that every creature in the house was sleeping—she could hear Nurse's even breathing close at hand—every one except herself, who needed sleep more than anyone to enable her to get through the coming day. It did not strike her that possibly Janey also might be lying open-eyed through the long hours.

Lady Louisa's mind wandered like a sullen, miserable tramp over her past life. She told herself that all had gone wrong with her, all had cheated her from first to last. It seems to be the doom of the egoist to crave for things for which he has no real value, on which when acquired he can only trample. Lady Louisa had acquired a good deal and had trampled heavily on her acquisitions, especially on her kindly, easy-tempered husband who had loved her. And how throughout her whole life she had longed to be loved!

To thirst voraciously to be loved, to have sufficient acumen to perceive love to be the only real bulwark, as it is, against the blows of fate; the only real refuge, as it is, from grief; the one sure consolation, as it is, in the recurring anguished ache of existence,—to perceive that life is not life without it, and then to find that love when appropriated and torn out of its shrine is no talisman, but only a wearisome, prosaic clog quickly defaced by being dragged in the dust up the thorny path of our egotism! Is there any disappointment so bitter, so devastating as that? Lady Louisa, poor soul, had endured it. She glanced for a moment at the photograph of her husband on the mantelpiece, with his hair brushed forward over his ears. Even death had not assuaged her long-standing grievance against him. Why had he always secretly preferred his nephew Roger to his own sons? Why did he die just after their eldest son Dick came of age? And why had not he left her Hulver for her life, instead of taking for granted that she would prefer to go back to her own house, Noyes Court, a few miles off? She had told him so, but he might have known she had never meant it. She had not wanted to go back to it. She had not gone back, though all her friends and Janey had especially wished it. She had hastily let it to Mr. Stirling the novelist, to show that she should do exactly as she liked, and had made one of those temporary arrangements that with the old are always for life. She had moved into the Dower House for a year, and had been in it seven years.

Her heart swelled with anger as she thought of the conduct of her eldest son after his father's death: and yet could anyone have been a brighter, more delightful child than Dicky? But Dicky had been a source of constant anxiety to her, from the day when he was nearly drowned in the mill-race at Riff to the present hour, when he was lying dying by inches of spinal paralysis at his aunt's house in Paris as the result of a racing accident. What a heartbreaking record his life had been, of one folly, one insane extravagance after another! And shame had not been wanting. He had not even made a foolish marriage, and left a son whom she and Janey could have taken from its mother and educated ; but there was an illegitimate child—a girl—whom Roger had told her about, by a village schoolmistress, an honest woman whom Dick had seduced under promise of marriage.

Perhaps, after all, Lady Louisa had some grounds for feeling that everything had gone against her. Dick was dying, and her second son Harry—what of him ? She was doggedly convinced that Harry was not " wanting " : that " he could help it if he liked." In that case, all that could be said was that he did not like. She stuck to it that his was a case of arrested development, in strenuous opposition to her husband, who had held that Harry's brain was not normal from the awful day when as a baby they first noticed that he always stared at the ceiling. Lady Louisa had fiercely convinced herself, but no one else, that it was the glitter of the old cut-glass chandelier which attracted him. But after a time even she had to own to herself, though never to others, that he had a trick of staring upwards where no chandelier was. Even now, at two-and-twenty, Harry furtively gazed upon the sky, and perhaps vaguely wondered why he could only do so by stealth—why that was one of the innumerable forbidden things among which he had to pick his way, and for which he was sharply reprimanded by that dread personage his mother.

Mr. Manvers on his death-bed had said to Dick in Lady Louisa's presence, " Remember, if you don't have a son, Roger ought to have Hulver. Harry is not fit."

She had never forgiven her husband for trying to denude Harry of his birthright. And to-night she felt a faint gleam of consolation in the surrounding dreariness in the thought that he had not been successful. When Dick died, Harry would certainly come in. On her last visit to Paris she had ransacked Dick's rooms at his training-stable. She had gone through all his papers. She had visited his lawyers. She had satisfied herself that he had not made a will. It was all the more important, as Harry would be very rich, that Janey should take entire and personal charge of him, lest he should fall into the hands of some designing woman. That pretty French adventuress, Miss Georges, who had come to live at Riff and whom Janey had made such friends with, was just the kind of person who might entangle him into marrying her. And then if Roger and Janey should eventually marry, Harry could perfectly well live with them. He must be guarded at all costs. Lady Louisa sighed. That seemed on the whole the best plan. She had looked at it all round. But Janey was frustrating it by refusing to do her part. She must fall into line. To-morrow she would send

for her lawyer and alter her will once more, leaving Noyes to Harry, instead of Janey, as she had done by a promise to her husband. Janey had no one but herself to thank for such a decision. She had forced it on her mother by her obstinacy and her colossal selfishness. What had she done that she of all women should have such selfish children ? Then Janey would have nothing of her own at all, and then she would be so dependent on Harry that she would have no alternative but to do her duty by him.

Lady Louisa sighed again. Her mind was made up. Janey must give way, and the nurse must be got rid of. Those were the two next things to be achieved. Then perhaps she would be suffered to rest in peace.

CHAPTER XV

" And Death stopped knitting at the muffling band. ' The shroud is done,' he muttered, ' toe to chin.' He snapped the ends, and tucked his needles in."

JOHN MASBFULD.

AFTER a sleepless night, and after the protracted toilet of the old and feeble, Lady Louisa tackled her task with unabated determination. She dictated a telegram to her lawyer, sent out the nurse for a walk, and desired Janey to bring Harry to her.

Harry, who was toiling over his arithmetic under the cedar, with the help of a tutor from Riebenbridge and a box of counters, obeyed with alacrity. He looked a very beaming creature, with " fresh morning face," as he came into his mother's room.

" Good morning, mamma."

" Good morning, my son."

The terrible ruler looked benign. She nodded and smiled at him. He did not feel as cowed as usual.

" You can go away, Janey, and you needn't come back till I ring."

" And now tell me all about the performing

dogs," said the terrible ruler in the bed, when Janey had left the room.

Harry saw that she was really interested, and he gave her an exact account, interrupted by the bubbling up of his own laughter, of a dog which had been dressed up as a man in a red coat, with a cocked hat and a gun. He could hardly tell her for laughing. The dread personage laughed too, and said, " Capital! Capital! " And he showed her one of the tricks, which consisted of sitting up on your hind legs with a pipe in your mouth. He imitated exactly how the dog had sat, which in a man was perhaps not quite so mirth-provoking as in a dog. Nevertheless, the dread personage laughed again.

It promised to be an agreeable morning. He hoped it would be a long time before she remembered his arithmetic and sent him back to it, that hopeless guess-work which he sometimes bribed Tommy the gardener's boy to do for him in the tool-shed.

" And then you got your gloves ! " said the dread personage suddenly. " How many pairs was it ? " Harry was bewildered, and stared blankly at her.

' You must remember how many pairs it was." Harry knit his poor brow, rallied his faculties, and said it was two pairs.

11 And now," said Lady Louisa, " you may have a chocolate out of my silver box, and let me hear all about—you know what," and she nodded confidentially at him. 9

But he only gaped at her, half frightened. She smiled reassuringly at him.

" Nurse told me all about it/' she said encouragingly. " That was why you weren't to tell me. She wanted it to be a great surprise to me."

" I wasn't to say a word," said Harry doubtfully,—" not a word—about that"

" No. That was just what Nurse said to me. You weren't to say a single word last night, until she had told me. But now I know all about it, so we can talk. Was it great fun ? "

" I don't know."

"It was great fun when I did it. How I laughed I"

" I didn't laugh. She told me not to."

" Well, no. Not at first. She was quite right. And what did her brother say ? Nurse said he went with you."

" Yes. We called for him, and he went with us, with a flower in his button-hole—a rose it was. He gave me one too."

Harry looked at his button-hole, as if expecting to see the rose still in it. But that sign of merry-making was absent.

Lady Louisa had on a previous occasion severely reprimanded Nurse for taking Harry to tea at her brother's house, a solicitor's clerk in Ipswich. Her spirits rose. She had detected her in an act of flagrant disobedience. And as likely as not they had all gone to a play together.

" Capital! " she said suavely. " He was just

the right person to go with. That was what I said to Nurse. And what did he talk about ? "

" He said, ' Mum's the word. Keep it all quiet till the old cat dies/ and he slapped me on the back and said, ' Mind that, brother-in-law/ He was very nice indeed."

A purple mark like a bruise came to Lady Louisa's clay-coloured cheeks. There was a long pause before she spoke again.

11 And did you write your name nicely, like Janey taught you ? " She spoke with long-drawn gasps, each word articulated with difficulty.

" Yes," said Harry anxiously, awed by the fixity of her eyes upon him. " I did indeed, mamma. I was very particular."

" Your full name ? "

" Yes, the man said my full name—Henry de la Pole Manvers."

" That was the man at the registry office? "

" Yes."

" And "—the voice laboured heavily and was barely audible—" did Nurse write her name nicely too ? "

11 Yes, and her brother and the man. We all wrote them, and then we all had tea at Frobisher's, — only it wasn't tea, — and Nurse's brother ordered a bottle of champagne. Nurse didn't want him to, but he said people didn't get married every day. And he drank our health, and I drank a little tiny sip, and it made me sneeze."

Lady Louisa lay quite motionless, the sweat upon her forehead, looking at her son, who smiled seraphically back at her.

And so Nurse had actually thought she could outwit her —had pitted herself against her ? She would shortly learn a thing or two on that head.

A great cold was invading her. And as she looked at Harry, it was as if some key, some master key, were suddenly and noiselessly turned in the lock. Without moving her eyes, she saw beyond him the door, expecting to see the handle turn, and Nurse or Janey to come in. But the door remained motionless. Nevertheless, a key somewhere had turned. Everything was locked tight—the room, the walls, the bed, herself in it —as in a vice.

11 Go back to your lessons," she said to Harry, " and send Janey to me." She felt a sudden imperative need of Janey.

But Harry, so docile, so schooled to obedience, made no motion to obey her. He only looked vacantly, expectantly at her.

She spoke again, but he paid no heed. She spoke yet again with anger, but this time he was fidgeting with the watch on her table and did not even look up. She saw him as if through a glass screen.

A wave of anger shook her.

" Leave the room this moment, and do as I tell you," she said, with her whole strength.

Had he suddenly became deaf ? Or had she ?

Was she ? A great fear took her. He put back the watch on its stand, and touched the silver box in which the chocolates were kept.

" May I have another—just one other ? " he said, opening it, his voice barely audible through the glass screen.

And then, glancing at her for permission, he was seized with helpless laughter.

" Oh, mamma ! You do look so funny, with your mouth all on one side—funnier than the dog in the hat."

His words and his laughter reached her, faint yet distinct, and she understood what had befallen her. Two large tears gathered in her anguished eyes and then slowly ran down her distorted face. Everything else remained fixed, as in a vice, save Harry, rocking himself to and fro, and snapping his fingers with delight.

CHAPTER XVI

" After all, I think there are only two kinds of people in the world, lovers and egotists. I fear that lovers must smile when they see me making myself comfortable, collecting refined luxuries and a pleasant society round myself, protecting myself from an uneasy conscience by measured ornamental acts of kindness and duty; mounting guard over my health and my seclusion and my liberty. Yes! I have seen them smile."—M. N.

THE violet dusk was deepening and the dew was falling as Annette crossed the garden under the apple trees on her return from the choir practice. There was a light in Aunt Maria's window, which showed that she was evidently grappling with the smoking embroglio which was racking two young hearts. Even a footfall in the passage was apt to scare that shy bird Aunt Maria's genius, so Annette stole on tiptoe to the parlour.

Aunt Harriet, extended on a sofa near a shaded lamp, looked up from her cushions with a bright smile of welcome, and held out both her hands.

Aunt Harriet was the youngest of three sisters, but she had not realized that that fact may in time cease to mean much. It was obvious that she had not yet kissed the rod of

middle age. She had been moderately good-

looking twenty years ago, and still possessed a willowy figure and a slender hand, and a fair amount of ash-coloured hair which she wore in imitation of the then Princess of Wales tilted forward in a dome of innumerable little curls over a longish pinkish face, leaving the thin flat back of her head unmitigated by a coil. Aunt Harriet gave the impression of being a bas-relief, especially on the few occasions on which she stood up, when it seemed as if part of her had become momentarily unglued from the sofa, leaving her spinal column and the back of her head behind.

She had had an unhappy and misunderstood —I mean too accurately understood— existence, during the early years when her elder sister Maria ruthlessly exhorted her to exert herself, and continually frustrated her mild inveterate determination to have everything done for her. But a temporary ailment long since cured and a sympathetic doctor had enabled her to circumvent Maria, and to establish herself for good on her sofa, with the soft-hearted Catherine in attendance. Her unlined face showed that she had found her niche in this uneasy world, and was no longer as in all her earlier years a drifter through life, terrified by the possibility of fatiguing herself. Greatly to her credit, and possibly owing to Catherine's mediation, Aunt Maria accepted the situation, and never sought to undermine the castle, not in Spain but on a sofa, which her sister had erected, and in which

she had found the somewhat colourless happiness of her life.

" Come in, my love, come in," said Aunt Harriet, with playful gaiety. " Come in and sit by me."

Her love came in and sat down obediently on the low stool by her aunt's couch, that stool to which she was so frequently beckoned, on which it was her lot to hear so much advice on the subject of the housekeeping and the management of the servants.

" I think, Annette, you ought to speak to Hodgkins about the Albert biscuits. I know I left six in the tin yesterday, and there were only four to-day. I went directly I was down to count them. It is not good for her to take the dining-room Alberts and then to deny it, as she did the other day. So I think it will be best if I don't move in the matter, and if you mention it as if you had noticed it yourself." Or, " There was a cobweb on my glass yesterday. I think, dearest, you must not overlook that. Servants become very slack unless they are kept up to their work." Aunt Harriet was an enemy of all slackness, idleness, want of energy, shirking in all its branches. She had taken to reading Emerson of late, and often quoted his words that " the only way of escape in all the worlds of God was performance."

Annette would never have kept a servant if she had listened to her aunt's endless promptings. But she did not listen to them. Her placid, rather happy-go-lucky temperament made her forget them at once.

" Have you had supper, dear child ? "

" Not yet. I will go now."

" And did you remember to take a lozenge as you left the church? "

" I am afraid I forgot."

" Ah ! my dear, it's a good thing you have some one to look after you and mother you. It's not too late to take one now."

" I should like to go and have supper now. I am very hungry."

" I rejoice to hear it. It is wonderful to me how you can do without a regular meal on choir nights. If it had been me, I should have fainted. But sit down again for one moment. I have something to tell you. You will never guess whom we have had here."

" I am sure I never shall." ' You know how much Maria thinks of literary people?"

" Yes."

" I don't care for them quite so much as she does. I am more drawn to those who have suffered, whose lives have been shattered like glass as my own life has been, and who gather up the fragments that remain and weave a beautiful embroidery out of them."

Annette knew that her aunt wanted her to say, " As you do yourself."

She considered a moment and then said, " You are thinking of Aunt Catherine."

Aunt Harriet was entirely nonplussed. She felt unable to own that she had no such thought. She sighed deeply, and said after a pause, " I don't want it repeated, Annette,—I learned long ago that it is my first duty to keep my troubles to myself, to consume my own smoke,—but my circulation has never been normal since the day Aunt Cathie died."

Then after a moment she added, with sudden brightness, as one who relumes the torch on which a whole household depends—

" But you have not guessed who our visitor was, and what a droll adventure it all turned out. How I did laugh when it was all over and he was safely out of hearing! Maria said there was nothing to laugh at, but then she never sees the comic side of things as I do."

" I begin to think it must have been Canon Wetherby, the clergyman who told you that story about the parrot who said ' Damn ' at prayers, and made Aunt Maria promise not to put it in one of her books."

" She will, all the same. It is too good to be lost. No, it was not Canon Wetherby. But you will never guess. I've never known you guess anything, Annette. You are totally devoid of imagination, and ah ! how much happier your life will be in consequence. I shall have to tell you. It was Mr. Reginald Stirling."

"The novelist?"

" Yes, and you know Maria was beginning to feel a little hurt because he hadn't called, as they are both writers. There is a sort of freemasonry in these things, and, of course, in a neighbourhood like this we naturally miss very much the extremely interesting literary society to which we were accustomed in London, and in which Maria especially shone. But anyhow he came at last, and he was quite delightful. Not much to look at. Not Mr. Harvey's presence, but most agreeable. And he seemed to know all about us. He said he went to Riff Church sometimes, and had seen our youngest sister in the choir. How I laughed after he was gone! I often wish the comic side did not appeal to me quite so forcibly. To think of poor me, who have not been to church for years, boldly holding forth in the choir, or Maria, dear Maria, who only knows ' God save the Queen ' because every one gets up : as Canon Wetherby said in his funny way, ' Does not know " Pop goes the Queen " from " God save the weasel/ 1 ' Maria said afterwards that probably he thought you were our younger sister, and that sent me off into fits again."

" I certainly sit hi the choir/ 1

"He was much interested in the house too, and said it was full of old-world memories."

" Did he really say that? " Annette's face fell.

"No. Now I come to think of it, / said that, and he agreed. And his visit, and his conversation about Mrs. Humphry Ward, comparing David Grieve and Robert Elsmere, quite cured dear Maria's headache, and we agreed that

neither of us would tell you about it in the absence of the other, so that we might make you guess. So remember, Annette, when Maria comes in, you don't know a word, a single word, of what I've told you."

Aunt Maria came in at that moment, and sat down on the other side of the fire.

Aunt Maria was a short, sacklike woman between fifty and sixty, who had long since given up any pretensions to middle age, and who wore her grey hair parted under a little cap. Many antagonistic qualities struggled for precedence in Aunt Maria's stout, uneasy face: benevolence and irritability, self-consciousness and absent-mindedness, a suspicious pride and the self-depreciation which so often dogs it; and the fatigue of one who daily and hourly is trying to be " an influence for good," with little or no help from temperament. Annette had developed a compassionate affection for both her aunts, now that they were under her protection, but the greater degree of compassion was for Aunt Maria.

" Aunt Harriet will have told you who has been to see us," she said as a matter of course.

Aunt Harriet fixed an imploring glance on Annette, who explained that she had seen a dogcart in the courtyard, and how later she had seen Mr. Stirling driving in it.

" I wished, Harriet," said Aunt Maria, without looking at her sister," that you had not asked him if he had read my books."

" But he had, Maria. He was only doubtful the first minute, till I told him some of the names, and then "

" Then the poor man perjured himself."

" And I thought that was so true how he said to you, (You and I, Miss Nevill, have no time in our hard-worked lives to read even the best modern fiction/ "

" I found time to read The Magnet" said Aunt Maria in a hollow voice.

At this moment the door opened and Hodgkins the parlour-maid advanced into the room bearing a tray, which she put down in an aggressive manner on a small table beside Annette.

" I am certain Hodgkins is vexed about something/' said Aunt Harriet solemnly, when that functionary had withdrawn. " I am as sensitive as a mental thermometer to what others are feeling, and I saw by the way she set the tray down that she was angry. She must have guessed that I've found out about the Alberts."

11 Perhaps she guessed that Annette was starving," said Aunt Maria.

CHAPTER XVII

" Life is like a nest in the winter, The heart of man is always cold therein."
Roumanian Folk Song.

THE lawyer who was to have altered Lady Louisa's will was sent away as soon as he arrived. No one knew why she had telegraphed for him. She had had a second stroke, and with it the last vestige of power dropped from her numb hands. She was unable to speak, unable to move, unable even to die.

Janey sat by her for days together in a great compassion, not unmixed with shame. Every one, Roger included, thought she was overwhelmed by the catastrophe which had befallen her mother, and he made shy, clumsy attempts at consolation, little pattings on the back, invitations to " come out and have a look at the hay harvest." But Janey was stunned by the thought that she was in danger of losing not her mother but her Roger, had perhaps already lost him ; and that her one friend Annette was unconsciously taking him from her. Her mother's bedside had become a refuge for the first time. As she sat hour after hour with Lady Louisa's cold hand in hers, it was in vain that she told herself that it was foolish, ridiculous, to attach importance to such a trivial incident as the fact that when Roger was actually at her door he should have made himself late by walking home with Annette. But she realized now that she had been vaguely anxious before that happened, that it had been a formless dread at the back of her mind which had nothing to do with her mother, which had made her feel that night of the choir practice as if she had reached the end of her strength. Is there any exhaustion like that which guards the steep, endless steps up to the shrine of love? Which of us has struggled as far as the altar and laid our offering upon it ? Which of us faint-hearted pilgrims has not given up the attempt half-way? But Janey was not of these, not even to be daunted by a fear that had taken shape at last.

We all know that jealousy fabricates its own " confirmations strong as proofs of Holy Writ." But with Janey it was not so much suspicion as observation, that close observation born of love, which if it is once dislinked from love not even Sir Galahad could endure scathless. With steady eyes she dumbly watched her happiness grow dim and dimmer. Roger was her all, and he was leaving her. His very kindness might have warned her as to his real feeling for her, and it seemed to Janey as if for months she had been shutting her eyes forcibly against the truth.

There is a great deal of talk nowadays about losing the one we love, and that attractive personality generally turns out to be some sagacious stranger who has the agility to elude us in the crowd. But Roger was as much an integral part of Janey's life as Hulver was part of his. Janey's life had grown round Roger. Roger's had grown round Hulver.

Small incidents spread over the last two months, since Annette had come to Riff, rose to her memory ; things too small to count by themselves hooked themselves like links one after another into a chain. For instance, the Ipswich Agricultural Show.

Janey had always gone to that annual event with Roger and Harry. And since the Blacks had come to Riff, they had accompanied them. It seemed pleasant to Janey to go in a little bunch together, and Mr. Black was good-natured to Harry and took him to the side shows, and Janey always had a new gown for the occasion. She had a new one this year, a pink one, and a white straw hat covered with pink roses. And Roger had said approvingly, " My word, Janey, you have done it this time ! " They had taken Annette with them, in a flowing pale amber muslin which made her hair and eyes seem darker than ever, and which Miss Black, in her navy-blue silk, pronounced at once in a loud aside to be theatrical. When they all arrived they divided, Annette owning she did not like the pigs and sheep. Janey at once said she preferred them, because she knew Roger did. If there was one thing more than another that Roger loved, it was to stand among the cattle pens, with his hat a little at the back of his head, exchanging oracular remarks with other agents and stock-breeders, who gathered with gratifying respect the pearls of wisdom which he let drop. For there was no sounder opinion in Lowshire on a brood mare or a two-year-old " vanner " than Roger.

It was always stiflingly hot among the cattle pens, and the pigs in their domestic life had no bouquet more penetrating than that which they brought with them to these public functions. Janey did not love that animal, of which it might with truth be said that its " best is yet to be," but she always accompanied Roger on these occasions, standing beside him, a neat, dainty little figure, by the hour together, giving her full attention to the various points of the animals as he indicated them to her. They did the same again this year. Roger said, " Come on, Janey," as usual, and hurried in the direction of the cattle pens, while Annette and Harry and Mr. Black wandered towards the flower tents. But when they had reached the pandemonium of the " live stock," Roger appeared dissatisfied. The animals, it seemed, were a poor lot this year. The flower of the Lowshire land agentry was absent. He didn't see Smith anywhere. And Blower was not about. He expressed the opinion frequently that they

must be " getting on," and they were soon getting on to such an extent that they had got past the reaping-machines, and even the dogcarts, and were back near the band-stand, Roger continually wondering what had become of the others. Janey, suddenly hot and tired, suggested that they should look for them. And they set out immediately, and elbowed their way through the crowded flower tents, and past side shows innumerable, till they finally came upon Mr. Black and Annette and Harry at an " Aunt Sally " ; Harry in a seventh heaven of enjoyment, Mr. Black blissfully content, and Annette under her lace parasol as cool as a water-lily. Janey never forgot the throb of envy and despair to which the sudden sight of Annette gave rise, as she smiled at her and made room for her on the bench beside her, while Roger, suddenly peaceful and inclined to giggle, tried his luck at the " Aunt Sally." They all stayed together in a tight bunch for the remainder of the day, the endless weary day which every one seemed to enjoy except herself. And at tea-time they were joined by Miss Black and her friend, an entirely deaf Miss Conder, secretary of the Lowshire Plain Needlework Guild, who had adhered to Miss Black since morning greetings had been exchanged at the station, and who at this, the first opportunity, deserted her for Janey. And when they all came back late in the evening, Roger had driven Annette home in his dogcart, while she and the Blacks and

Harry, who could hardly be kept awake, squeezed into the wagonnette. And when Janey got home she tore off the pink gown and the gay hat, and wondered why she was tired out. She knew now, but she had not realized it at the time. She had somehow got it into her head, and if Janey once got an idea into her little head it was apt to remain there some time, that Annette and Mr. Black were attracted to each other. In these days, as she sat by her mother, Janey saw that that idea had led her astray. Mr. Black's hapless condition was sufficiently obvious. But perhaps Annette did not care for Mr. Black? Perhaps she preferred Roger ? And if she did

The reed on which Janey's maimed life had leaned showed for the first time that heartbreaking tendency inherent in every reed, to pierce the hand of the leaner. Strange, how slow we are to learn that everything in this pretty world is fragile as spun glass, and nothing in it is strong enough to bear our weight, least of all that reed shaken in the wind—human love. We may draw near, we may hearken to its ghostly music, we may worship, but we must not lean.

Janey was not a leaner by nature. She was one on whom others leaned. Nevertheless, she had counted on Roger.

CHAPTER XVIII

" So fast does a little leaven spread within us—so incalculable is the effect of one personality on another."— GEORGE ELIOT.

JANEY'S set face distressed Roger.

Presently he had a brilliant idea. Miss Georges was the person to cheer her, to tempt her out of her mother's sick-room. So the next time he was going to Red Riff to inspect some repairs in the roof—the next time was the same afternoon—he expounded this view at considerable length to Annette, whom he found thinning the annuals in a lilac pinafore and sunbonnet in the walled garden.

She sat down on the circular bench round the apple tree while he talked, and as he sat by her it seemed to him, not for the first time, that in some mysterious way it was a very particular occasion. There was a delightful tremor in the air. It suggested the remark which he at once made that it was a remarkably fine afternoon. Annette agreed, rather too fine for thinning annuals, though just the weather for her aunts to drive over to Noyes to call on Mr. Stirling Now that Roger came to look at Annette he perceived that she herself was part of the

delicious trouble in the air. It lurked in her hair, and the pure oval of her cheek, and her eyes—most of all in her eyes. He was so taken aback by this discovery that he could only stare at the sky. And yet if the silly man had been able to put two and two together, if he had known as much about human nature as he did about reaping-machines, he would not have been in the dark as to why he was sitting under the apple tree at this moment, why he had ordered those new riding-breeches, why he had them on at this instant, why he had begun to dislike Mr. Black, and why he had been so expeditious in retiling the laiterie after the tree fell on it. If he had had a grain of self-knowledge, he would have realized that there must indeed be a grave reason for these prompt repairs which the Miss Nevills had taken as a matter of course.

For in the ordinary course of things tiles could ha'rdly be wrested out of Roger, and drainpipes and sections of lead guttering were as his life-blood, never to be parted with except as a last resort after a desperate struggle. The estate was understaffed, underfinanced, and the repairs were always in arrear. Even the estate bricklayer, ruthlessly torn from a neighbouring farm to spread himself on the Miss Nevills' roof, opined to his nephew with the hod, that " Mr. Roger must be uncommon sweet on Miss Georges to be in such a mortial hurry with them tiles."

Annette's voice recalled Roger from the contemplation of the heavens.

11 I will go down to-day, after tea," she was saying, " and I will persuade Janey to come and sit in the hay-field. It is such a pretty thing a hay-field. I've never seen hay in—in what do you call it ? "

" In cock."

" Yes. Such a funny word ! I've never seen hay in cock before."

Roger smiled indulgently. Annette's gross ignorance of country-life did not pain him. It seemed as much part of her as a certain little curl on the white nape of her neck.

Down the lane a child's voice came singing—

" If I could 'ave the one I love, 'Ow 'appy I should be ! "

" That's Charlie Nokes," said Roger, feeling he ought to go, and singularly disinclined to move, and casting about for a little small-talk to keep him under this comfortable apple tree. " His father used to sing that song at Harvest Homes before he took to the drink. Jesse Nokes. He's dead now. He and my cousin Dick, the present squire, used to get into all kinds of scrapes together when they were boys. I've seen them climb up that vine and hide behind the chimney-stack when Uncle John was looking for them with his whip. They might have broken their necks, but they never thought of that. Poor Jesse ! He's dead. And Dick's dying."

It was the first time Roger had ever spoken to her of the present owner of Hulver, the black sheep of the family, of whose recklessness and folly she had heard many stories from his foster-mother, Mrs. Nicholls. Janey, in spite of their intimacy, never mentioned him.

And partly because he wanted to remain under the apple tree, partly because he was fond of Janey, and partly because a change of listeners is grateful to the masculine mind, Roger talked long about his two cousins, Janey and Dick Manvers : of her courage and unselfishness, and what a pity it was that she had not been the eldest son of the house. And then he told her a little of the havoc Dick was making of his inheritance and of the grief he had caused his mother, and what, according to Roger, mattered still more, to Janey.

" Janey loved Dick," he said, " and I was fond of him myself. Everybody was fond of him. You couldn't help liking Dick. There was something very taking about him. Can't say what it was, but one felt it. But it seems as if those taking people sometimes wear out all their takingness before they die, spend it all like money, so that at last there is nothing left for the silly people that have been so fond of them and stuck so long to them. Dick is like that. He's worn us all out, every one, even Janey. And now he's dying. I'm afraid there's no one left to care much—except, of course "

He stopped short.

" I've just been to see him in Paris,' 1 he went on. " Didn't you live in Paris at one time ? I wonder if you ever came across him ? "

Annette shook her head.

" I never met a Mr. Manvers that I know of."

" But he dropped the Manvers when he started his racing-stables. He had the decency to do that. He always went by his second name, Le Geyt."

" LeGeyt?"

" Yes ; Dick Le Geyt. Lady Louisa's mother was a Le Geyt of Noyes, you know, the last of the line. She married Lord Stour, as his second wife, and had no son. So her daughter, Lady Louisa, inherited Noyes. 11

" Dick Le Geyt?"

"Yes. Did you ever meet him? But I don't suppose you did. Dick never went among the kind of people you would be likely to associate with."

Annette was silent for a moment, and then said—

" Yes, I have met him. I used to see him sometimes at my father's cabaret." She saw he did not know what a cabaret was, and she added, " My father keeps a public-house in the Rue du Bac." Roger was so astonished that he did not perceive that Annette had experienced a shock.

11 Your father I " he said. " A publican ! "

" He was a courier first," she said, speaking with difficulty, like one stunned but forcing herself to attend to some trivial matter. " That was how my mother met him. And after her death he set up a little drinking-shop, and married again—a woman in his own class of life. I lived with them for a year, till—last September."

" Good Lord !" said Roger, and he said no more. He could only look at Annette in sheer astonishment. The daughter of a publican ! He was deeply perturbed. The apple tree had quite ceased to be comfortable. He got slowly to his feet, and said he must be going. She bade him " good-bye " absently, and he walked away, thinking that no other woman in Lowshire would have let him go after four o'clock without offering him a cup of tea.

Just when she thought he was really gone she found he had come back and was standing before her.

" Miss Georges," he began, awkwardly enough, ' I dare say I have no business to offer advice, but you don't seem to know country-life very well. Never seen hay in cock before, I think you mentioned. So perhaps you would not think it cheek of me if I said anything."

11 About the hay ? "

" No, no. About what you've just told me."

11 About my father keeping a public-house? "

" Yes. None of my business," — he had become plum colour,—" but "

She looked blankly at him. She felt unable

to give him sufficient attention to help him out. He had to flounder on without assistance.

" If you mentioned that fact to anyone like Miss Black, it would go the round of the parish in no time.' 1

" Would that matter ? "

Roger was nonplussed for a moment. Her ignorance was colossal.

" Some things are better not talked about/ 1 he said. " I have been telling you of poor Dick, but there were things in his life that were better not talked about, so I did not mention them. 1 '

His words transfixed her. Was it possible that he was warning her that he was aware of her adventure with Dick ? At any rate, she gave him her full attention now.

She raised her eyes to his and looked search-ingly at him. And she saw with a certainty that nothing could shake, that he knew nothing, that he was only trying to save her from a petty annoyance.

" The Miss Nevills have always been very close about your father," he added. " You can ask them, but I think you would find they wouldn't be much pleased if his—profession was known down here. It might vex them. So many vexatious things in this world that can't be helped, aren't there ? And if there are any that can, so much the better. That was all I came back to say. I should not volunteer it, if I were you. It seemed to drop

out so naturally that I thought you might have said the same to Miss Black."

" Certainly I might. I do hate concealments of any kind." Annette spoke with conviction.

" So do I," said Roger whole-heartedly. " I've hushed up too many scrawls not to hate them. But this isn't a concealment. It's— it's—you see, Miss Black does run round with her tongue out and no mistake, and Uncle John's advice when I settled down here as his agent was, ' Never say more than you must.' So I just pass it on to you, now that you've settled down at Riff too."

And Roger departed for the second time. She watched him go, and a minute later heard him ride out of the courtyard.

She sat quite still where he had left her, gazing in front of her, so motionless that the birds, disturbed by Roger's exodus, resumed possession of the grass-plot at once.

The plebeian sparrows came hopping clumsily as if they were made of wood, propped up by their stiff tails. A bulging thrush with wide speckled waistcoat hastened up and down, throwing out his wing each time he darted forward. A thin water-wagtail came walking with quick steps, and exquisite tiny movements of head and neck and long balancing tail. A baby-wagtail, brown and plump and voracious, bustled after it, shouting, " More ! More ! " the instant after its overworked, partially bald parent had stuffed a billful down its yellow throat.

Annette looked with wide eyes at the old dim house with its latticed windows and the vine across it—the vine which Dick had climbed as a lad.

Dick was Mr. Manvers of Hulver.

The baby-wagtail bolted several meals, fluttering its greedy little wings, while Annette said to herself over and over again, half stupefied—

" Dick is Mr. Manvers. Dick is Janey's brother."

She was not apprehensive by nature, but gradually a vague alarm invaded her. She must tell Mrs. Stoddart at once. What would Mrs. Stoddart say? What would she do? With a slow sinking of the heart, Annette realized that that practical and cautious woman would probably insist on her leaving Riff. Tears came into her eyes at the thought. Was it then unalloyed bliss to live with the Miss Nevills, or was there some other subtle influence at work which made the thought of leaving Riff intolerable ? Annette did not ask herself that question. She remembered with a pang her two friends Janey and Roger, and the Miss Blinketts, and Mrs. Nicholls, and her Sunday-school class, and the choir. And she looked at the mignonette she had sown, and the unfinished annuals, and the sweet peas which she had raised in the frame, and which would be out in another fortnight.

She turned and put her arms round the little old apple tree, and pressed her face against the bark.

" I'm happy here/ 1 she said. " I've never been so happy before. I don't want to go."

CHAPTER XIX

" In the winter, when all the flowers are dead, the experienced Bee Keeper places before His hive a saucer of beer and treacle to sustain the inmates during the frost. And some of the less active bees, who have not used their wings, but have heard about honey, taste the compound, and rinding it wonderfully sustaining and exactly suited to their aspirations, they religiously store it, dark and sticky, in waxen cells, as if it were what they genuinely believe it to be—the purest honey.

" But the other surly, unsympathetic bees with worn-out wings contend that honey is not come by as easily as that: that you must fly far, and work hard, and penetrate many flower-cups to acquire it. This naturally arouses the indignation of the beer and treacle gatherers.

" And the Bee Keeper as He passes His hive hears His little people buzzing within, and—smiles."—M. N.

" AND now/' said Aunt Harriet, the same evening,—" now that we have made Mr. Stirling's acquaintance and been to tea with him, and may expect to see him frequently, I think we ought to take a little course of his books. What do you say, Maria ? Eh ! Annette ? You seem strangely apathetic and inert this evening, my dear. So different from me at your age. I was gaiety and energy itself until my health failed. You might read aloud some extracts from The Magnet, instead of the Times. It is a book which none of us can afford to disregard.

How I cried over it when it came out! I wrote

to him after I had finished it, even though I did not know him. Authors like it, don't they, Maria ? I felt very audacious, but I am a child of impulse. I have never been able to bind myself down with conventional ideas as I see others do. I felt I simply must tell him what that book had been to me, what it had done for me, coming like a ray of light into a darkened room/' Mrs. Stoddart had read aloud The Magnet to Annette at Teneriffe, and it was intimately associated with her slow reawakening to life. It had had a part, and not a small part, in sending her back humbled and contrite to her aunts. But she felt a deep repugnance to the thought of hearing their comments upon it.

She took the offered book reluctantly, but Aunt Harriet's long thin finger was already pointing to a paragraph.

" Begin at ' How we follow Self at first,' the top of the page," she said. And she leaned back among her cushions. Aunt Maria took up her knitting, and Annette began to read :—

" How we follow Self at first! How long we follow her! How pallid, how ephemeral is all else beside that one bewitching form I We call her by many beautiful names—our career, our religion, our work for others. The face of Self is veiled, but we follow that mysterious rainbow-tinted figure as some men follow art, as some men follow Christ, leaving all else behind. We follow her across the rivers. If the stepping-stones are alive and groan beneath our feet, what of that? We follow her across the hills. Love weeps and falls behind, but what of that? The love which will not climb the hills with us is not the love we need. Our friends appeal to us and one by one fall behind. False friends I Let them go. Our ideals are broken and left behind. Miserable impediments and hindrances ! Let them go too.

"For some of us Self flits veiled to the last, and we trudge to our graves, looking ever and only at her across the brink. But sometimes she takes pity on us. Sometimes she turns and confronts us in a narrow place, and lifts her veil. We are alone at last with her we love. The leprous face, the chasms where the eyes should be, the awful discoloured hand are revealed to us, the crawling horror of every fold of that alluring drapery.

" Here is the bride. Take her !

" And we turn, sick unto death, and flee for our lives.

" After that day, certain easy self-depreciations we say never again while we have speech. After that day our cheap admission of our egotism freezes on our lips. For we have seen. We know."

" We have seen. We know," repeated Aunt Harriet solemnly. " That last bit simply changed my life. If I had a talent for writing like you, Maria, which of course I have not, that is just the kind of thing I should have said myself to help other sufferers. Unselfishness, that must be the key-note of our lives. If the stepping-stones are alive and groan beneath our feet, what of that ? How often I have said those words to myself when the feet of the world have gone over me, poor stepping-stone, trying hard, trying so hard not to groan. And if I am to be perfectly honest just for once, you know, dear Maria, you and Annette do trample somewhat heavily at times. Of course you are absorbed in your work, and Annette is young, and you don't either of you mean it. I know that, and I make allowances for you both. I am making allowances all the time. But I sometimes wish you could remember that the poor stepping-stone is alive."

There was a moment's silence. Annette got up and gently replaced the couvre-pied which had slipped from the stepping-stone's smart high-heeled shoes. Aunt Harriet wiped away a delicious tear.

" Our ideals are broken and left behind," she went on. " Only the invalid knows how true that is. Dear me ! When I think of all the high ideals I had when I was your age, Annette, who don't seem to have any! But perhaps it is happier for you that you haven't. Though Mr. Stirling looks so strong I feel sure that he must at one time have known a sofa-life. Or perhaps he loved some one like Elizabeth Barrett Browning, who was as great a prisoner to her couch as I am. He simply couldn't have written ii those lines otherwise. I often think as I lie here in solitude, hour after hour, how different my life might have been if anyone like Browning had sought me out—had But it's no use repining: all these things are ordered for the best. Go on, my dear, go on."

When the reading was over and Aunt Harriet, still emotional, had gone to bed, after embracing them both with unusual fervour, Annette opened the window as her custom was, and let in the soft night ah*. Aunt Harriet was a lifelong foe to fresh air. Aunt Maria gave a sigh of relief. She was stout and felt the heat.

The earth was resting. The white pinks below the window gave forth their scent. The low moon had laid a slanting black shadow of the dear old house and its tall chimney-stacks upon the silvered grass.

Annette's heart throbbed. Must she leave it all? She longed to go to her own room and think over what had happened, but she had an intuitive feeling that Aunt Maria had been in some mysterious way depressed by the reading aloud, and was in need of consolation.

" I think," said Aunt Maria after a time, " that Mr. Stirling rather exaggerates, don't you ?— that he has yielded to the temptation of picturesque overstatement in that bit about following Self."

"It seems to me—just right."

11 You don't feel he is writing for the sake of effect ? "

11 No. Oh no."

" I am afraid I do a little. But then the picture is so very highly coloured, and personally I don't care much for garish colouring."

Annette did not answer.

" I should like to know what you think about it, Annette."

Whenever Aunt Maria used that phrase, she wanted confirmation of her own opinion. Annette considered a moment.

" I think he has really seen it exactly as he says. I think perhaps he was selfish once, and— and had a shock."

" He is quite right to write from his experience," continued Aunt Maria. " I have drawn largely from mine in my books, and I am thankful I have had such a deep and rich experience to draw from. Experience, of course, must vary with each one of us. But I can't say I have ever felt what he describes. Have you ? "

" Yes."

" The veiled figure meeting you in a narrow place and raising its veil ? "

" Yes."

Aunt Maria was momentarily taken aback. When our opinions do not receive confirmation from others we generally feel impelled to restate them at length.

" I have never looked at selfishness like that," she said, " as something which we idealize. I have always held that egotism is the thing of all others which we ought to guard against. And egotism seems to me ugly—not beautiful or rainbow-tinted at all. I tried to show in Crooks and Coronets what an obstacle it is to our spiritual development, and how happiness is to be found in little deeds of kindness, small sacrifices for the sake of others, rather than in always considering ourselves.' 1

Annette did not answer. She knew her aunt's faith in spiritual homoeopathy.

" I have had hundreds of letters," continued the homoeopath uneasily, " from my readers, many of them perfect strangers, thanking me for pointing out the danger of egotism so fearlessly, and telling me how much happier they have been since they followed the example of Angela

Towers in Crooks and Coronets in doing a little act of kindness every day."

If Aunt Maria were alive now she would have been thrilled by the knowledge that twenty years after she had preached it the Boy Scouts made that precept their own.

" Perhaps the man who was following the veiled figure did little kindnesses too, in order to feel comfortable," said Annette half to herself. Fortunately her aunt did not hear her.

" I yield to no one in my admiration of Mr. Stirling," continued Miss Nevill, " but he suggests no remedy for the selfishness he describes. He just says people flee for then* lives. Now, my experience is that they don't flee, that they don't see how selfish they are, and need helpful suggestions to overcome it. That is just what

I have tried to do in my books, which I gather he has never opened."

There was a subdued bitterness in her aunt's voice which made Annette leave her seat by the window and sit down beside her.

" You have plenty of readers without Mr. Stirling," she said soothingly.

It was true. Miss Nevill had a large public. She had never lived, she had never come in close contact with the lives of others, she had no perception of character, and she was devoid of humour. She had a meagre, inflexible vocabulary, no real education, no delicacy of description, no sense of language, no love of nature. But she possessed the art of sentimental facile narration, coupled with a great desire to preach, and a genuine and quenchless passion for the obvious. And the long succession of her popular novels, each exactly like the last, met what a large circle of readers believed to be its spiritual needs : she appealed to the vast society of those who have never thought, and who crave to be edified without mental effort on their part. Her books had demanded no mental effort from their author, and were models of unconscious tact in demanding none from their readers, and herein, together with their evident sincerity, had lain part of the secret of their success. Also, partly because her gentle-people— and her books dealt mainly with them—were not quite so unlike gentle-people as in the majority of novels. If she did not call a spade a spade,

neither did she call an earl an earl. Old ladies adored her novels. The Miss Blinketts preferred them to Shakespeare. Canon Wetherby dipped into them in his rare moments of leisure. Cottage hospitals laid them on the beds of their convalescents. Clergymen presented them as prizes. If the great Miss Nevill had had a different temperament, she might have been a happy as she was a successful woman ; for she represented culture to the semi-cultivated, and to succeed in doing that results in a large income and streams of flattering letters. But it does not result in recognition as a thinker, and that was precisely what she hankered after. She craved to be regarded as a thinker, without having thought. It chagrined her that her books were not read by what she called " the right people/'— that, as she frequently lamented, her work was not recognized. In reality it was recognized—at first sight. The opening chapter, as Mr. Stirling had found that morning, was enough. The graver reviews never noticed her. No word of praise ever reached her from the masters of the craft. She had to the full the adulation of her readers, but she wanted adulation, alas ! from the educated, from men like Mr. Stirling rather than Canon Wetherby. Mr. Stirling had not said a word about her work this afternoon, though he had had time to refresh his memory of it, and she had alluded to it herself more than once. For the hundredth time Aunt Maria felt vaguely disturbed and depressed. The reading

aloud of The Magnet had only accentuated that depression.

Annette's hand felt very soft and comforting in hers. The troubled authoress turned instinctively towards possible consolation nearer at hand,

11 I will own/' she said tentatively, " that when I see you, my dear Annette, so different

from what you were when you left us two years ago, so helpful, and so patient with poor Harriet, who is trying beyond words, so considerate and so thoughtful for others, I will own that I have sometimes hoped that the change might have been partly, I don't say entirely, but partly brought about by Crooks and Coronets, which I sent to you at Teneriffe, and into which I had poured all that was best in me. When you rejoined us here it seemed as if you had laid its precepts to heart." Aunt Maria looked at her niece almost imploringly.

Annette was not of those who adhere to a rigid truthfulness on all occasions.

She stroked her aunt's hand.

"It was borne hi on me at Teneriffe, after I was ill there, how selfish I had been," she said, and her voice trembled. " I ought never to have left you all. If only I had not left you all! Then I should not be—I shouldn't have—but I was selfish to the core. And my eyes were only opened too late."

' No, my dear, not too late. Just in the nick of time, at the very moment we needed you most, after dear Cathie's death. You don't know what a comfort you have been to us."

" Too late for Aunt Cathie," said Annette hoarsely. " Poor, kind, tired Aunt Cathie, who came to me in my room the last night and asked me not to leave her, told me she needed my help. But my mind was absolutely set on going. I cried, and told her that later on I would come back and take care of her, but that I must go. Self in her rainbow veil beckoned and—and I followed. If Aunt Cathie was the stepping-stone which groaned beneath my feet, what of that ? What did I care ? I passed over it, I trampled on it without a thought."

The subdued passion in Annette's voice stirred anew the vague trouble in Aunt Maria's mind.

For a moment her own view of life, even her heroine's puny and universally admired repentance, tottered, dwindled. For a brief moment she saw that the writer of The Magnet made a great demand on his reader, and that Annette had passionately responded to it. For a moment Mr. Stirling's gentle, ruthless voice seemed to overthrow her whole position, to show her to herself as petty and trivial. For a moment she even doubted whether Crooks and Coronets had really effected the great change she perceived in Annette, and the doubt disheartened her still more. She withdrew resolutely into the stronghold of her success, and rose slowly to her feet.

" Well/' she said, " it's time to go to bed. Close the shutters, Annette. It's very natural you should be impressed by The Magnet. I should have been at your age. Young people are always attracted by eloquence. But as one gets older I find one instinctively prefers plainer language, as one prefers plainer clothes, less word-painting, and more spiritual teaching."

It was already late, but Annette sat up still later writing a long letter to Mrs. Stoddart.

CHAPTER XX

" Yourself are with yourself the sole consortress In that unleaguerable fortress; It knows you not for portress."

FRANCIS THOMPSON.

I HAVE often envied Lesage's stratagem in which he makes Le diable boiteux transport his patron to a high point in the city, and then obligingly remove roof after roof from the houses spread out beneath his eyes, revealing with a sublime disregard for edification what is going on in each of them in turn. That is just what I should like to do with you, Reader, transport you to the top of, shall we say, the low church tower of Riff, and take off one red roof after another of the clustering houses beneath us. But I should not choose midnight, as Lesage did, but tea-time for my visitation, and then if you appeared bored, I would quickly whisk off another roof.

We might look in at Roger's cottage near the church first of all, and see what he is doing.

On this particular afternoon, some three weeks after his conversation with Annette under the apple tree, I am sorry to record that he was doing nothing. That was a pity, for there was a great deal waiting to be done. July and a new quarter were at hand. Several new leases had to be looked over, the death of one of his farmers had brought up the old hateful business of right of heriot, the accounts of the Aldeburgh house property were in at last and must be checked. There was plenty to do, but nevertheless Roger was sitting in his office-room, with his elbow on his last labour-sheet, and his chin i_. his hand. He, usually so careful, had actually blotted the names of half a dozen labourers. His housekeeper, the stoutest woman in Riff, sister to the late Mr. Nicholls, had put his tea near him half an hour before. Mr. Nicholls' spinster sister was always called "Mrs. Nicholls." But it was the wedded Mrs. Nicholls who had obtained the situation of Roger's housekeeper by sheer determination for the unwedded lady of the same name, and when Roger had faintly demurred at the size of his housekeeper designate, had informed him sternly that " she was stout only in appearance."

It was a pity he had let his tea grow cold, and had left his plate of thick, rectangular bread-and-butter untouched.

Roger was a person who hated thought, and he was thinking, and the process was fatiguing to him. He had for years " hustled " along like a sturdy pony on the rounds of his monotonous life, and had been fairly well satisfied with it till now. But lately the thoughts which would have been invading a more imaginative man for a long time past had at last reached him, had filtered down through the stiff clay of the upper crust of his mind.

Was he going on for ever keeping another man's property assiduously together, doing two men's work for one man's pay ? When his uncle made him his agent he lived in the house at Hulver, and his horses were kept for him, and the two hundred a year was a generous allowance. But Dick had not increased it when he succeeded. He had given him the cottage, which was in use as an estate office, rent free, but nothing else. Roger had not liked to say anything at first, even when his work increased, and later on Dick had not been "to be got at." And the years were passing, and Roger was thirty-five. He ought to be marrying if he was ever going to marry at all. Of course, if Dick were in a state of health to be appealed to at close quarters—he never answered letters—he would probably act generously. He had always been open-handed. But Dick, poor beggar, was dead already as far as any use he could be to himself or others.

Roger shuddered at the recollection of the shapeless, prostrate figure, with the stout, vacant face, and the fat hand, that had once been so delicate and supple, which they had wanted to guide to do it knew not what.

Roger could not see that he had any future. But then he had not had any for years past, so why was he thinking about that now ? Annette was the reason. Till Annette came to Riff he had always vaguely supposed that he and Janey would " make a match of it " some day. Janey was the only person he really knew. I do not mean to imply for a moment that Roger in his pink coat at the Lowshire Hunt Ball was not a popular partner. He was. And in times past he had been shyly and faintly attracted by more than one of his pretty neighbours. But he was fond of Janey. And now that his uncle was dead, Janey was, perhaps, the only person left for whom he had a rooted attachment. But it seemed there were disturbing women who could inspire feelings quite different from the affection and compassion he felt for his cousin. Annette was one of them. Roger resented the difference, and then dwelt upon it. He distrusted Annette's parentage. " Take a bird out of a good nest." That was his idea of a suitable marriage. Never in his wildest moments would he have thought of marrying a woman whose father was a Frenchman, much less a Frenchman who kept a public-house. He wasn't thinking of such a thing now—at least, he told himself he wasn't. But he had been deeply chagrined at Annette's mention of her father all the same, so deeply that he had not repeated the odious fact even to Janey, the recipient of all the loose matter in his mind.

How kind Annette had been to poor Janey during these last weeks ! Janey had unaccountably and dumbly hung back at first, but Annette was not to be denied. Roger, with his elbow on his labour-sheet, saw that whatever her father might be, the least he could do would be to ride up to Riff at an early date and thank her.

It is only a step from Roger's cottage to the Dower House.

All was silent there. Janey and Harry had gone up to Hulver to sail his boat after tea, and the house was deserted. Tommy, the gardener's boy, the only person to whom Harry had confided his marriage, was clipping the edges of the newly-mown grass beneath Lady Louisa's window.

And Lady Louisa herself ?

She lay motionless with fixed eyes, while the nurse, her daughter-in-law, read a novel near the open window.

She knew what had happened. She remembered everything. Her hearing and sight were as clear as ever. But she could make no sign of understanding or recognition. A low, guttural sound she could sometimes make, but not always, and the effort was so enormous that she could hardly induce herself to make it. At first she had talked unceasingly, unable to remember that the words which were so clear to herself had no sound for those bending over her, trying to understand what she wished. Janey and the doctor had encouraged her, had comforted her, had made countless experiments in order to establish means of communication with her, but without avail.

" Would you like me to read, mother ? See, I am holding your hand. Press it ever so little, and I shall know you would like a little reading."

No faintest pressure.

" Don't trouble to answer, mother, but if you would like to see Roger for a few minutes, shut your eyes."

The eyes remained open, fixed. Lady Louisa tried to shut them, but she could not.

" Now I am going to hold up these large letters one after another. If there is something you wish me to do, spell it to me. Make a sound when I reach the right letter. I begin with A. Now we come to B. Here is C."

But after many fruitless attempts Janey gave up the letters. Her mother groaned at intervals, but when the letters were written down they did not make sense. No bridge could span the gulf. At last the doctor advised Janey to give up trying to span it.

" Leave her in peace," he said in Lady Louisa's hearing, that acute hearing which was as intact as her eyesight.

So Lady Lcuisa was left in peace.

She saw the reins and whip which she had held so tightly slip out of her hands. She who had imposed her will on others all her life could impose it no longer. She was tended by a traitor whom she hated, yet she was unable to denounce her, to rid herself of her daily, hourly presence.

A wood pigeon cooed tranquilly in the cedar, and Lady Louisa groaned.

The nurse put down her book, and came and stood beside the bed. The two enemies looked at each other, the younger woman boldly meeting the impotent hatred of her patient's eyes.

"It's no use, milady," she said, replacing a little cushion under her elbow. "You're down, and I'm up, and you've got to make up your mind to it. Harry told me you'd got it out of him. Are you any the happier for knowing I'm your daughter-in-law? I'd meant to spare you that. It was that as brought on the stroke. Very clever you were to wheedle it out of Harry, but it didn't do you much good. You'd turn me out without a character if you could, wouldn't you? But you can't. And listen to me. You won't ever be any better, or I shouldn't talk like this. I dare say I'm pretty bad, but I'd never say there wasn't a chance while there was the least little scrap of one left. But there isn't, not one scrap. It's all over with your high and mighty ways, and riding rough-shod over everybody, and poor Miss Manvers. It's no use crying. You've made others cry often enough. Now it's your turn. And don't go and think I'm going to be cruel to you because you've been cruel to others. I'm not. I'm sorry enough for you, lying there like a log, eating your heart out. I'm going to make you as comfortable as ever I can, and to do my duty by you. And when you're gone I'm going to make Harry happier than he's ever been under your thumb. So now you understand."

Lady Louisa understood. Her eyes, terrible, fierce as a wounded panther's, filled with tears. She made no other sign.

The nurse wiped them away.

CHAPTER XXI

"The less wit a man has, the less he knows that he wants it." — GEORGE ELIOT.

THE Vicarage is within a stone's throw of the Dower House. On this particular afternoon Mr. and Miss Black were solemnly seated opposite each other at tea, and Mr. Black was ruefully reflecting, as he often did at meal-times, on his sister's incapacity as a housekeeper.

We sometimes read in the biographies of eminent men how trains and boats always eluded those distinguished personages, in spite of their pathetic eagerness to overtake them; how their luggage and purses and important papers fled from them; how their empty chairs too frequently represented them on state occasions.

Miss Black was not eluded by such bagatelles as trains and omnibuses, but by things of greater importance, by new-laid eggs, and fresh butter, and cottage loaves. No egg until it was of advanced middle age would come within a mile of Miss Black. The whole village was aware that old Purvis sold her "potted eggs" at "new-laid" prices, and that she never detected the lime on them. Scones and tea-cakes and loaves with "kissing crust" remained obdurately huddled in the baker's cart at the Vicarage back door. All that ever found their way into the house were those unappropriated blessings, those emotionless rectangular travesties of bread called "tin loaves."

Coffee and Miss Black were not on speaking terms. After years of deadly enmity she had relinquished the fruitless struggle, and gave her brother coffee essence instead for breakfast— two spoonfuls to a cup of tepid milk.

Fire and water would not serve Miss Black. The bath water was always cold at the Vicarage, and the drinking water was invariably warm. Butter, that sensitive ally of the housekeeper, bore her a grudge. Miss Black said all the Riff butter was bad. In London she had said the same. Biscuits became demoralized directly they set tin in the house. The first that emerged from the box were crisp, delicious, but in a day or two they were all weary, tough, and tasteless. They were kept on plates on sideboards in the sun, or thrust into mousy cupboards. She left off ordering gingerbread nuts at last, which her brother liked, because they all stuck together like putty. She attributed this peculiarity to the proximity of the Rieben.

Miss Black was no more perturbed by the ostracism in which she lived as regards the vegetable and mineral kingdom than Napoleon was by the alliance of Europe against him. She combined a high opinion of herself with a rooted conviction that everything vexatious or disagreeable was inherent in the nature of things— a sort of original sin. It was in the fallen nature of butter to be rancid, and eggs to be laid stale, and milk to be sour, and villagers to cheat, and old people to be fretful, and pretty women (like Annette) to be vain and unscrupulous, and men (like her brother) to care inordinately about food and to be enslaved by external attractions. She expected these things, and many more, as she stumped through life, and she was not disappointed.

" I think you are wrong, Walter," she said, masticating a plasmon biscuit, " in making Miss Georges take that bit in the anthem as a solo. I went to see Mrs. Cocks this afternoon, and we got talking of the choir, and I am sure she did not like it."

" I cannot steer my course entirely by Mrs. Cocks."

" Of course not. But she told me that in Mr. Jones's time "

11 I am rather tired of hearing of Mr. Jones and his times."

" In his time all the trebles took the solo together, to prevent any jealousy or ill-feeling."

11 I can't prevent jealousy of Miss Georges," said Mr. Black, looking coldly at his sister, and then still more coldly at the cup of tea she handed him, made quarter of an hour before by the young servant who, as the Miss Blinketts who had trained her had faithfully warned Miss Black, " mistook bubbling for boiling."

The tea was the consistency of treacle, and the cream his sister poured into it instantly took the contorted worm-like shapes which sour cream does take. Miss Black drank hers slowly, not finding it good, but thinking it was like all other tea.

" You won't make the jealousy less by putting her forward an everything."

" It irritates me to hear Miss Georges' voice muffled up with Mrs. Cocks and Jane Smith. I don't suppose Riff Church has ever had such a voice in it since it was built."

" I'm sure I can't tell about that. But Miss Georges has been partly trained for a public singer."

" Has she ? I did not know that."

11 The truth is we know very little about her. I am not sure we ought not to have made more inquiries before we admitted her to the choir and the Sunday school."

" My dear, pure good-nature on her part is responsible for her being in either. And could anything be more ultra respectable than her aunts?"

" We don't know who her father was. I should not wonder if he were an actor, her manner of singing is so theatrical. Not quite a good example for the other trebles. She draws attention to herself."

" She can't help that, Angela. That is partly due to her appearance, for which she is not responsible."

Mr. Black, patient and kindly by nature, showed to greater advantage with his sister than with Annette, because he never attempted to show Miss Black the sort of man he was. You could not be two minutes in her society without realizing that she saw no more difference between one person and another than she did between fresh eggs and stale. Men were men to her, as eggs were eggs. And that was all about it.

" She is responsible for a good deal of the attention she courts," said Miss Black scornfully, and with a modicum of truth on her side. " She need not let her hair stand out over her ears, or make those two little curls in the nape of her neck. And did you notice her absurd hat ? "

" I noticed nothing absurd about it."

" When every one is wearing trimmed hats she must needs make herself conspicuous in a perfectly plain straw with no trimming at all, except that black ribbon tied under her chin. Everybody was staring at her last Sunday."

" That I can well believe."

" I asked her where she had got that nice garden hat."

" Is it possible ? How angry you would have been if she had asked you where you got yours ! "

Mr. Black glanced for the first time at a battered but elaborate arrangement sprinkled with cornflowers, sitting a little crooked, like a badly balanced plate, on the top of his sister's narrow head.

" She wasn't the least angry. There was nothing to be offended at. And she said her aunt in Paris sent it her, who was a milliner."

" How like her to say that—to volunteer it ! " said Mr. Black, aware that his sister was watching how he took the news of Annette's connection with trade. " But we must be careful how we repeat it. In this amazing little world of Riff it might be against her to have a milliner for an aunt."

" I don't see that Riff is more amazing than other places," said Miss Black, who had already circulated the story of the dressmaking aunt with the same diligence which she showed in the distribution of the parish magazine. " I hope we can all be civil to Miss Georges, even if her aunt is a dressmaker, and her father lower still in the social scale. She has no De before her name. And Georges is a very common surname."

" Indeed ! "

" Perhaps you are thinking of asking her to change it," said his sister, whose temper was liable to boil up with all the suddenness of milk.

' I had not got so far as that," he said, rising.

' You must remember, Angela, that you see a possible wife for me in every woman I exchange a word with. It is very flattering that you should think so many might be prevailed on to share my little Vicarage, but the Church only allows me one wife, and the selection I believe rests with me."

" I know that. It's so silly to talk as if I expected anything different.' 1

" All I can say is that if I could delude myself into believing that Miss Georges put on that hat or any other hat with a view to attracting me, I should feel some alacrity in finishing my Sunday sermon, which I must now do without any alacrity at all."

Miss Black swallowed the remains of her plasmon biscuit, and said in the voice of one accustomed to the last word—

" Miss Georges is very good-looking, of course. No one admires that sort of pale, clear complexion and calm manner more than I do. But you must remember that they are merely the result of a constitution free from an excess of uric acid. Non-gouty subjects always look like that."

CHAPTER XXII

" Give me the sweet cup wrought of the earth from which I was born, and under which I shall he dead."— ZONAS.

FROM the church tower, Reader, you can see beyond the mill and the long water meadows the little hamlet of Swale.

That old house in the midst, with its wonderful twisted chimneys and broken wall, was once the home of the extinct Welyshams of Swale. But the name of Welysham, embedded in the history of Lowshire and still renowned in India, is forgotten in Riff. Their old house, fast falling into ruins, is now used as a farm, until Roger can get leave to restore it, or pull it down. The sky looks in at the upper rooms. No one dare go up the wide oak staircase, and Mrs. Nicholls' chickens roost on the carved balustrade of the minstrels' gallery.

We will go there next.

Mrs. Nicholls, the devoted nurse of all the Manvers family and the principal treble in the choir, had married at a portly age the tenant-farmer at Swale, and Annette was having tea with her on this particular afternoon, and hearing a full description, which scorned all omissions, of the last illness of Mr. Nicholls, who had not been able " to take a bite in his head " of anything solid for many weeks before his death.

11 And so, miss," said Mrs. Nicholls philosophically, " when he went I felt it was all for the best. It's a poor thing for a man to live by suction."

Annette agreed.

" Swale seems quite empty this afternoon," she said, possibly not unwilling to change the subject. " There is hardly a soul to be seen."

" I expect they've all gone to Sir Harry's 'lection tea," said Mrs. Nicholls. " I used to go while Nicholls was alive, and very convenient it was ; but Sir Harry don't want no widders nor single spinsters—only wives of them as has votes."

Politics were not so complicated twenty years ago as they are now. Those were the simple days when Sir Harry Ogden, the Member, urbanely opined that he was for Church and State, and gave tea shortly before the election to the wives of his constituents. And the ladies of Swale and Riff, and even the great Mrs. Nicholls, thought none the worse of their Member because there was always a sovereign at the bottom of the cup.

" Mr. Black wants to start a Mothers' Meeting in Swale," continued Annette. " He asked me to talk it over with you. I know he is hoping for your nice parlour for it, so beautiful as you always keep it."

Mrs. Nicholls was softened by the compliment to her parlour, the condition of which was as well known as that Queen Victoria was on the throne, but she opined that there had been a deal too much " argybargy " already among the Swale matrons about the Mothers' Meeting, and that she did not see her way to joining it.

Annette, who had been deputed by Mr. Black to find out the mysterious cause of Mrs. Nicholls' reluctance, remarked meditatively, " I don't know how the Vicar will get on without you, Mrs. Nicholls."

" No, miss," said Mrs. Nicholls, " of course not. He was here only yesterday, and he says to me, ' Mrs. Nicholls, the Swale folk oughter all heng together, and we look to you.' And I says, (Sir, it's not for me to chunter with you ; but it's no manner of use setting me up as a queen in Swale when there's Mrs. Tomkins as bounceful as can be, as has been expecting homage ever since she and her spring-cart came in last Lammas, which none of us don't feel obligated to bow down to her."

" Of course not. But there are others besides Mrs. Tomkins. There are the Tamsies, your next-door neighbours. They are quiet, hardworking people, with a lot of little ones. She would be very thankful, I know, to join the Mothers' Meeting, if the Vicar can start it."

" Mrs. Tamsy," said Mrs. Nicholls judicially.

" I dare say Mrs. Tamsy would like anything she can get, whether it's out of my pig-tub or her own. That don't make no differ to Mrs. Tamsy, nor what's put on the hedge to dry—if so be as any thing's blowed to her side. She's that near she'd take the pence off the eyes of her mother's corp. No, miss ! I'd do a deal for the Vicar, but I won't have Mrs. Tamsy in my place, nor I won't set foot in hers. Not that I ain't sorry for her, with Tamsy coming home roaring on a Saturday night, and hectoring and bullocking about till the children has to sleep in the hen-roost."

And in the course of conversation Mrs. Nicholls at last divulged to Annette, what she had kept bottled up from Mr. Black, and indeed from every one, that the real reason that a Mothers' Meeting could not be instituted in the small circle of the Swale matrons, even if the gathering did not include Mrs. Tamsy, was because of old Mr. Thornton's death. Mr. Thornton, it seemed, had been " an octogeranium and the last sediment of his family, and not one of his own kin to put him in his coffin." The Swale ladies had taken the last duties on themselves, and there had been " unpleasantness at the laying out," so that friendly relations had been suspended between them ever since the funeral.

Annette sighed as she left Mrs. Nicholls and set out across the meadows towards Riff. She was to meet Janey in the Hulver gardens, and
help her to pick the snap-dragons, now blooming riotously there.

But one small sigh for the doomed Mothers' Meeting was the only tribute Annette paid to it. Her thoughts reverted quickly to other subjects.

Her placid, easy-going mind was troubled.

The long letter written at night to Mrs. Stoddart three weeks ago had never been posted. The following morning had brought a hurried line from her friend saying that she was that moment starting on a yachting trip with her son. She mentioned that she was coming down to Annette's neighbourhood in a month's time, on a visit to Mr. Stirling at Noyes, when she hoped for opportunities of seeing her.

Annette had dropped her own letter into the fire, not without a sense of relief. She had hated the idea of immediate action, and she had been spared it. She would go on quietly until she could confer with Mrs. Stoddart. But in spite of the momentary respite the fear remained at the back of her mind that when Mrs. Stoddart did know about the Manvers family she would almost certainly insist on Annette's leaving Riff. Annette could see for herself that her position there was untenable. But the longing to remain grew, nevertheless. She vaguely, foolishly hoped that some way of remaining might yet be found. For she was drawn towards Riff, as she had never been drawn to any other place, partly no doubt because, owing to her
aunt's death, all her energies had been called out there for the first time in her life. It had been no sinecure to take Aunt Cathie's place. She had taken it, and she had filled it. She was no longer a pale, useless, discontented girl, cooped up in an airless London house with two self-centred, elder women whom she secretly despised for immolating their sister. Now that her aunts were under her protection and absolutely dependent on her, and, if they had but known it, at her mercy, she had become at first tolerant of them, and then compassionate and amused, and finally affectionate. If she had kept her own life entirely apart from them, they were not aware of it. For neither of the Miss Nevills had yet discovered that though they themselves were not alive others might be, and Annette had done nothing since her return to them to break that illusion so rudely shaken by her departure. In their opinion, Annette had now " settled down," and each aunt was secretly of opinion that her niece's existence was supported by copious draughts from the deep

wells of her own wisdom and experience. But perhaps Annette had other incentives for clinging to Riff.

Sometimes as we go through life we become conscious of a mysterious instinctive attraction towards certain homely people, and certain kindly places, for which we cannot account, to which we can only yield. They seem to belong to us, to have a special significance for us. When

Annette first saw Janey and Roger she felt that she had known them all her life, that they had long been part of her existence. When first she walked with them beside the Rieben she seemed to recognize every turn of the stream. The deep primrosed lanes welcomed her back to them. Had she wandered down them in some previous existence ? When she gathered her first posy of lady's-smock in the long water meadow near the mill, the little milk-white flowers said, " Why have you been away from us so long?" And when, a few days later, she first stood with Janey in the April sunshine on the wide terrace of Hulver, the stately shuttered house had seemed to envelop her with its ancient peace, and to whisper to her, " I am home."

Annette reached the bridge by the mill, and looked across the tranquil water to the village clustering round the church, and the old red-gabled Manor house standing among its hollies.

Her heart throbbed suddenly.

Surely the angel with the sword would not drive her away again 1

CHAPTER XXIII

" Thou vacant house, moated about by peace."

STEPHEN PHILLIPS.

MR. STIRLING and his nephew were standing in the long picture gallery of Hulver, looking at the portrait of Roger Manvers of Dunwich, who inherited Hulver in Charles the Second's time.

" His grandmother, Anne de la Pole, that pinched-looking old woman in the ruff, would never have left it to her daughter's son if she had had anyone else to leave it to," said Mr. Stirling. " She built Hulver in the shape of an E in honour of her kinswoman Queen Elizabeth. That prim little picture below her portrait shows the house when it was new. It must have looked very much the same then as it does now, except that the hollies were all trimmed to fantastic shapes. Look at the birds and domes and crowns."

" I like them better as they are now," said his nephew, a weak-looking youth with projecting teeth, his spectacled eyes turning from the picture to the renowned avenue of hollies, now stooping and splitting in extreme old age.

" I have often wondered what homely Roger

Manvers, the burgess of Dunwich, must have felt when old Anne actually left him this place after her only son was drowned. I can so well imagine him riding over here, a careful, sturdy man, not unlike the present Roger Manvers, and having a look at his inheritance, and debating with himself whether he would leave Dunwich and settle here."

" And did he ? "

" Yes. The sea decided that for him. A year later it swept away the town of Dunwich as far as Maison Dieu. And it swept away Roger Manvers' pleasant house, Montjoy. And he moved across the borders of Suffolk to Low-shire with all he had been able to save from his old home, and established himself here. I like the way he has hung those wooden - looking pictures of his burgess forbears in their furred cloaks and chains among the brocaded D'Urbans and De la Poles. Roger Manvers tells me that it was old Roger who first took the property in hand, and heightened the Kirby dam, and drained Mendlesham Marsh, and built the Riff almshouses. The De la Poles had never troubled themselves about such matters. And to think of that wretched creature the present owner tearing the old place limb from limb, throwing it from him with both hands! It makes me miserable. I vow I will never come here again."

The caretaker had unshuttered a few among the long line of windows, and the airlessness, the ghostly outlines of the muffled furniture, the dust which lay grey on everything, the faint smell of dry rot, all struck at Mr. Stirling's sensitive spirit and oppressed him. He turned impatiently to the windows.

If it is a misfortune to be stout, even if one is tall, and to be short, even if one is slim, and to be fifty, even if one is of a cheerful temperament, and to be bald, even if one has a well-shaped head, then Mr. Stirling, who was short and stout, and bald as well, and fifty into the bargain, was somewhat heavily handicapped as to his outer man. But one immense compensation was his for an unattractive personality. He never gave it a moment's thought, and consequently no one else did either. His body was no more than a travelling-suit to him. It was hardy, durable, he was comfortable in it, grateful to it, on good terms with it, worked it hard, and used it to the uttermost. That it was not more ornamental than a Gladstone bag did not trouble him.

" Put it all in a book," said his nephew absently, whose eyes were glued to the pictures. " Put it in a book, Uncle Reggie."

Mr. Stirling had long since ceased to be annoyed by a remark which is about as pleasant to a writer as a suggestion of embezzlement is to a bank manager.

" Have you seen enough, Geoff? Shall we go? " he said.

" Wait a bit. Where's the Raeburn ? "

" ' Highland Mary '? Sold. A pork butcher in America bought her for a fabulous sum. I believe Dick Manvers lost the whole of it on one race. If there is coin in the next world, he will play ducks and drakes with it upon the glassy sea."

" Sold ! Good God ! " said his nephew, staring horrorstruck at his uncle. " How awful! Pictures ought not to belong to individuals. The nation ought to have them." He seemed staggered. " Awful!" he said again. " What a tragedy 1"

11 To my mind, that is more tragic," sr.id Mr. Stirling bluntly, pointing to the window.

In the deserted garden, near the sundial, Janey was standing, a small nondescript figure in a mushroom hat, picking snap-dragons. The gardens had been allowed to run wild for lack of funds to keep them in order, and had become beautiful exceedingly in consequence. The rose-coloured snap-dragons and amber lupins were struggling to hold their own in their stone-edged beds against an invasion of willow weed. A convolvulus had climbed to the sundial, wrapping it round and round, and had laid its bold white trumpet flowers on the leaded disk itself. Janey had not disturbed it. Perhaps she thought that no one but herself sought to see the time there. The snap-dragons rose in a great blot of straggling rose and white and wine-red round her feet. She was picking them slowly, as one whose mind was not following her hand. At a little distance Harry was lying at his full length on the flags beside the round stone-edged fountain, blowing assiduously at a little boat which was refusing to cross. In the midst of the water Cellini's world-famed water nymph reined in her dolphins.

A yellow stone-crop had found a foothold on the pedestal of the group, and flaunted its raw gold in the vivid sunshine amid the weather-bitten grey stone, making a fantastic broken reflection where Harry's boat rippled the water. And behind Janey's figure, and behind the reflection of the fountain in the water, was the cool, sinister background of the circular yew hedge, with the heather pink of the willow weed crowding up against it.

The young man gasped.

" But it's—it's a picture," he said. And then, after a moment, he added, " Everything except the woman. Of course she won't do."

Geoff's curiously innocent prominent eyes were fixed. His vacant face was rapt. His uncle looked sympathetically at him. He knew what it was to receive an idea " like Dian's kiss, unasked, unsought."

The caretaker, whose tea-time was already delayed, coughed discreetly in the hall.

" Come, Geoff," said Mr. Stirling, remorsefully but determinedly, taking his nephew's arm. " We can't remain here for ever."

11 It's all right except the woman," said Geoff, not stirring. " Every scrap. It hits you in the eye.^Look how the lichen has got at the dolphins. All splendour and desolation, and the yew hedge like a funeral procession behind. Not a bit of sky above them : the only sky reflected in the water." His voice had sunk to a whisper.

" When you are my age/' said Mr. Stirling, " it is just the woman, not some fanciful angel with a Grecian profile and abnormally long legs, but that particular little brown-haired creature with her short face whom you brush aside, who makes the tragedy of the picture. When I think of what that small courageous personage endures day by day, what her daily life must be —but what's the use of talking? Twenty can't hear a word fifty is saying—isn't meant to. Wake up, Geoff. There is another lady in the case. It is past the caretaker's tea-time. You must learn to consider the fair sex, my dear boy. We are keeping her from her tea. Look, Miss Manvers has seen us. We'll join her in the gardens."

One of Mr. Stirling's pleasantest qualities was that he never remembered he was a man of letters. Consequently it was not necessary for him to show that he was still a boy at heart and that he could elaborately forget that he was a distinguished novelist by joining in sailing Harry's boat. Harry scrambled to his feet and shook hands with both men at Janey's bidding, and then he looked wistfully at Geoff as a possible playfellow and smiled at

him, an ingratiating smile. But Geoff at twenty, two years younger than Harry, Geoff the artist, the cultured inquirer after famous Raeburns, the appraiser of broken reflections and relative values, only gaped vacantly at him, hands in pockets, without seeing him.

Harry puffed out an enormous sigh and looked back at his boat, and then he clapped his hands suddenly and ran to meet Annette, who was coming slowly towards them across the grass.

Mr. Stirling's eyes and Janey's followed him, and Mr. Stirling felt rather than saw that Janey winced as she looked gravely at the approaching figure.

Geoff's hat was at the back of his sugar-cone of a head. His mild face was transfixed.

" Mrs. Le Geyt," he said, below his breath.

" Our life is like a narrow raft, Afloat upon the hungry sea. Thereon is but a little space, And all men, eager for a place, Do thrust each other in the sea— And each man, raving for a place, Doth cast his brother in the sea."

HALF an hour later, when Annette had left them, Mr. Stirling and his nephew turned with Janey towards the tall Italian gates, which Harry was dutifully holding open for them. As Geoff shambled beside him, glancing backwards in the direction of the path across the park which Annette had taken, Mr. Stirling half wished that his favourite sister's only child stared less at pretty women, that he had less tie and hair, and rather more backbone and deportment.

11 Uncle Reggie," blurted out Geoff, " that Miss Georges ! "

"Well?"

" Has she divorced him ? Is that why she's called Miss Georges ? "

"I suppose she's called Miss Georges for the same reason that you are called Geoffrey Lestrange," said his uncle. "Because it happens to be her name."

"But she is Mrs. Le Geyt," continued Geoff, looking with wide-open, innocent eyes from his uncle to Janey. "Mrs. Dick Le Geyt. I know it. I knew her again directly. I saw her when they were staying at Fontainebleau on their honeymoon. I've never forgotten her. I wanted to draw her. I thought of asking him if I might, but he was rather odd in his manner, and I didn't, and the next day he was ill, and I went away. But they were down in the visitors' book as Mr. and Mrs. Le Geyt, and I heard him call her Annette, and "

Mr. Stirling suddenly caught sight of Janey's face. It was crimson, startled, but something in it baffled him. It had become rigid, and he saw with amazement that it was not with horror or indignation, but as if one in torture, terrified at the vision, saw a horrible way of escape over a dead body.

"You are making a mistake, Geoff," he said sternly. "You never get hold of the right end of any stick. You don't in the least realize what you are saying, or that Mr. Le Geyt is Miss Manvers' brother."

"I only wish," said Janey, with dignity and with truth, "that my poor brother were married to Miss Georges. There is no one I should have liked better as a sister-in-law. But you are mistaken, Mr. Lestrange, in thinking such a thing. To the best of my belief he is not married."

"They were at Fontainebleau together as husband and wife," said Geoff. "They really were. And she had a wedding ring on. She has not got it on now. I looked, and—and "

But Mr. Stirling swept him down.

" That's enough. You must forgive him, Miss Manvers. He has mistaken his vocation. He ought not to be a painter, but a novelist. Fiction is evidently his forte. Good evening. Good-bye, Harry. Thank you for opening the gate for us. We will take the short cut across the fields to Noyes. Good-bye. Good-bye."

And Mr. Stirling, holding Geoff by the elbow, walked him off rapidly down the lane.

"Uncle Reggie," said the boy," I think I won't go to Japan to-morrow after all. I think I'll stop on here. I can get a room in the village, and make a picture of the fountain and the lichen and the willow weed, with Mrs. Le Geyt picking flowers. She's just what I want. I suppose there isn't any real chance of her being so kind as to stand for me, is there?—she looks so very kind,—in the nude, I mean. It's quite warm. But if she wouldn't consent to that, that gown she had on, that mixed colour, cobalt with crimson lake in it "

" Called lilac for short," interpolated Mr. Stirling.

"It would be glorious against the yews, and knocking up against the grey stone and that yellow lichen in the reflection. The whole thing would be—stupendous. I see it."

Geoff wrenched his elbow away from his uncle's grip, and stopped short in the path, looking at Mr. Stirling, through him.

"I see it," he said, and his pink, silly face became pale, dignified, transfigured.

Mr. Stirling's heart smote him.

" Geoff," he said gently, taking his arm again, and making him walk quietly on beside him, " listen to me. There are other things hi the world to be attended to besides pictures."

" No, there aren't."

" Yes, there are. I put it to you. You have made a statement about Miss Georges which will certainly do her a great deal of harm if it is repeated. You blurt out things about her which are tantamount to making a very serious accusation against her character, and then in the same breath you actually suggest that you should make use of her in your picture—when you have done your level best to injure her reputation. Now, as one man of the world to another, is that honourable, is it even' cricket' ? "

Geoff's face became weak and undecided again. The vision had been shattered.

Mr. Stirling saw his advantage, and pressed it with all the more determination because he perceived that Geoff at any rate was firmly convinced of the truth of what he had said, incredible as it seemed.

" You will take no rooms in this village," he said with decision, " and you will start for Japan to-morrow as arranged. I shall see you off,

and before you go you will promise me on your oath never to say another word to anyone, be they who they may, about having seen Miss Georges at Fontainebleau, or any other ' bleau,' in that disreputable Dick Le Geyt's company."

Janey's heart beat violently as she walked slowly home.

During the last few weeks she had sternly faced the fact that Roger was attracted by Annette, and not without many pangs had schooled herself to remain friends with her. There had been bitter moments when a choking jealousy had welled up in her heart against Annette. She might have let Roger alone. Beautiful women always hypocritically pretended that they could not help alluring men. But they could. Annette need not have gratified her vanity by trying to enslave him.

But after the bitter moment Janey's sturdy rectitude and sense of justice always came to her rescue.

f< Annette has not tried," she would say stolidly to herself. " And why shouldn't she try, if she likes him ? I am not going to lose her if she does try. She doesn't know I want him. She is my friend, and I mean to keep her, whatever happens."

Whatever happens. But Janey had never dreamed of anything like this happening. As she walked slowly home with her bunch of snapdragons, she realized that if Roger knew what

she and Mr. Stirling knew about Annette, he would leave her. It was not too late yet. His mind was not actually made up—that slow mind, as tenacious as her own. He was gravitating towards Annette. But if she let it reach his ears that Annette had been Dick's mistress he would turn from her, and never think of her as a possible wife again. After an interval he would gradually revert to her, Janey, without having ever realized that he had left her. Oh ! if only Roger had been present when that foolish young man had made those horrible allegations 1 —if only he had heard them for himself I Janey reddened at her own cruelty, her own disloyalty.

But was it, could it be true that Annette with her clear, unfathomable eyes had an ugly past behind her ? It was unthinkable. And yet— Janey had long since realized that Annette had a far wider experience of men and women than she had. How had she gained it, that experience, that air of mystery which, though Janey did not know it, was a more potent charm than her beauty ?

Was it possible that she might be Dick's wife after all, as that young man had evidently taken for granted ? No. No wife, much less Annette, would have left her husband at death's door, and have fled at the advent of his relations. His mistress might have acted like that, had actually acted like that; for Janey knew that when her aunt arrived at Fontainebleau a woman who till then had passed as Dick's wife

and had nursed him devotedly had decamped, and never been heard of again.

Was it possible that Annette had been that woman ? Mr. Lestrange had been absolutely certain of what he had seen. His veracity was obvious. And Annette's was not a face that one could easily forget, easily mistake for anyone else. In her heart Janey was convinced that he had indeed seen Annette with her brother, passing as his wife. And she saw that Mr. Stirling was convinced also.

She had reached the garden of the Dower House, and she sank down on the wooden seat round the cedar. The sun had set behind the long line of the Hulver woods, and there was a flight of homing rooks across the amber sky.

Then Annette must be guilty, in spite of her beautiful face and her charming ways l Janey clasped her hands tightly together. Her outlook on life was too narrow, too rigid, to differentiate or condone. Annette had been immoral.

And was she, Janey, to stand by, and see Roger, her Roger, the straightest man that ever walked, and the most unsuspicious, marry her brother's mistress ? Could she connive at such a wicked thing ? Would Roger forgive her, would she ever forgive herself, if she coldly held aloof and let him ruin 1pj& life, drench it in dishonour, because she was too proud to say a word ? It was her duty to speak, her bounden duty. Janey became dizzy under the onslaught of a sudden wild tumult within her. Was it grief ?

Was it joy ? She only knew that it was anguish.

Perhaps it was the anguish of one dying of thirst to whom the cup of life is at last held, and who sees even as he stretches his parched lips towards it that the rim is stained with blood.

CHAPTER XXV

" We sometimes think we might have loved more in kinder circumstances, if some one had not died, or if some one else had not turned away from us. Vain self-deception! The love we hare given is all we had to give. If we had had more in us it would have come out. The circumstances of life always give scope for love if they give scope for nothing else. There is no stony desert in which it will not grow, no climate however bleak in which its marvellous flowers will not open to perfection."—M. N.

Two days later, when Janey was pacing in the lime walk of the Hulver gardens, Mr. Stirling joined her. She had known him slightly ever since he had become her mother's tenant and their neighbour at Noyes, but her acquaintance with him had never gone beyond the thinnest conventional civility. The possibility that Mr. Stirling might have been an acquisition in a preposterously dull neighbourhood had not occurred to Janey and Roger. They did not find Riff dull, and they were vaguely afraid of him as " clever." The result had been that they seldom met, and he was quickly aware of Janey's surprise at seeing him.

He explained that he had been to call on her at the Dower House, and the servant said she had gone up to the gardens, and finding the gate

unlocked he had ventured to follow her. She saw that he had come for some grave reason, and they sat down on the green wooden seat which followed the semicircle in the yew hedge. Far off at the other end of the lime walk was another semicircular seat. There had been wind in the night, and the rough grass, that had once been a smooth-shaven lawn, and the long paved walk were strewn with curled amber leaves as if it were autumn already.

Mr. Stirling looked with compassion at Janey's strained face and sleepless eyes.

" I have come to see you," he said, " because I know you are a friend of Miss Georges."

He saw her wince.

" I am not sure I am," she said hoarsely, involuntarily.

" I am quite sure," he said.

There was a moment's silence.

" I came to tell you that my nephew has started for Japan, and that he has promised me upon his oath that he will never speak again of what he gabbled so foolishly. He meant no harm. But stupid people generally manage to do a good deal. The worst of Geoff's stupidity was that it was the truth which he blurted out."

" I knew it," said Janey below her breath. " I was sure of it."

" So was I," said Mr. Stirling sadly. " One can't tell why one believes certain things and disbelieves others. But Geoff's voice had that mysterious thing the ring of truth in it. I knew at once you recognized that. That is why I am here."

Janey looked straight in front of her.

" Of course I hoped, you and I both hoped/ 1 he continued, " that Geoff might have been mistaken. But he was not. He was so determined to prove to me that he was not that he unpacked one of his boxes already packed to start for Japan, and got out his last year's notebooks. I kept one of them. He did not like it, but I thought it was safer with me than with him."

Mr. Stirling produced out of a much-battered pocket a small sketch-book with an elastic band round it, and turned the leaves. Each page was crowded with pencil studies of architecture, figures, dogs, children, nursemaids ; small elaborate drawings of door-knockers and leaden pipe-heads ; vague scratches of officials and soldiers, the individuality of each caught in a few strokes. He turned the pages with a certain respectful admiration.

" He has the root of the matter in him," he said. " He will arrive."

Janey was not impressed. She thought the sketches very unfinished.

Then he stopped at a certain page. Neither of them could help smiling. The head waiter, as seen from behind, napkin on arm, dish on spread hand, superb, debonair, stout but fleet.

Alphonse was scribbled under it, Fontaine-bleau, Sept. the tenth, and the year. 14

Mr. Stirling turned the leaf, turned three or four leaves, all with Mariette scrawled on them. Mariette had evidently been the French chambermaid, and equally evidently had detained Geoff's vagrant eye.

Another page. A man leaning back in his chair laughing. Dick Le Geyt was written under it.

" Is it like him ? " asked Mr. Stirling.

" It's him," said Janey.

Yet another page. They both looked in silence at the half-dozen masterly strokes with Mrs. Le Geyt written under them.

11 It is unmistakable," Mr. Stirling said. " It is not only she, but it is no one else."

His eyes met Janey's. She nodded.

He closed the little book, put its elastic band round it, and squeezed it into his pocket.

11 Why did you bring that to show me ? " she said harshly. It seemed as if he had come to tempt her.

11 I knew," he said, " that for the last two days you must have been on the rack, torn with doubt as to the truth of what my miserable nephew had affirmed. You look as if you had not slept since. Anything is better than suspense. Well, now you know it is true."

" Yes, it is true," said Janey slowly, and she became very pale. Then she added, with difficulty, " I knew—we all knew—that Dick had had some one—a woman—with him at Fontainebleau when he was taken ill. His valet told my aunt he had not gone—alone. And the hotel-keeper told her the same. She ran away when Aunt Jane arrived. Aunt Jane never saw her. We never knew who she was."

" Till now/' said Mr. Stirling softly.

Two long-winged baby-swallows were sitting on their breasts on the sunny flagged path, resting, turning their sleek heads to right and left. Mr. Stirling watched them intently.

" Why should anyone but you and I ever know?" he said, with a sigh, after they had flown. He had waited, hoping Janey would say those words, but he had had to say them himself instead.

She did not answer. She could not. A pulse in her throat was choking her. This, then, was what he had come for, to persuade her to be silent, to hush it up. All men were the same about a pretty woman. A great tumult clamoured within her, but she made no movement.

" I may as well mention that I am interested in Miss Georges," he went on quietly. " Don't you find that rather ridiculous, Miss Manvers ? An elderly man of fifty, old enough to be her father. It is quite absurd, and very undignified, isn't it ? You are much too courteous to agree with me. But I can see you think it is so, whether you agree or not. Wise women often justly accuse us silly susceptible men of being caught by a pretty face. I have been caught by a sweet face. I never exchanged a word with Miss Georges till yesterday, so I have not had the chance of being attracted by her mind. And it is not her mind that draws me, it is her face. I have known her by sight for some time. I go to church in order to see her. I called on her two aunts solely in order to make her acquaintance. The elder one, the portentous authoress, is the kind of person whom I should creep down a sewer to avoid ; even the saintly invalid does not call out my higher nature."

Mr. Stirling became aware that Janey was lost in amazement. Irony is singularly unsuited to a narrow outlook.

He waited a moment, and then went on, choosing his words carefully, as if he were speaking to some one very young—

" It is quite a different thing to be attracted, and to have any hope of marriage, isn't it? I have, and had, no thought of marrying Miss Georges. I am aware that I could not achieve it. Men of my age do not exist for women of her age. But that does not prevent my having a deep desire to serve her. And service is the greater part of love, isn't it ? I am sure you know that, whose life is made up of service of others."

" I am not sure I do," she said stiffly. She was steeling herself against him.

If he found her difficult, he gave no sign of it. He went on tranquilly—

" As one grows old one sees, oh I how clearly one sees that the only people whom one can be any real use to are those whom one loves— with one's whole heart. Liking is no real use. Pity and duty are not much either. They are better than nothing, but that is all. Love is the one weapon, the one tool, the one talisman. Now we can't make ourselves love people. Love is the great gift. I don't, of course, mean the gift of a woman's love to a man, or of a man's to a woman. I mean the power to love anyone devotedly, be they who they may, is God's greatest gift to us His children. And He does not give it us very often. To some He never gives it. Many people go through life loved and cherished who seem to be denied His supreme blessing—that of being able to love, of seeing that wonderful light rest upon a fellow-creature. And as we poor elders look back, we see that there were one or two people who crossed our path earlier in life whom we loved, or could have loved, and whom we have somehow lost : perhaps by their indifference, perhaps by our own temperament, but whom nevertheless we have lost. When the first spark is lit in our hearts of that mysterious flame which it sometimes takes us years to quench, one does not realize it at the time. I did not. Twenty-five years ago, Miss Manvers, before you were born, I fell in love. I was at that time a complete egoist, a very perfect specimen, with the superficial hardness of all crustaceans who live on the defensive, and wear their bones outside like a kind of

armour. She was a year or two younger
than I was, just about Miss Georges' age. Miss Georges reminds me of her. She is taller and more beautiful, but she reminds me of her all the same. I was not sure whether she cared for me. And I had a great friend. And he fell in love with her too. And I renounced her, and withdrew in his favour. I went away without speaking. I thought I was acting nobly. He said there was no one like me. Thoreau had done the same, and I worshipped Thoreau in my youth, and had been to see him in his log hut. I was sustained in my heartache by feeling I was doing a heroic action. It never struck me I was doing it at her expense. I went abroad, and after a time she married my friend. Some years later, I heard he was dying of a terrible disease in the throat, and I went to see him. She nursed him with absolute devotion, but she would not allow me to be much with him. I put it down to a kind of jealousy. And after his death I tried to see her, but again she put difficulties in the way. At last I asked her to marry me, and she refused me."

" Because you had deserted her to start with," said Janey.

" No ; she was not like that. Because she was dying of the same disease as her husband. She had contracted it from him. That was why she had never let me be much with him, or afterwards with her. When I knew, I was willing to risk it, but she was not. She had
her rules, and from them she never departed. She let me sit with her in the garden, and to the last she was carried out to her long chair so that I might be with her. She told me it was the happiest time of her life. I found that from the first she had loved me, and she loved me to the last. She never reproached me for leaving her. She was a simple person. I told her I had done it on account of my friend, and she thought it very noble of me, and said it was just what she should have expected of me. There was no irony in her. And she slipped quietly out of life, keeping her ideal of me to the last."

" I think it was noble too," said Janey stolidly.

" Was it ? I never considered her for a moment. I had had the desire to serve her, but I never served her. Instead, I caused her long, long unhappiness—for my friend had a difficult temperament—and suffering and early death. I never realized that she was alive, vulnerable, sensitive. I should have done better to have married her and devoted myself to her. I have never wanted to devote myself to any woman since. We should have been happy together. And she might have been with me still, and we might have had a son who would just have been the right age to marry Miss Georges."

' You would not have wanted him to marry her now," said Janey hoarsely. " You would not want her to marry anyone you were fond of."

Among a confusion of tangled threads Mr. Stirling saw a clue—at last.

A dragon-fly alighted on the stone at his feet, its long orange body and its gauze wings gleaming in the vivid sunshine. It stood motionless save for its golden eyes. Even at that moment, his mind, intent on another object, unconsciously noted and registered the transparent shadow on the stone of its transparent wings.

" I think," he said, " if I had had a son who was trying to marry her, I should have come to you just as I have come now, and I should have said, ' Why should anyone but you and I ever know ? ' "

" No. No, you wouldn't," said Janey, as if desperately defending some position which he was attacking. " You would want to save him at all costs."

" From what ? From the woman he loves ? I have not found it such great happiness to be saved from the woman I loved."

Janey hesitated, and then said—

11 From some one unworthy of him."

Mr. Stirling watched an amber leaf sail to the ground. Then he said slowly—

" How do I know that Annette is unworthy of him ? She may have done wrong and still be worthy of him. Do you not see that if I decided she was unworthy and hurried my son away, I should be acting on the same principle as I did in my own youth, the old weary principle which has pressed so hard on women, that you can treat a fellow-creature like a picture or a lily, or a sum of money ? I handed over my love just as if she had been a lily. How often I had likened her to one ! But she was alive, poor soul, all the time, and I only found it out when she was dying, years and years afterwards. Only then did my colossal selfishness confront me. She was a fellow-creature like you and me. What was it Shy lock said ? ' If you prick us, do we not bleed ? ' Now, for aught we know to the contrary, Annette may be alive. "

His grave eyes met hers, with a light in them, gentle, inexorable.

" Unless we are careful we may make her bleed. We have the knife ready to our hands. If you were in her place, and had a grievous incident in your past, would anything wound you more deeply than if she, she your friend, living in the same village, raked up that ugly past, and made it public for no reason ? "

" But there is a reason," said Janey passionately,— " not a reason that everyone should know, God forbid, but that one person should be told, who may marry her in ignorance, and who would never marry her if he knew what you and I know—never, never, never ! "

" And what would you do in her place, in such a predicament ? "

" I should not be in it, because when he

asked me to marry him I should tell him everything."

" Perhaps that is j ust what she will do. Knowing her intimately as you do, can you think that she would act meanly and deceitfully ? I can't."

Janey avoided his searching glance, and made no answer.

" You can't either," he said tranquilly. " And do you think she would lie,about it ? "

" No," said Janey slowly, against her will.

" Then let us, at any rate, give her her chance of telling him herself."

He got up slowly, and Janey did the same. He saw that her stubbornness though shaken was not vanquished, and that he should obtain no assurance from her that she would be silent.

" And let us give this man, whoever he may be, his chance too," he said, taking her hand and holding it. He felt it tremble, and his heart ached for her. He had guessed. " The chance of being loyal, the chance of being tender, generous, understanding. Do not let us wreck it by interference. This is a matter which lies between her and him, and between her and him only. It may be the making of him. It would have been the making of me if I could but have taken it— my great chance—if I had not preferred to sacrifice her, in order to be a sham hero."

CHAPTER XXVI

" Look long, look long in the water Melisande,

Is there never a face but your own ? There is never a soul you shall know Melisande, Your soul must stand alone, All alone in the world Melisande, Alone, alone."

ETHEL CLIFFORD.

THE long evening was before Janey. Since her stroke, her mother " retired for the night/' as the nurse called it, at nine instead of ten. And at nine, Janey came down to the drawing-room and established herself with her work beside the lamp. Harry, whom nothing could keep awake after his game of dominoes, went to bed at nine also.

But to-night, as she took up her work, her spirit quailed at the long array of threadbare thoughts that were lying in wait for her. She dared not think any more. She laid down her work, and took up the paper. But she had no interest in politics. There seemed to be nothing in it. She got up, and taking the lamp in her hand crossed the room and looked at the books in the Chippendale bookcase, the few books which her mother had brought with her from Hulver. They were well chosen, no doubt, but somehow Janey did not want them. Shakespeare ? No. Longfellow ? No. She was tired of him, tired even of her favourite lines, " Life is real, life is earnest." Tennyson? No. Pepys' Diary ? She had heard people speak of it. No. Bulwer's novels, Jane Austen's, Maria Edgeworth's, Sir Walter Scott's ? No. Crooks and Coronets ? She had only read it once. She might look at it again. She liked Miss Nevill's books. She had read most of them, not intentionally, but because while she was binding them in brown paper for the village library, she had found herself turning the leaves. She especially liked the last but one, about simple fisher-folk. She often wondered how Miss Nevill knew so much about them. If she had herself been acquainted with fishermen, she would have realized how little the dignified authoress did know. Somehow, she did not care to read even one of Miss Nevill's books to-night.

The Magnet, by Reginald Stirling. She hesitated, put out her hand, and took the first of the three volumes from the shelf. She had skimmed it when it came out five years ago, because the Bishop, when he stayed with them for a confirmation, had praised it. Janey had been surprised that he had recommended it when she came to read it, for parts of it were decidedly unpleasant. She might look at it again. She had no recollection of it, except that she had not liked it. Her conversation with Mr. Stirling had agitated her, but it had also stirred her. Though she did not know it, it was the first time she had come into real contact with an educated and sensitive mind, and one bent for the moment on understanding hers. No one as a rule tried to understand Janey. It was not necessary. No one was interested in her. You might easily love Janey, but you could not easily be interested in her.

The book was dusty. It was obvious that The Magnet had not proved a magnet to anyone in the Dower House.

She got out an old silk handkerchief from a drawer and dusted it carefully. Then she sat down by the lamp once more and opened it. Ninetieth thousand. Was that many or few to have sold ? It seemed to her a good many, but perhaps all books sold as many as that. She glanced at the first page.

" To A BLESSED MEMORY."

That, no doubt, was the memory of the woman of whom he had spoken. She realized suddenly that it had cost him something to speak of that. Why had he done it ? To help Annette ? Every one wanted to help and protect Annette, and ward off trouble from her. No one wanted to help or guard her—Janey.

11 No one ? " asked Conscience.

Janey saw suddenly the yellow leaves on the flags. She had not noticed them at the time. She saw the two baby-swallows sitting on their breasts on the sun-warmed stone. She had not noticed them at the time. She saw suddenly, as in a glass, the nobility, the humility, and the benevolence of the man sitting beside her, and his intense desire to save her from what he believed to be a cruel action. She had noticed nothing at the time. She had been full of herself and her own devastating problem. She saw that he had pleaded with her in a great compassion as much on her own account as on Annette's. He had stretched out a hand to help her, had tried to guard her, to ward off trouble from her. This required thought. Janey and Roger could both think, though they did not do so if they could help it, and he did his aloud to Janey by preference whenever it really had to be done. Janey's mind got slowly and reluctantly to its feet. It had been accustomed from early days to walk alone.

A step crunched the gravel, came along the terrace, a well-known step. Roger's face, very red and round-eyed behind a glowing cigarette end, appeared at the open window.

" I saw by the lamp you had not gone to bed yet. May I come in ? " Coming in. " My I It is like an oven in here."

" I will come out," said Janey.

They sat down on the terrace on two wicker chairs. It was the first time she had been alone with him since she had met Geoff Lestrange. And as Roger puffed at his cigar-

ette in silence she became aware that he had something on his mind, and had come to unburden himself to her. The moon was not yet risen, and the church tower and the twisted pines stood as if cut out of black velvet against the dim pearl of the eastern sky.

" I came round this afternoon," said Roger in an aggrieved tone, " but you were out."

It seems to be a fixed idea, tap-rooted into the very depths of the masculine mind, that it is the bounden duty of women to be in when they call, even if they have not thought fit to mention their flattering intentions. But some of us are ruefully aware that we might remain indoors twenty years without having our leisure interrupted. Janey had on many occasions waited indoors for Roger, hut not since he had seen Annette home after the choir practice.

" You never seem to be about nowadays," he said.

" I was in the Hulver gardens."

1 Yes, so I thought I would come round now."

Roger could extract more creaking out of one wicker garden chair than any other man in Lowshire, and more crackling out of a newspaper, especially if music was going on : that is, unless Annette was singing. He was as still as a stone on those occasions.

" How is Aunt Louisa ? "

11 Just the same."

" Doctor been? "

" No."

' I was over at Noyes this morning about the bridge. Stirling gave me luncheon. I don't know where I'm going to get the money for it, with Aunt Louisa in this state. It's her business to repair the bridge. It's going to cost hundreds."

Janey had heard all this before many times. She was aware that Roger was only marking time.

(When I was over there," continued Roger, ' I saw Bartlet, and he told me Mary Deane—you know who I mean?"

" Perfectly."

" I heard the child, the little girl, had died suddenly last week. Croup or something. They ought to have let me know. The funeral was yesterday."

" Poor woman ! "

" She and the old servant between them carried the little coffin themselves along the dyke and across the ford. Wouldn't let anyone else touch it. I heard about it from Bartlet. He ought to have let me know. I told him so. He said he thought I did know. That's Bartlet all over. And he said he went up to see her next day, and—and she was gone."

"Gone?"

11 Yes, gone. Cleared out ; and the servant too. Cowell said a man from Welysham had

called for their boxes. They never went back to the house after the funeral. I ought to have been told. And to-day I get this/' Roger pulled a letter out of his pocket and held it out to her. He lit a match, and by its wavering light she read the few lines, in an educated hand :—

" I only took the allowance from you when Dick became too ill to send it, on account of Molly. Now Molly is dead, I do not need it, or the house, or anything of Dick's any more. The key is with Cornell.—M."

" Poor woman 1" said Janey again.

" It's a bad business/' said Roger. " She was—there was something nice about her. She wasn't exactly a lady, but there really was something nice about her. And the little girl was Dick over again. You couldn't help liking Molly."

" I suppose she has gone back to her own people?"

Roger shook his head.

" She hasn't any people—never knew who her parents were. She was—the same as her child. She loved Dick, but I don't think she ever forgave him for letting Molly be born out of wedlock. She knew what it meant. It embittered her. It was not only her own pride which had been wounded, and she was a proud woman. But Molly ! She resented Molly being illegitimate."

" Oh, Roger, what will become of her ? "

" Goodness knows."

11 Dick oughtn't^ have done it," said Roger slowly, as if he were enunciating some new and 15 startling hypothesis. " But to do him justice I do believe he might have married her if he'd lived. I think if he cared for anybody it was for her. Dick meant well, but he was touched in his head. She ought not to have trusted him. Not quite like other people; no memory : and never in the same mind two days running."

There was a short silence. But Roger had got under way at last. Very soothing at times is a monologue to the weary masculine mind.

" I used to think," he went on, " that Dick was the greatest liar and swindler under the sun. He went back on his word, his written word, and he wasn't straight. I'm certain he ran a ramp at Leopardstown. That was the last time he rode in Ireland. You couldn't trust him. But I begin to think that from the first he had a bee in his bonnet, poor chap. I remember Uncle John leathering him within an inch of his life when he was a boy because he said he had not set the big barn alight. And he had. He'd been seen to do it by others as well as by me.

I saw him, but I never said. But I believe now he wasn't himself, sort of sleep-walking, and he really had clean forgotten he'd done it. And do you remember about the Eaton Square house ? "

Of course Janey remembered, but she said,

II What about that? "

" Why, he wrote to me to tell me he had decided to sell it only last August, a month before his accident, as he wanted cash. He had clean forgotten he had sold it two years ago and had had the money. Twenty thousand it was."

Puff! Puff!

" Jones, his valet, you know! "

" Yes."

" Jones told me privately when I was in Paris a month ago that Dick couldn't last much longer. Gangrene in both feet. The wonder is he has lived so long. Aunt Louisa will get her wish after all. You'll see he will die intestate, and everything will go to Harry. Pity you weren't a boy,

Janey. Dick can't make a will now, that's certain, though I don't believe if he could and wanted to, Lady Jane would let him. But whatever happens, the family ought to remember Jones when Dick's gone, and settle something handsome on him for life. Jones has played the game by Dick."

Janey thought it was just like Roger to be anxious about the valet, when his own rightful inheritance was slipping away from him. For Roger came next in the male line after Dick, if you did not count Harry.

There was a long silence.

11 When Dick does go," said Roger meditatively,—" moon looks jolly, doesn't it, peeping out behind the tower ?—I wonder whether we shall have trouble with the other woman, the one who was with him when he was taken ill."

11 At Fontainebleau ? "

" Yes. I hear she was not at all a common person either, and as handsome as paint."

At the back of his mind Roger had a rueful, half-envious feeling that really the luck had been with Dick : one pretty woman after another, while he, Roger, plodded along as good as gold and as dull as ditch water, and only had to provide for the babes of these illicit unions. It did not seem fair.

11 Perhaps there is another child there," he said.

11 Oh no, no !" said Janey, wincing.

" It's no use saying,' Oh no, no 1' my good girl. It may be,' Oh yes, yes !' The possibility has to be faced." Roger spoke as a man of the world. " There may be a whole brood of them for aught we know."

11 Do you think he may possibly have married this—second one ? " said Janey tentatively.

" No, I don't. If he had, she wouldn't have bolted. Besides, if Dick had married anyone, I do believe it would have been Mary Deane. Well, she's off our hands, poor thing. She won't trouble us again, but I don't expect we shall get off as easy with number two."

CHAPTER XXVII

" Erfahrungen haben 1st nichts, aber aus alien Erfahrnngen ein reines Herz gerettet zu haben, Alles." L. HABICHT.

IT was the second week in August. Mrs. Stoddart had arrived at Noyes, and had driven over to see Annette, and to make the acquaintance of the Miss Nevills.

She was an immediate success with them, possibly because she intended to be one, and knew how to set about it.

The Miss Nevills had two worlds, the social and the literary, and each one had " right people" in it. In the social world the right people were of course those who belonged to the same social order as themselves, who were connected with, or related to, or friends of Nevills, or were connected with, or related to, or friends of the connections and relatives and friends of Nevills. Mrs. Stoddart allowed her visiting list to be probed, and quickly established herself as one of the right people. She knew people they knew. Her sister Lady Brandon was a frequent visitor at the Deanery of St. Botolph's, where they had lunched during the Church Congress. And it was her niece who became the second Mrs.

Templeton when the first Mrs. Templeton, known of the Miss Nevills, died.

If, Reader, you have ever engaged in the back-breaking, hand-blistering task of eradicating a scattered and well-established colony of nettles, you have no doubt discovered that a nettle—except a few parvenus, growth of the last rains—does not live to itself alone. It possesses endless underground ramifications and knotted connections with other groups and neighbouring groves of nettles. Get hold of the root of one, and you pull up a long string resetted at intervals with bunches of the same stimulating family. So it was with the social world of the Miss Nevills. There was always what they called " a link," and one of Aunt Harriet's chief interests in life was the establishment of these links in the case of each newcomer, though nothing much happened when it was established.

Just as you and I, Reader, in our vulgar, homely way, strike up an eager acquaintanceship, even form a friendship with equally communicative strangers on steamers, in omnibuses, in trains, because we have both stayed in the same hotel at Lauter-brunnen, or go to the same dentist, or derive benefit from the same pre-digested food, so the Miss Nevills continually established links by more aristocratic avenues with the assiduity of Egyptologists.

But much of the pleasure of Mrs. Stoddart's visit was damped by the fact which she dis-
erectly concealed till almost the last moment, that she was the bearer of an invitation from Mr. Stirling to Annette to spend a few days at Noyes during her own visit there. Aunt Maria was wounded to the quick. She had made up her mind to cultivate Mr. Stirling, to steep herself in long literary conversations with him, to read aloud certain important chapters of The Silver Cross to him, on which his judgment would be invaluable. And here was Annette, who had not an idea in her mind beyond housekeeping and gardening and singing in the choir, here was Annette preferred before her. Aunt Maria yearned to be admitted to the society of the " right people " in the literary world as well as the social one. She had been made much of by the camp followers of literature, who were always prodigal of their invitations. And a few uneasy vanities, such as the equally ignored Mr. Harvey, found a healing comfort as she did herself in their respectful adulation. But all the time she knew that she was an outsider in the best literary circles. There was no one more democratic than the author of Crooks and Coronets when she approached the literary class. She was, to use her own phraseology, " quite ready " to meet with urbanity anyone distinguished in the world of letters, quite regardless of family. But they apparently were not equally ready to meet her—at least, not to meet her a second time. Mr. Stirling was a writer of considerable importance, and Aunt Maria

was magnanimously prepared to overlook the fact that his father had been a small shopkeeper in Hammersmith.

But he preferred Annette's society to hers.

Mrs. Stoddart hastened to lay a soothing unguent on the sensitive spirit of the celebrated authoress. It quickly transpired that the invitation to Annette had been mainly the result of Mrs. Stoddart's own suggestion.

" I begged him to let me have Annette with me for a few days/' she said, " and he was most kind about it. He is one of my oldest friends."

Aunt Maria, somewhat mollified, yielded a dignified consent, and an incident which had had its painful moment was closed. The next day the news reached the Miss Blinketts with the afternoon delivery of milk that the carriage from Noyes Court had come to Red Riff, and that Annette had departed in it with a small dress-box at her feet, and a hat-box on the vacant seat beside her.

Noyes Court is not an old house as old houses go in Lowshire, not like Loudham close by, which has looked into its lake since Edward the Third's time. Noyes was built by Hakoun Le Geyt, to whom Henry the Eighth gave Noyes Priory and the estates belonging thereto. And Hakoun erected a long black and white timbered house, with elaborately carved beams and doorways, on the high ground above the deserted Priory. And possibly he took most of the lead from the Priory roof, and certainly he took some of the carved hammerbeams, for they have the word " Maria " running along them, as you may see to this day. For when Cardinal Wolsey came to visit him, the Priory was already a ruin. Perhaps Hakoun was a man of foresight, and may have realized that the great Cardinal, who was coming to Noyes on the quest of suppressing some of the Lowshire monasteries in order to swell the revenues of his new college at Ipswich, might lay his clutching hand on anything that still remained in the condemned Priory, and so thought it politic to appropriate what he could while opportunity offered.

However that may have been, Noyes is rich in ancient lattice and stained glass, and curious lead-work and gargoyle. And in the minstrels' gallery you may see how cunningly the carved angels and griffons have been inserted at intervals in the black oak balustrade.

Hakoun must have been a man of taste, though he was a parvenu in spite of his fine coat-of-arms : some said he was nothing better than one of Catherine of Aragon's pages, who became a favourite with England's stout young King when poor Catherine was herself in favour. But he had the wit to consolidate his position in Lowshire by marrying into one of its greatest families, the beautiful Jane de Ludham. Her father it was, Ralph de Ludham, who had made the passage through Sweet Apple Tree marsh because the hated Priors of Noyes hindered people

passing through their lands. And his son-in-law, eager to conciliate his Lutheran father-in-law and his country neighbours, gave the stones of the Priory to build the new bridge over the Rieben which stands to this day. From the earliest times, almost from the Conquest, there had been trouble about the bridge. The Priors of Noyes were bound to keep it in good repair by reason of the lands they held on both sides of it. But the Priors had never troubled themselves to carry out their duty, and there was a grim justice in the fact that the very fabric of their Priory fulfilled the obligation which they themselves had ignored when the last of them was in his tomb, and a young Frenchman had taken possession of their lands.

The young Frenchman made good his hold on Noyes, and his successors prospered, marrying steadily into the Lowshire families, excepting a certain unlucky Richard who must needs wed a French maid-of-honour of Charles the Second's Court, and, as some averred, the daughter of that witty monarch. There is a charming portrait of Henriette of many curls in the gallery which certainly has a look of the Stuarts, hanging opposite her ill-fated Richard, who soon after the marriage got himself blown up with Lord Sandwich in the Royal James.

Mrs. Stoddart and Annette were sitting in the walled herb garden which Henriette in her widowhood had made, who had put with pardon-

able vanity her initials twined in gilded iron in the centre of the iron gate which led down to it from the terrace above. The little enclosed garden lay bathed in a misty sunshine. Beyond it, the wide lawns were still all silvered with dew in the shadows of the forest trees, which seemed to be advanced posts of the great forest gathered like an army on the other side of the river. The ground fell away before their eyes, in pleasaunce and water meadows, to where in the distance you could just discern the remains of the Prior\'7d'- near the bridge which had cost it so dear.

Even that " new " bridge was now old, and was showing ominous signs of collapse, and Annette's eyes followed the movements of tiny workmen crawling over it. The distant chink of trowel and hammer reached them through the haze of the windless summer morning.

It was evident that the two women had had a long conversation, and that Mrs. Stoddart was slowly turning over something point by point in her mind.

' You realize, Annette," she said at last, ' that you can't go on living at Riff now you know who the Manvers are ? "

' I was afraid you would say that."

" But surely you see it for yourself, whether I say it or not ? "

Annette did not answer. ' There are no two ways about it. You must break with the Manvers root and branch,"

Annette coloured painfully.

" Must I ? "

" Doesn't your own common sense, ii you would only use it, tell you the same ? "

" I am very fond of Janey Manvers." 1 That can't be helped."

"You see," said Annette slowly, " Janey and Roger are the two people I like best anywhere, except you. You don't know," turning her grave eyes to her companion, " how good they are."

" I never like people myself because they are good."

"No, I know. And it's very lucky for me you don't. And then, I dare say, you have always known numbers of good people. But it's different for me. I haven't. I've never been with good people except Aunt Cathie and you."

" If the sacred Miss Nevills could hear you now ! "

" I used to think I hated goodness. But I see now that it was the theory of it, the talking about it, that sickened me. Janey and Roger never talk about it. And then, when I had broken away from the aunts and went to Paris, the life there was really evil under a thin veil which soon got torn. And then I came here, and met Janey and Roger, and got to know them well."

"He is Mr. Le Geyt's younger brother, I suppose ? "

" No, first cousin."

" That short-nosed, sunburnt, silent man we met at the bridge yesterday ? "

" Yes."

" I liked his looks."

" He is straight," said Annette, " and so is Janey. I always think of them together, because they are so alike. They might be brother and sister, and I'm sure they are as fond of each other as if they were. They aren't clever, of course, like you and Mr. Stirling, but then I'm not clever myself. They are just the kind of people I like."

" My poor child, I am afraid you must give them up."

"I'd rather give up anybody than them, except you."

" It isn't a question of what you'd rather do or not do. Now you know who they are, you cannot continue on terms of friendship with them. I don't want to force my will upon you. I only want to advise you for the best. Don't you see for yourself, without my insisting on it, that you will involve yourself hi an impossible situation if you continue your friendship with them ? If I were not here to point that out, surely, surely you could see it for yourself? Annette, if I were not here, if you had no one to advise you, what would you do ? "

" I would tell them," said Annette. " I won't, because I've promised you not to tell anyone, but if I were "

" Free ? " suggested Mrs. Stoddart.

" Yes, if I were free, I should tell them both.'"

Mrs. Stoddart let her knitting fall into her lap, and stared at her companion.

" And what good, in the name of fortune, would come of that ? "

" I don't know that any particular good would come of it, but I should feel happier in my mind. I never had any wish to tell the aunts. I don't know exactly why, but you don't somehow want to tell them things. But ever since I've known that Dick was Janey's brother I've wanted to tell her—her and Roger. It seems to come between me and them like a cloud. You see, they like me, and I like them. There is nothing kept back in their lives, and they think I'm the same as them. I feel as if I ought to tell them."

" But, my dear, if I know anything of people like the Manvers, especially when embedded in the country, it is that they would be terribly shocked, and the disclosure would make an estrangement at once."

"It might," Annette agreed. " I think you're right. I'm afraid it would. But I should like to tell them, all the same."

" They would not be wide-minded enough to understand."

" They're not wide-minded, I know that, and of course they may feel I've been here under false pretences."

11 They certainly would. Wouldn't it be better to do as I advise—to leave Riff ? You must lose them either way, Annette. Then why not lose them by going away, instead of telling them first and then having to go away ?—for, of course, you could not remain. It would give less pain all round."

Annette locked her hands together.

" I would rather they knew the truth about me."

" The truth!" said Mrs. Stoddart, who, like most shrewd women, did not relish opposition. 11 The truth I And who will get at the truth if you tell that story of your act of supreme folly ? Who will believe that you were not Dick Le Geyt's mistress ? The truth ! Do you think it is the truth about you that I have taken such trouble to conceal ? "

" Yes, partly," said Annette. " And I have often wondered lately if it had not been a mistake."

" Why particularly lately ? "

" Because of Roger Manvers."

"The young man at the bridge? I wondered whether he was in love with you when we were talking to him. But I did not think it mattered if he was."

" It matters to me."

" You mean you are actually thinking of him ? Of course, he is most estimable, and a gentleman, one can see that at a glance, but isn't he a trine dull, borne?"

" I think I could get on better with a dull person, if he was kind and honourable, than a clever one I've had one clever one—who wasn't honourable. You see, I'm only good-looking. I'm nothing else. That's why I like being with the Miss Blinketts and Mrs. Nicholls. I forgot perhaps you don't know Mrs. Nicholls is the washerwoman. A clever man would get tired of me, or bored with me, and he would expect so much, understandings and discriminations and things which I could not give, or only by a dreadful effort. If I married Roger, he would be pleased with me as I am."

" I have no doubt he would."

" And I should be pleased with him too."

11 I am not so sure of that."

" I am, but for some time past I have wished he knew anything there was to know against me."

" Well, but, Annette, you know we agreed— you had my full approval—that you should tell everything to the man you were engaged to. 1 '

" I thought that all right at the time—at least, I mean I never thought about it again. But, of course, I did not know Roger then, and I had not realized how cruel it would be to him to go farther and farther, and think more and more of me, and get it firmly rooted in his mind that he would like to marry me,—it takes a long time for him to get his mind fixed,—and then, when I had accepted him and he was feeling very comfortable, to have this—this ugly thing—sprung upon him."

" I don't see how that can be helped."

" Yes, if he had been told very early in the day, he might have withdrawn,—-of course he would have withdrawn if he had believed the worst,—but it would not have cost him much. He would have felt he had had a lucky escape. But as it is," Annette's voice wavered, " I am afraid

Roger will be put to expense."

" Has he said anything ? "

" Yes. No. I mean he said something the other day, but it was by the weir, and I know he thought I did not hear. I was listening to the water, and it made a noise. I heard every word, but I did not like to say so, because I saw he was rather surprised at himself, taken aback."

Mrs. Stoddart cogitated.

At last she said, " My dear, I know what is wise, and that is what I have advised you. But I also know that I am a managing woman, and that one must not coerce the lives of others. You are not what is called wise. And you never will be. But I perceive that you have some kind of course to steer your ship by, and I must even let you steer it. We can't both stand at the helm, Annette. I think you do not see the rocks ahead, which I have taken such trouble to avoid, but at any rate I have pointed them out. I take my hands off the wheel. I give you back your promise."

Mr. Stirling and Roger were coming through the slender iron gates with their scrolled initials, 16

from which the white hanging clusters of the 11 Seven Sisters " had to be pushed back to allow them to pass.

" There are worse things than rocks," said Annette, looking at Roger. But she had become very white.

CHAPTER XXVIII

" Early in the day it was whispered that we should sail in a boat, only thou and I, and never a soul in the world \ would know of this our pilgrimage to no country and to no end."—RABINDRA NATH TAGORE.

MR. STIRLING had no curiosity—that quality which in ourselves we designate as interest in our fellow-creatures, even while we are kneeling at a keyhole.

But his interest in others amounted to a passion. He drew slowly through his hand a little chain, looking at each link with kindly compassion. The first link had been the expression in Janey's eyes when his nephew had unconsciously maligned Annette. The sudden relief as from pain, the exultation in those gentle, patient eyes, had brought him instantly to her side as her ally against herself. And in his interview with her, the commonplace pitiful reason had spread itself out before him. She loved some one, probably Mr. Black, or her cousin Roger—at any rate some one who was drifting into love with Annette. He felt confident when he left Janey that she would not use her weapon against Annette as a means to regain her lover—that Annette was safe as far as she was concerned. Janey was not of those

who blindfold their own eyes for long. He had, he knew, removed the bandage from them. That was all that was necessary.

And now here was Roger, kindly, sociable Roger, whom he had always got on with so well,—in spite of the secret contempt of the country-bred man for a man who neither shoots not hunts,—here was Roger suddenly metamorphosed into a laconic poker, hardly willing to exchange a word with himself or Annette at luncheon. Mr. Stirling perceived, not without amusement, that Roger was acutely jealous of him, and drew the last link of the chain through his hand. Then it was Roger to whom Janey Manvers was attached, Roger who was in love with Annette? That good-looking Mr. Black apparently did not come into the piece at all. The situation had, after all, a classic simplicity. Two women and one man. He had seen something not unlike it before. And he smiled as he remembered how Miss Blinkett once supplied him unasked with sundry details of the affiance-ment of her cousin the Archdeacon with the Bishop's sister, and her anxious injunction when all was divulged that he must not on any account put it into a book. That promise he had kept without difficulty, but not in Miss Blinkett's eyes, who, when his next novel appeared, immediately traced a marked resemblance between the ardent love-making of the half-Italian hero and the gratified comments of the Archdeacon while allowing himself to be

towed into harbour by the blameless blandishments of the Bishop's sister.

Would Roger in turn think he had been " put in " ? Mr. Stirling realized that it was only too likely. For he knew to his cost how deeply embedded in the mind of the provincial male is the conviction that there is nothing like him under the sun. In the novel which Mr. Stirling had recently finished, he had drawn, without a hairbreadth's alteration, the exact portrait of a married brother-novelist, as an inordinately pompous old maid of literary fame. When the book appeared this character called forth much admiration from the public in general, and the brother-novelist in particular ; but it caused a wound so deep and so rankling in the bosom of Aunt Maria that all intercourse was broken off between her and Mr. Stirling for ever, in spite of the fact that he was able to assure her—only she never believed it—that his novel was in the press before he made her acquaintance. But this is a digression.

Mr. Stirling showed some absence of mind during luncheon, and then owned that he was in a small difficulty about the afternoon. He had promised to drive Mrs. Stoddart and Annette to the old cross at Haliwell. But the victoria only held two comfortably, and the horse which was to have taken him in the dogcart had fallen lame.

' I think I shall commandeer you and your dogcart," he said to Roger. " Take a few hours' holiday for once, Manvers, and do us all

a good turn at the same time. We can put some cushions in your cart, so that Miss Georges will be sufficiently comfortable."

Roger was electrified, but he made no sign. He mumbled something about a foreman, he hung back, he was able to reassure himself afterwards by the conviction that he had appeared most unwilling, as indeed he did ; but very deep down within him he felt a thrill of pleasure. He was tired to death, though he did not know it, of the routine of his life, though he clung to it as a bird will sometimes cling to its cage. He had had enough of farm buildings and wire fencing, and the everlasting drainage of land, the weary water-logged Lowshire land. His eyes became perfectly round, and he looked at his plate with his most bottled-up expression. But he was pleased. Fortunately for Annette, she knew that. It did not strike him that she might be disconcerted by his apparent unwillingness to escort her. His savage irritation against Mr. Stirling as " a clever chap who could talk a bird out of a tree " was somewhat mollified. Perhaps, after all, he was interested in Mrs. Stoddart, a widow of about his own age. Roger shot a furtive glance from under his tawny eyelashes at Mrs. Stoddart, suddenly bolted a large piece of peach, and said he thought he could manage it.

It was a still August afternoon, and Roger drove Annette through the sunny countryside.

The cool breath of the sea blew softly in their faces, travelling towards them across the low-lying woods and cornfields. For there are few hills in Lowshire. It is a land of long lines : long lines of tidal river and gleaming flats, and immense stretches of clover—clover which is a soft green for half the summer, and then a sea of dim blue pink. The heather and the gorse-land creep almost down among the fields, with here and there a clump of pines taking care of tiny cottages so muffled in the gorse that you can only see the upper windows, or keeping guard round quaint little churches with flint towers. And everywhere in the part of Lowshire where the Rieben winds, there are old bridges of red blue brick shouldering up among the buttercups, and red cows, with here and there a blue one, standing without legs in the long grass. And scattered far apart, down deep blackberried lanes, lie the villages of pink-plastered cottages clustering together, red roof by red roof, with a flinty grey church in the midst.

The original artist who designed and painted Lowshire must have always taken a dab of blue in his brush just when he had filled it with red, to do the bridges and the old farms and barns and the cows. For in Lowshire the blues and the reds are always melting into each other like the clover.

Roger and Annette were heading towards the sea, and so you would have thought would be their companion the Rieben. But the Rieben

was in no hurry. It left them continually to take the longest way, laying itself out in leisurely curves round low uplands, but always meeting them again a few miles farther on, growing more stately with every detour. Other streams swelled it, and presently wharves and townships stretched alongside of it, and ships came sailing by. It hardly seemed possible to Annette that it could be the same little river which one low arch could span at Riff.

At last they turned away from it altogether, and struck across the wide common of Gallow-score amid its stretches of yellowing bracken; and Roger showed her where, in past times, a gibbet used to hang, and told her that old Cowell the shepherd, the only man who still came to church in smock-frock and blue stockings, had walked all the way from Riff to Gallowscore, as a lad, to see three highwaymen hanging in chains on it. The great oak had been blown down later, gibbet and all, and the gibbet had never been set up again.

A walking funeral was toiling across the bracken in the direction of the church on the edge of the common, and Roger drew up and waited bareheaded till it had passed. And he told Annette of the old iniquitous Lowshire " right of heriot " which came into force when a tenant died, and how his uncle Mr. Manvers, the last lord of the manor, had let it lapse, and how Dick, the present owner, had never enforced it either.

11 I couldn't have worked the estate if he had/' said Roger simply. " Lady Louisa told Dick he ought to stick to it, and make me enforce it, but I said I should have to go if he did. The best horse out of his stable when a man died, and the best cow out of his field. When Dick understood what heriot meant he would not do it. He was always open-handed."

Annette looked at the little church tolling its bell, and at the three firs gathered round it.

" There is a place like this in The Magnet" she said. " That is why I seem to know it, though I've never seen it before. There ought to be a Vicarage just behind the firs, with a little garden enclosed from the bracken."

" There is," said Roger, and then added, with gross ingratitude to its author, " I never thought much of The Magnet. I like the bits about the places, and he says things about dogs that are just right, and—robins. He's good on birds. But when it comes to people ! "

Annette did not answer. It was not necessary. Roger was under way.

" And yet," he added, with a tardy sense of justice, " Stirling's in some ways an understanding man. I never thought he'd have made allowance for old Betty Hesketh having the wood mania and breaking up his new fence, but he did. Such a fuss as Bartlet kicked up when he caught her at his wood-stack 1 Of course he caught her at it. Old folks can't

help it. They get wood mania when they're childish, if they've known the pinch of cold for too many years. And even if their sheds are full of wood—Betty has enough to last her lifetime—they'll go on picking and stealing. If they see it, they've got to have it. Only it isn't stealing. Mr. Stirling understood that. He said he'd known old ladies the same about china. But the people in his books !" Roger shook his head.

[< Didn't you like Jack and Hester in The Magnet? I got so fond of them."

"I don't remember much about them. I dare say I should have liked them if I had felt they were real, but I never did. It's always the same in novels. When I start reading them I know beforehand everybody will talk so uncommonly well—not like "

" You and me," suggested Annette.

" Well, not like me, anyhow. And not like Janey and the kind of people I know—except perhaps Black. He can say a lot."

" I have felt that too," said Annette, " especially when the hero and heroine are talking. I think how splendidly they both do it, but I secretly feel all the time that if I had been in the heroine's place I never could have expressed myself so well, and behaved so exactly right, and understood everything so quickly. I know I should have been silent and stupid, and only seen what was the right thing to say several hours later, when I had gone home."

Roger looked obliquely at her with an approving eye. Here indeed was a kindred soul!

"In The Magnet" he said, with a sudden confiding impulse, " the men do propose so well. Now in real life they don't. Poor beggars, they'd like to, but they can't. Most difficult thing, but you'd never guess it from The Magnet. Just look at Jack !—wasn't that his name ?— how he reels it all out! Shows how much he cares. Says a lot of really good things—not copybook, I will say that for him. Puts it uncommonly well about not being good enough for her, just as Mr. Stirling would himself if he were proposing. That's what I felt when I read it. Jack never would have had the nerve to say all that, but of course a clever chap like Mr. Stirling, sitting comfortably in his study, with lots of time and no woman to flurry him, could make it up."

Annette did not answer. Perhaps she did not want to flurry him.

" I could never say anything like that," said Roger, flicking a fly off Merrylegs' back, " but

I might feel it. I do feel it, and more."

" That is the only thing that matters," said Annette, with a tremor in her voice.

11 This is not the moment! " whispered Roger's bachelor instinct, in sudden panic at its imminent extinction. "I'd better wait till later in the afternoon," he assented cautiously to himself.

II A dogcart's not the place."

They crossed the common, and drove through an ancient forest of oak and holly in which kings had hunted, and where the last wolf in England had been killed.

And Roger told her of the great flood in the year of Waterloo, when the sea burst over the breakwater between Haliwater and Kirby, and carried away the old Hundred bridge, and forced the fishes into the forest, where his grandfather had seen them weeks afterwards sticking in the bushes.

When they emerged once more into the open the homely landscape had changed. The black-berried hedges were gone, replaced by long lines of thin firs, marking the boundaries between the fields. Sea mews were wheeling and calling among the uncouth hummocked gorse, which crowded up on either side of the white poppy-edged road. There was salt in the air.

Roger pointed with his whip.

11 The Rieben again," he said.

But could this mighty river with its mile-wide water be indeed the Rieben ? Just beyond it, close beside it, divided only by a narrow thong of shingle, lay the sea.

And Roger told Annette how at Mendlesham Mill the Rieben had all but reached the sea, and then had turned aside and edged along, stubbornly, mile after mile, parallel with it, almost within a stone's throw of it.

" But it never seems all to fall in and have done with it," he said, pointing to where it melted away into the haze, still hugging the sea, but always with the thong of shingle stretched between.

The Rieben skirting the sea, within sound of it, frustrated by its tides, brackish with its salt, but still apart, always reminded Roger of Lady Louisa. She too had drawn very near, but could not reach the merciful sea of death. A narrow ridge of aching life, arid as the high shingle barrier, constrained her, brackish month by month, from her only refuge. But Roger could no more have expressed such an idea in words than he could have knitted the cable-topped shooting-stockings which Janey made him, and which he had on at this moment.

The carriage in front had stopped at a lonely homestead among the gorse. On a low knoll at a little distance fronting the marsh stood an old stone cross.

Mrs. Stoddart and Mr. Stirling had already taken to their feet, and were climbing slowly through the gorse up the sandy path which led to the Holy Well. Roger and Annette left the dogcart and followed them.

Presently Mr. Stirling gave Mrs. Stoddart his hand.

Roger timidly offered his to Annette. She did not need it, but she took it. His shyness stood him in good stead. She had known bolder advances

Hand in hand, with beating hearts, they went, and as they walked the thin veil which hides

the enchanted land from lonely seekers was withdrawn. With awed eyes they saw " that new world which is the old " unfold itself before them, and smiled gravely at each other. The little pink convolvulus creeping in the thin grass made way for them. The wild St. John's wort held towards them its tiny golden stars. The sea mews, flapping slowly past with their feet hanging, cried them good luck ; and the thyme clinging close as moss to the ground, sent them delicate greeting, " like dawn in Paradise."

Annette forgot that a year ago she had for a few hours seen a mirage of this ecstasy before, and it had been but a mirage. She forgot that the day might not be far distant when this kindly man, this transfigured fellow-traveller, might leave her, when he who treated her now with reverence, delicate as the scent of the thyme, might not be willing to make her his wife, as that other man had not been willing.

But how could she do otherwise than forget ? For when our eyes are opened, and the promised land lies at our feet, the most faithless of us fear no desertion, the most treacherous no treachery, the coldest no inconstancy, the most callous no wound ; much less guileless souls like poor unwise Annette.

She had told Mrs. Stoddart that she would never trust anyone again, and then had trusted her implicitly. She had told herself that she would never love again, and she loved Roger.

A certain wisdom, not all of this world, could never be hers, as Mrs. Stoddart had said, but neither could caution, or distrust, or half-heartedness, or self-regard. Those thorny barricades against the tender feet of love would never be hers either. Ah, fortunate Annette ! It seems, after all, as if some very simple, unsuspicious folk can do without wisdom, can well afford to leave it to us, who are neither simple nor trustful.

Still hand in hand, they reached the shoulder of the low headland, and sat down on the sun-warmed, gossamer-threaded grass.

The ground fell below their eyes to the long staked marsh-lands of the Rieben, steeped in a shimmer of haze.

Somewhere, as in some other world, sheep-bells tinkled, mingled with the faint clamour of sea-birds on the misty flats. The pale river gleamed ethereal as the gleaming gossamer on the grass, and beyond it a sea of pearl was merged in a sky of pearl. Was anything real and tangible? Might not the whole vanish at a touch?

They could not speak to each other.

At last she whispered—

" The sea is still there."

She had thought as there was a new heaven and a new earth that there would be no more sea. But there it was. God had evidently changed His mind.

A minute speck appeared upon it.

NOTWITHSTANDING

Roger pulled himself together.

11 That's the Harwich boat," he said, " or it may be one of Moy's coaling-ships. I rather think it is."

He gazed with evident relish at the small puff of smoke. He experienced a certain relief in its advent, as one who descries a familiar face in a foreign crowd. He said he wished he had brought his glasses, as then he could have identified it. And he pointed out to her, far away in the mist, the crumbling headlands of the Suffolk coast, and the church tower of Dunwich, half lost in the sea haze, waiting for the next storm to engulf it.

Recalled to a remembrance of their destination by the coal-boat, they rose and walked slowly on towards the old stone cross standing bluntly up against a great world of sky. Mr. Stirling and Mrs. Stoddart were sitting under it ; and close at hand a spring bubbled up, which slipped amid tumbled stone and ling to a little pond, the margin fretted by the tiny feet of sheep, and then wavered towards the Rieben as circuitously as the Rieben wavered to the sea.

There was nothing left of the anchorite's cell save scattered stones, and the shred of wall on which Mrs. Stoddart was sitting. But a disciple of Julian of Norwich had dwelt there once, Mr. Stirling told them, visited, so the legend went, by the deer of the forest when the moss on their horns fretted them, and by sick wolves with

thorns in their feet, and by bishops and princes and knights and coifed dames, with thorns in their souls. And she healed and comforted them all. And later on Queen Mary had raised the cross to mark the spot where the saint of the Catholic Church had lived, as some said close on a hundred years.

11 It is a pity there are no saints left nowadays," said Mr. Stirling, " to heal us poor sick wolves.' 1

" But there are," said Annette, as if involuntarily, " only we don't see them until we become sick wolves. Then we find them, and they take the thorn away."

A baby-kite, all fluff, and innocent golden eyes, and callow hooked beak, flew down with long, unsteady wings to perch on the cross and preen itself. Presently a chiding mother's note summoned it away. Mr. Stirling watched it, and wondered whether the link between Mrs. Stoddart and Annette, which he saw was a very close one, had anything to do with some dark page of Annette's past. Had Mrs. Stoddart taken from her some rankling thorn ?—healed some deep wound in her young life ? He saw the elder woman's eyes looking with earnest scrutiny at Roger.

" The girl believes in him, and the older woman doubts him," he said to himself.

Annette's eyes followed a narrow track through the gorse towards a distant knoll with a clump of firs on it.

11 I should like to walk to the firs," she said. 17

Roger thought that an excellent idea, but he made no remark. Mr. Stirling at once said that it could easily be done if she were not afraid of a mile's walk. The knoll was farther than it looked.

Mrs. Stoddart said that she felt unequal to it, and she and Mr. Stirling agreed to make their way back to the carriage, and to rejoin Roger and Annette at Mendlesham Mill.

The little stream was company to them on their way, playing hide-and-seek with them, but presently Roger sternly said that they must part from it, as it showed a treacherous tendency to boggy ground, and they struck along an old broken causeway on the verge of the marsh, disturbing myriads of birds congregated on it.

" Shall I do it now ? " Roger said to himself. He made up his mind that he would speak when they reached the group of firs, now close at hand, with a low grey house huddled against them. He had never proposed before, but he stolidly supposed that if others could he could.

The sun had gone in, and a faint chill breath stirred the air.

" But where is the river gone to ? " said Annette.

Roger, who had been walking as in a dream, with his eyes glued to the firs, started. The river had disappeared. The sun came out again and shone instead on drifting billows of mist, like the clouds the angels sit on in the picture-books.

" It is the sea roke," he said; " we must hurry."

" It won't reach Mrs. Stoddart, will it? " said Annette breathlessly, trying to keep up with his large stride. " Damp is so bad for her rheumatism."

" She is all right/' he said almost angrily. " They have wraps, and they are half-way home by now. It's my fault. I might have known, if I had had my wits about me, when Dunwich looked like that, the roke would come up with the tide."

He took off his coat and put it on her. Then he drew her arm through his.

" Now," he said peremptorily, " we've got to walk—hard."

All in a moment the mist blotted out everything, and he stopped short instantly.

" It will shift," he said doggedly. " We must wait till it shifts."

He knew well the evil record of that quaggy ground, and of the gleaming, sheening flats— the ruthless oozy flats which tell no tales. The birds which had filled the air with their clamour were silent. There was no sound except the whisper everywhere of lapping water, water stealing in round them on all sides, almost beneath their feet. The sound meant nothing to Annette, but Roger frowned.

The tide was coming in.

" The roke will shift," he said again doggedly.

And it did. The tawny clouds, yellow where the sun caught them, drifted past them and parted. They saw the homely earth beneath

their feet, the tiny pink convolvulus peering up at them.

" Do you see that bunch of firs ? " he said.

" Yes."

" Well, we've got to get there. We must run for it."

They ran together towards it over the slippery sedge, and up the still more slippery turf. The sun came out brilliantly, and she laughed and would have slackened to look at the fantastic world sailing past her; but he urged her on, his hand gripping her elbow. And he was right. By the time they reached the trees they were in a dense white darkness, and the nearest fir whipped them across the face.

Annette was frightened, and it was Roger's turn to laugh—a short, grim laugh, with considerable relief in it.

" Ha I That's right," still holding her elbow tightly, and reaching out with the other hand. " We've fired into the brown and no mistake. Here's the middle tree. Two more this side. Then down. Mind your footing, and hold on to me."

They slid down into a dry ditch—at least, Roger said it was dry. " And good luck, too," he said. " Made that ditch myself to carry off the snowwater. Awful lot of water off the bank in winter." He pulled her up the other side, and then stopped and felt about him.

" The garden wall should be here," he said. " Empty house. Take shelter in it. Yes."

He groped, and met with resistance. " Here it is."

They stumbled slowly along beside a wall. " Lot of nettles, I'm afraid. Sorry, but can't be helped," as they plunged into a grove of them. " Here we are."

His hand was on an iron gate which gave and opened inwards. She felt a house rising close above them. Roger relinquished her, with many injunctions to stand still, and she heard his steps going away along a flagged path.

Annette was not country-bred, and she had not that vague confidence in her mother earth which those who have played on her surface from childhood never lose in later life. She was alarmed to find herself alone, and she shivered a little in the dripping winding-sheet of the mist. She looked round her and then up. High in heaven a pale disk showed for a moment and was blotted out. The sun !—it was shining somewhere. And far away, in some other world, she heard a lark singing, singing, as it soared in the blue.

A key in a lock turned, and a door close at hand grated on its hinges.

" Wait till I light a match," said Roger's welcome voice.

The match made a tawny blur the shape of a doorway, and she had time to reach it before it flickered out.

Roger drew her into the house, and closed the door.

CHAPTER XXIX

" There's no smoke in the chimney, And the rain beats on the floor ;

There's no glass in the window, There's no wood in the door ;

The heather grows behind the house, And the sand lies before.

No hand hath trained the ivy,

The walls are gray and bare ; The boats upon the sea sail by,

Nor ever tarry there; No beast of the field comes nigh, Nor any bird of the air."

MARY COLERIDGE.

IT was black dark inside the house, instead of the white darkness outside.

Knocking Annette carefully against pieces of furniture, Roger guided her down a narrow passage into what felt like a room. Near the ceiling were two bars of white where the fog looked in over the tops of the shutters.

He struck another match, and a little chamber revealed itself, with faded carpet and a long mirror. But no sooner was it seen than it was gone.

" Did you see that chair near you ? " said Roger. " I haven't many matches left."

" There is a candle on the mantelpiece/' she said.

Roger was amazed at Annette's cleverness. He had not seen it himself, but she had. He exulted in the thought.

He lit it, and the poor little tall drawing-room came reluctantly into view, with its tarnished mirror from which the quicksilver had ebbed, and its flowered wall-paper over which the damp had scrawled its own irregular patterns. The furniture was of the kind that expresses only one idea and that a bad one. The foolish sofa, with a walnut backbone showing through a slit in its chintz cover, had a humped excrescence at one end like an uneasy chair, and the other four chairs had servilely imitated this hump, and sunk their individuality, if they ever had any, to be " a walnut suite." A glass-fronted chiffonier had done its horrid best to "be in keeping " with the suite. On the walls were a few prints of race-horses stretched out towards a winning-post ; and steel engravings of the Emperor of the French in an order and the Empress Eugenie all smiles and ringlets served as pendants to two engravings of stags by Landseer.

Annette took off Roger's coat and laid it on a chair.

" Some one has been very unhappy here," she said, below her breath.

Roger did not hear her. He was drawing together the litter of waste-paper in the grate. And then — careful man 1—having ascertained with the poker that the register was open, he set a light to it.

The dancing, garish firelight made the sense of desolation acute.

" Who lived here ? " said Annette.

Roger hesitated a moment, and then said—

" A Mrs. Deane."

" Was she very old ? "

11 Not very—not more than twenty-seven."

" And is she dead ? "

Roger put some more paper on the fire, and held it down with the poker.

" No. She has left. Her child died here a month ago."

" Poor soul! Her only child ? "

" Yes."

" And her husband ? Is he dead too ? "

Roger thought a moment, and then said slowly, " As good as dead."

He looked round the room and added, " Dick Manvers lent her the house. It used to be the agent's, but no one has lived in it since I can remember. It has always been to let furnished, but no one ever took it. People seem to think it is rather out of the way."

The rollicking, busy flame died down and left them in the candle-light once more. But after a few moments the ghostly pallor above the shutters deepened. Roger went to them and opened them. They fell back creaking, revealing a tall French window. The fog was eddying past, showing the tops of the clump of firs, and then hiding them anew. He gazed intently at the drifting waves of mist.

" The wind is shifting/' he said. " It will blow from the land directly, and then the roke will go. I shall run down to the farm and bring the dogcart up here."

After all, he should have to propose in the dogcart. Men must have proposed and have been accepted in dogcarts before now. Anyhow, he could not say anything in this house when he remembered who had lived here, and the recent tragedy that had been enacted within its walls.

" You must put on your coat again," she said, bringing it to him. " And mayn't I come with you ? Wouldn't that be better than bringing the cart up here ? "

" Oh, Merry legs can see anywhere. Besides, there's the ford; I doubt you could get over it dry-shod, and I shall have to go a couple of miles round. And you've had walking enough. I shan't be gone more than half an hour. I dare say by then the sun will be full out."

" I would rather come with you."

" You're not afraid to stay here, are you ? There is nothing to hurt you, and that candle will last an hour. I don't believe there's even a live mouse in the place."

" I am sure there isn't. Everything here is dead and broken-hearted. I would rather go with you."

Roger's face became the face of a husband, obstinacy personified. She did not realize that they had been in danger, that he had felt anxiety for her, and that he had no intention of being so acutely uncomfortable again if he could help it.

" You will stay quietly here," he said doggedly. 11 This is the most comfortable chair."

She sat down meekly in it at once, and smiled at him—not displeased at being dragooned.

He smiled back, and was gone. She heard him go cautiously along the passage, and open and shut the front door.

The light was increasing steadily, and a few minutes after he had left the house the sun came pallidly out, and a faint breeze stirred the tops of the fir trees. Perhaps this was the land breeze of which he had spoken. A sense of irksomeness and restlessness laid hold on her. She turned from the window, and wandered into the little entrance hall, and unbarred a shutter to see if Roger were coming back. But no one was in sight on the long, straight, moss-rutted road that led to the house. She peered into the empty kitchen, and then, seeing a band of sunlight on the staircase, went up it. Perhaps she should see Roger from one of the upper windows. There were no shutters on them. She glanced into one after another of the little cluster of dishevelled bedrooms, with crumpled newspapers left over from a hurried packing still strewing the floors. The furniture was

massive, early Victorian, not uncomfortable, but direfully ugly.

There was one fair-sized south bedroom, and on the window-sill was a young starling with outspread, grimy wings. Annette ran to open the window, but as she did so she saw it was dead, had died beating against the glass trying to get out into the sunshine, after making black smirches on the v r alls and ceiling.

Everything in this one room was gay and pretty. The curtains and bed-hangings were of rosebud chintz. Perhaps the same hand that had made them had collected from the other rooms the old swinging mirror with brass rosettes, and the chest of drawers with drop handles, and the quaint painted chairs. Annette saw the crib in the corner. This room had been the nursery. It was here, no doubt, that Mrs. Deane had watched her child die. Some of the anguish of the mother seemed to linger in the sunny room with its rose-coloured curtains, and something, alas ! more terrible than grief had left its traces there.

A devastating hand, a fierce destructive anger had been at work. Little pictures had evidently been torn down from the wall and flung into the fire. The fireplace was choked high with half-burned debris—small shoes, pinafores, and toys. A bit of a child's linen picture-book had declined to burn, and hung forlornly through the bars, showing a comic picture of Mrs. Pig driving home from market. A green wheel

had become unfastened, and had rolled into the middle of the room when the wooden horse and cart were thrust into the fire.

" She must have cried all the time," said Annette to herself, and she shivered. She remembered her own mad impulse of destruction.

" It's no use being angry," she whispered to the empty walls. "No use. No use."

The photograph frames had evidently been swept into the fire too, all but one, for there was broken glass in the fender and on the floor. But one framed photograph stood on the mantelpiece, the man in it, smiling and debonair, looking gaily out at Annette and the world in general. Under it was written in a large clear hand, " Daddy."

It was Dick Le Geyt, but younger and handsomer than Annette had ever known him. She looked long at it, slowly realizing that this, then, had been the home of Dick's mistress, the Mary of whom he had spoken and her child, to whom he had done a tardy justice in his will, the will she had helped him to make. The child, Dick's child, was dead. Its empty crib was in the corner. Its memorials had perished with it.

All that was left now of that little home was Dick's faded photograph smiling in its frame, purposely, vindictively left when all the others had been destroyed. Mary Deane had not cared to take it with her when she cut herself adrift from her past. She had not had the

clemency to destroy it with the rest. She had left it to smile mockingly across the ruins of the deserted nursery. While Annette stood motionless the fierce despair of the mother became almost visible to her : the last wild look round the room and at the empty crib, the eyes averted from the smiling face on the mantelpiece, and then—the closed door and the lagging, hurrying footfall on the stairs.

" It's no use being angry," she whispered again. " Even Dick knew that. No use. No use."

And with pitying hands she took Dick's photograph out of the frame and tore it up small, and thrust the pieces among the charred remains of his child's toys. It was all she could do for him.

Oh ! if she had but known Mary Deane, if she could but have come to her, and put her arms round her and told her that Dick had not been as heartless as she thought, that he had remembered her at the last, and as far as he could had made a late amends for all the evil he had done her.

But the child was dead, and Mary Deane herself was gone. Gone whither ? She had flung away in anger and despair, as she, Annette, had once flung away. Perhaps there had been no Mrs. Stoddart to care for Mary in her hour of need.

Annette's heart sank as if a cold hand had been laid upon it.

The peaceful, radiant faith and joy of a few hours ago—where were they now ? In their place, into this close, desolate room with the dead bird on the sill, came an overwhelming fear.

Men were cruel, ruthless creatures, who did dreadful things to women under the name of love.

As at a great distance, far far away in the depths of childhood, she heard her mother sobbing in the dark. Almost her only recollection of her mother was being waked in the night by that passionate sobbing. The remembrance of her father came next, sordid, good-humoured, mercenary, and she shuddered. No wonder her mother had cried so bitterly! Close behind it followed the sensitive, sensual face of the musician who had offered to train her. And then, sudden and overwhelming, blotting out everything else, came the beautiful young lover whom she had cast forth from her heart with passion a year ago. All the agony and despair which she had undergone then surged back upon her, seemed to rush past her to join forces with the cold desolation lingering in the empty room. Annette hid her face in her hands. She had put it all behind her. She had outlived it. But the sudden remembrance of it shook her like a leaf.

In that grim procession Dick came last—poor, poor Dick ! He had not been wicked, but he had done wicked things. He had betrayed and broken faith. He had made as much desolation

and anguish as if he had been hard-hearted. Oh ! why did women love men ? Why did they trust them ?

Annette stood a long time with her face in her hands. Then she went out and closed the door behind her. The sun was shining bravely, and she longed to get out of this death-shadowed house into the warm, living sunshine. She went back to the drawing-room, her quiet step echoing loudly down the passage, and looked out of the long window. But the outlook was not calculated to lessen her oppression.

Close at hand, as she knew, were gracious expanses of sea and sky and gleaming river. But a stone wall surrounded the house, and on the top of it a tall wooden fence had been erected, so high that from the ground floor you could not look over it. This wooden fence came up close to the house on every side, so close that there was only just room for the thin firs and a walnut tree to grow within the narrow enclosure, their branches touching the windows.

Annette did not know that the wall and the fence and the trees were there to protect the house from the east wind, which in winter swept with arctic ferocity from the sea.

In the narrow strip between the fenced wall and the house Mary Deane had tried to make a little garden. Vain effort! The walnut tree and the firs took all si*n from the strip of flower-bed against the wall of the house, where a few Michaelmas daisies and snap-dragons hung their

heads. She had trained a rose against the wall, but it clung more dead than alive, its weak shoots slipping down from its careful supports. She had made a gravel path beside it, and had paced up and down it. How worn and sunk that path was! There was not room for two to go abreast in it. One footfall had worn that narrow groove, narrow almost as a sheep track in the marsh. And now the path was barely visible for the dead leaves of the walnut, falling untimely, which had drifted across it, and had made an eddy over the solitary clump of yellow snapdragon.

Annette drew back the bolt of the window, and stepped out. The air, chill with the mist which had silvered everything, was warm compared to the atmosphere of the house.

She drew a long breath, and her mind, never accustomed to dwell long upon herself, was instantly absorbed in freeing the snap-dragon from the dead leaves which had invaded it. Two birds were bathing themselves sedulously in the only sunny corner at the end of the garden. Annette saw that their bath also was choked with leaves, and when she had released the snapdragon, she applied her energies to the birds' bath.

But she had hardly removed a few leaves from it when she stopped short. It was a day of revelations. The birds' bath was really a lake: a miniature lake with rocks in it, and three tin fishes, rather too large it must be owned to

be quite probable, and a tin frog spread out in a swimming attitude, and four ducks all jostling each other on its small expanse. It was a well-stocked lake. Tears rose in Annette's eyes as she explored still farther, lifting the drifted leaves gently one by one.

They covered a doll's garden about a yard square. Some one, not a child, had loved that garden, and had made it for a beloved child. The enclosure with its two-inch fence had no grass in it, but it had winding walks, marked with sand and tiny white stones. And it had a little avenue of French lavender which was actually growing, and which led to the stone steps on the top of which the house stood, flanked by shells. It was a wooden house, perhaps originally a box; of rather debased architecture, it must be conceded. But it had windows and a green door painted on it, and a chimney. On the terrace were two garden-seats, evidently made out of match-boxes; and outside the fence was a realistic pigsty with two china pigs in it, and a water-butt, and a real haystack. Close at hand lay a speckled china cow, and near it were two seated crinkly white lambs.

Annette kneeling by the lake, crying silently, was so absorbed in tenderly clearing the dead leaves from the work of art, and in setting the cow on its legs again, that she did not hear a step on the path behind her. Roger had come back and was watching her. 18

When she discovered the two lambs sitting facing each other, she seized them up, and kissed them, sobbing violently.

Something in Annette's action vaguely repelled him as he watched her. It was what he would have defined as "French." And though he had swallowed down the French father, he hated all symptoms of him in Annette. It was alien to him to kiss little china lambs. Janey would never have done that. And Janey was the test, the touchstone of all that was becoming in woman.

And then all in a moment the tiny wave of repulsion was submerged in the strong current of his whole being towards her. It was as if some dormant generous emotion had been roused and angered by his petty pin-prick opposition to put out its whole strength and brush it away.

11 Don't cry," said Roger gruffly. But there were tears in his small round eyes as well as in hers.

"Oh, Roger," said Annette, speaking to him for the first time by his Christian name, " have you seen it, the fishes and the ducks, and the pigsty, and the little lambs and everything ? "

Roger nodded. He had watched that property in course of construction. He might have added that he had provided most of the animals for it. But if he had added that, he would not have been Roger.

" And she's burnt everything in the nursery,"

continued Annette, rising and going to him, the tears running down her face. " The toys and everything. And she's torn down the little pictures from the wall and broken them and thrown them on the fire. And I think she only left the garden because—poor thing—because she forgot it."

Roger did not answer. He took her in his arms, and said with gruff tenderness, as if to a child, " Don't cry."

She leaned against him, and let his arms fold her to him. And as they stood together in silence their hearts went out to each other, and awe fell upon them. All about them seemed to shake, the silvered firs, the pale sunshine, the melancholy house, the solid earth beneath their feet.

" You will marry me, won't you, Annette ? " he said hoarsely.

Remembrance rushed back upon her. She drew away from him, and looked earnestly at him with tear-dimmed, wistful eyes.

The poor woman who had lived here, who had worn the little path on which they were standing, had loved Dick, but he had not married her. She herself, for one brief hour, had loved some one, but he had had no thought of marrying her. Was Roger, after all, like other men ? Would he also cast her aside when he knew all, weigh her in the balance, and find her not good enough to be his wife ?

There was a loud knocking at the door, and

the bell pealed. It echoed through the empty house.

Roger started violently. Annette did not move. So absorbed was she that she heard nothing, and continued gazing at him with unfathomable eyes. After one bewildered glance at her, he hurried into the house, and she followed him half dazed.

In the hall she found him reading a telegram while a dismounted groom held a smoking horse at the door. At the gate the dogcart was waiting, tied to the gate-post.

Roger crushed the telegram in his hand, and stared out of the window for a long moment. Then he said to. Annette—

" Janey has sent me on this telegram to say her brother Dick is dead. It has been following me about for hours. I must go at once/'

He turned to the groom. " I will take your horse. And you will drive Miss Georges back to Noyes in the dogcart."

The man held the stirrup, and Roger mounted, raised his cap gravely to Annette, turned his horse carefully in the narrow path, and was gone.

CHAPTER XXX

" Even the longest lane has a turning, though the path trodden by some people is so long and so straight that it seems less like a lane than ' a permanent way.' "— ELLEN THORNEYCROFT FOWLER.

TIME moves imperceptibly at Riff, as imperceptibly as the Rieben among its reeds.

To Janey it seemed as if life stood stock-still. Nevertheless, the slow wheel of the year was turning. The hay was long since in, standing in high ricks in the farmyards, or built up into stacks in lonely fields with a hurdle round them to keep off the cattle. The wheat and the clover had been reaped and carried. The fields were bare, waiting for the plough. It was the time of the Harvest Thanksgiving.

Janey had been at work ever since breakfast helping to decorate the church, together with Harry and Miss Black, and her deaf friend Miss Conder, the secretary of the Plain Needlework Guild. Miss Conder's secretarial duties apparently left her wide margins of leisure which were always at the disposal of Miss Black.

Except for the somewhat uninspiring presence of Miss Black and Miss Conder and her ear trumpet, it had all been exactly as it had been ever since Janey could remember.

As she stood by the Ringers' Arch it seemed to her as if she had seen it all a hundred times before : the children coming crowding round her, flaxen and ruddy, with their hot little posies tied with grass,—the boys made as pretty posies as the girls,—and Hesketh, " crome from the cradle," limping up the aisle with his little thatched stack under his arm ; and Sayler with his loaf; and the farmers' wives bringing in their heavy baskets of apples and vegetables.

Sometimes there is great joy in coming home after long absence and finding all exactly as we left it and as we have pictured it in memory. We resent the displacement of a chair, or the lopping of one of the cedar's boughs, and we note the new tool-shed with an alien eye.

But it is not always joyful, nay, it can have an element of despair in it, to stay at home, and never go away, and see the wheel of life slowly turn and turn, and re-turn, and yet again re-turn, always the same, yet taking every year part of our youth from us. The years must come which will strip from us what we have. Yes, we know that. But life should surely give us something first, before it begins to take away.

Janey was only five-and-twenty, and it seemed to her that already the plundering years had come. What little she had was being wrested from her. And an immense distaste and fatigue of life invaded her as she made her lily and maiden-hair cross for the font. How often she had made it, as she was making it now! Should she go on for ever, till she was sixty, making crosses for the font at Harvest Homes, and putting holly in the windows at Christmas, and " doing the reading-desk " with primroses at Easter ?

Harry working beside her, concocting little sheaves out of the great bundle of barley which Roger had sent in the night before, was blissfully happy. He held up each sheaf in turn, and she nodded surprise and approbation. It seemed to her that after all Harry had the best of the bargain, the hard bargain which life drives with some of us.

It was all as it had always been.

Soon after eleven, Miss Amy Blinkett, a little fluttered and self-conscious, appeared as usual, followed up the aisle by a wheelbarrow, in which reposed an enormous vegetable marrow with " Trust in the Lord " blazoned on it in red flannel letters. These " marrer texes," as the villagers called them, were in great request, not only in Riff, but in the adjoining parishes; and it was not an uncommon thing for " Miss Amy's marrer "to be bespoken, after it had served at Riff, for succeeding Harvest Homes in the neighbourhood. It had been evolved out of her inner consciousness in her romantic youth, and in the course of thirty years it had grown from a dazzling novelty to an important asset, and was now an institution. Even the lamentable

Mr. Jones, who had "set himself against" so many Riff customs, had never set himself against " Miss Amy's marrer." And an admiring crowd always gathered round it after service to view it reclining on a bed of moss beneath the pulpit.

By common consent, Miss Amy had always been presented with the largest vegetable marrow that Riff could produce. But this year none adequate for the purpose could be found, and considerable anxiety had been felt on the subject. Mrs. Nicholls, who sent in the finest, had to own that even hers was only about fourteen inches long. " No bigger nor your foot," as she expressed it to Janey. Fortunately, at the last moment Roger obtained one from Sweet Apple Tree, about the size of a baby, larger than any which had been produced in Riff for many years past. That Sweet Apple Tree could have had one of such majestic proportions when the Riff marrows had failed, was not a source of unmixed congratulation to Riff. It was feared that the Sweet Appiers " might get cocked up."

The suspense had in the meanwhile given Miss Amy a sharp attack of neuralgia, and the fact that the marrow really came up to time in the wheelbarrow was the result of dauntless and heroic efforts on her part.

This splendid contribution was wheeled up the aisle, having paused near the font to receive Janey's tribute of admiration, and then a few

minutes later, to her amazement, she saw it being wheeled down again, Miss Amy walking very erect in dignified distress beside it. With cold asperity, and without according it a second glance, Miss Black had relegated it—actually relegated " Miss Amy's marrer "—to the Ringers' Arch. The other helpers stopped in their work and gazed at Miss Black, who, unconscious of the doubts of her sanity which had arisen in their minds, continued rearing white flowers against the east window, regardless of the fact that nothing but their black silhouettes were visible to the congregation.

At this moment Mr. Black came into the church, so urbane, and so determined to show that he was the kind of man who appreciated the spirit in which the humblest offerings were made, that it was some time before Janey could make him aware of the indignity to which Miss Amy's unique work of art had been subjected.

" But its grotesqueness will not be so obvious at the Ringers' Arch," he said. " It's impossible, of course, but it has been a labour of love, I can see that, and I should be the last man in the world to laugh at it."

He had to work through so many sentiments which did him credit that Janey despaired of making him understand, of ever getting him to listen to her.

" Miss Blinkett's marrow is always under the pulpit," she repeated anxiously. " No, the Ringers' Arch is not considered such an im-

portant place as the pulpit. The people simply love it, and will be disappointed if they don't see it there as usual. And Miss Blinkett will be deeply hurt. She is hurt now, though she does not show it."

At last her words took effect, and Mr. Black was guided into becoming the last man to wound the feelings of one of his parishioners. Greatly to Janey's relief, the marrow was presently seen once more to ascend the aisle, was assisted out of its wheelbarrow by Mr. Black himself and installed on a bed of moss at the pulpit foot ; Miss Black standing coldly aloof during the transaction, while Miss Conder, short-sighted and heavy-footed, walked backwards into an arrangement of tomatoes and dahlias in course of construction round the reading-desk.

Mr. Black and his sister had had an amicable discussion the evening before as to the decoration of the church, and especially of the pulpit, for this their first Harvest Thanksgiving at Riff. They had both agreed, with a cordiality which had too often been lacking in their conversations of late, that they would make an effort to raise the decoration to a higher artistic level than in the other churches in the neighbourhood, some of which had already celebrated their Harvest Thanksgivings. Miss Black had held up to scorn the naive attempts of Heyke and Drum, at which her brother had preached the sermon, and he had smiled indulgently and had agreed with her.

But Riff was his first country post, and he had not been aware until he stepped into it, of the network of custom which surrounded Harvest decoration, typified by Miss Blinkett's vegetable marrow. With admirable good sense, he adjusted himself to the occasion, and shutting his ears to the hissing whispers of his sister, who for the hundredth time begged him not to be weak, gave himself up to helping his parishioners in their own way. This way, he soon found, closely resembled the way of Heyke and Drum, and presently he was assisting Mrs. Nicholls to do " Thy Will be Done " in her own potatoes, backed by white paper roses round the base of the majestic monument of the Welyshams of Swale, with its two ebony elephants at which Harry always looked with awe and admiration.

As he and Janey were tying their bunches of barley to its high iron railings, a telegram was brought to her. Telegrams were not so common twenty years ago as they are now, and Janey's heart beat. Her mind flew to Roger. Had he had some accident ? She knew he had gone to Noyes about the bridge.

She opened it and read it, and then looked fixedly at Harry, stretching his hand through the railing to stroke the elephants and whisper gently to them. She almost hated him at that moment.

She folded up the telegram and sought out Mr. Black, who, hot and tired, and with an earwig
exploring down his neck, was now making a cardboard dais for Sayer's loaf of bread.

" My brother Dick is dead," she said. " I must go home at once. Harry can stay and finish the railings. He knows exactly how to do them, and he has been looking forward to helping for days."

Harry looked towards her for approval, and her heart smote her. It was not his fault if his shadowy existence was the occasion of a great injustice. She went up to him and patted his cheek, and said, " Capital, capital ! What should we do without you, Harry ? "

11 I'm taking my place, aren't I ? " he said, delighted. " That's what Nurse is always saying. I must assert myself and take my place."

CHAPTER XXXI

" Remember, Lord, Thou didst not make me good. Or if Thou didst, it was so long ago I have forgotten—and never understood, I humbly think."

GEORGE MACDONALD.

ON a sunny September day Dick the absentee was gathered to his fathers at Riff.

Is there any church in the world as beautiful as the old church of Riff where he was buried ?— with its wonderful flint-panelled porch ; with the chalice, host, and crown carved in stone on each side of the arched doorway as you go in ; beautiful still in spite of the heavy hand of Cromwell's men who tore all the dear little saints out of their niches in the great wooden font cover, which mounts richly carved and dimly painted like a spire, made of a hundred tiny fretted spires, to the very roof of the nave, almost touching the figures of the angels leaning with outstretched wings from their carved and painted hammerbeams. In spite of all the sacrilege of which it has been the victim, the old font cover with the coloured sunshine falling aslant upon it through the narrow pictured windows remains a tangle of worn, mysterious splendour. And the same haggard, forlorn beauty rests on the remains of the carved screen, with its company of female saints painted one in each panel.

Poor saints I savagely obliterated by the same Protestant zeal, so that now you can barely spell out their names in semicircle round their heads : Saint Cecilia, Saint Agatha, Saint Osyth.

But no desecrating hand was laid on the old oaken benches with their carved finials. Quaint intricate carvings of kings and queens, and coifed ladies kneeling on tasselled cushions, and dogs licking their own backs,—outlandish dogs with curly manes and shaved bodies and rosetted tails,—and harts crowned and belted with branching antlers larger than their bodies, and knights in armour, and trees with acorns on them so big that each tree had only room for two or three, and the ragged staff of the Earls of Warwick with the bear. All these were spared, seeing they dealt with man and beast, and not with God and saint. And by mistake Saint Catherine and her wheel and Saint Margaret and her dragon were overlooked and left intact. Perhaps because the wheel and the dragon were so small that the destroyers did not recognize that the quaint little ladies with their parted hair were saints at all. And there they all are to this day, broken some of them, alas !—one of them surreptitiously mutilated by Dick as a small boy,-^but many intact still, worn to a deep black polish by the hands of generation after generation of the sturdy people of Riff taking hold of them as they go into their places.

The Manvers monuments and hatchments jostle each other all along the yellow-plastered walls : from the bas-relief kneeling figure of the first Roger Manvers, Burgess of Dunwich, to the last owner, John Manvers, the husband of Lady Louisa Manvers.

But their predecessors, the D'Urbans and de Uffords, had fared ill at the hands of Dowsing and his men, who tore up their brasses with " orate pro anima " on them, and hacked their " popish " monuments to pieces, barely leaving the figures of Apphia de Ufford, noseless and fingerless, beside her lord, Nicholas D'Urban of Valenes. One Elizabethan brass memorial of John de la Pole, drowned at Walberswick, was spared, representing a skeleton, unkindly telling others that as he is we soon shall be, which acid inscription no doubt preserved him. But you must look up to the hammerbeams if you care to see all that is left of the memorials of the D'Urbans and De la Poles and the de Uffords, where their shields still hang among the carved angels.

Dick had not been worthy of his forbears, and it is doubtful whether if he had had any voice in the matter he would have wished to be buried with them. But Roger brought his coffin back to Riff as a matter of course.

His death had caused genuine regret among the village people, if to no one else. They had all known him from a boy. There had been a reckless bonhomie about him which had endeared him to his people, in a way that Roger, who had to do all the disagreeable things, could not expect. In time past, Dick had fought and ferreted and shared the same hunk of cake and drunk out of the same mug with half the village lads of Riff. They had all liked him, and later on in life, if he would not or could not attend to their grievances or spend money on repairs, he always " put his hand in his pocket " very freely whenever he came across them. Even the local policeman and the bearers decorously waiting at the lych-gate had sown their few boyish wild oats in Dick's delightful company. He was indis-solubly associated with that short heyday of delirious joy ; he had given them their one gulp from the cup of adventure and escapade. They remembered the taste of it as the hearse with its four plumed black horses came in sight between the poplars along the winding road from Riebenbridge. Dick had died tragically at thirty-three, and the kindly people of Riff were sorry.

Janey and Roger were the only chief mourners, for at the last moment Harry had been alarmed by the black horses, and had been left behind under the nurse's charge. They followed the coffin up the aisle, and sat together in the Squire's seats below the step. Close behind them, pale and impassive, sitting

alone, was Jones the valet, perhaps the only person who really mourned for Dick. And behind him again was a crowd of neighbours and family friends, and the serried ranks of the farmers and tenants.

In the chancel was the choir, every member present except Mrs. Nicholls, Dick's foster-mother, who was among the tenantry. So the seat next to Annette was empty, and to Mr. Stirling down by the font it seemed as if Annette were sitting alone near the coffin.

Janey sat and stood and knelt, very pale behind her long veil, her black-gloved hands pinching tightly at a little Prayer Book. She was not thinking of Dick. She had been momentarily sorry. It is sad to die at thirty-three. It was Roger she thought of, for already she knew that no will could be found. Roger had told her so on his return from Paris two days ago. A sinister suspicion was gradually taking form in her mind that her mother on her last visit to Dick in Paris had perhaps obtained possession of his will and had destroyed it, in the determination that Harry should succeed. Janey reproached herself for her assumption of her mother's treachery, but the suspicion lurked nevertheless like a shadow at the back of her mind. Was poor Roger to be done out of his inheritance ? for by every moral right Hulver ought to be his. Was treachery at work on every side of him ? Janey looked fixedly at Annette. Was she not deceiving 19

him too ? How calm she looked, how pure, and how beautiful! Yet she had been the mistress of the man lying in his coffin between them. Janey's brain seemed to shake. It could not be. But so it was. She shut her eyes and prayed for Roger, and Dick, and Annette. It was all she could do.

Roger, beside her, kept his eyes fixed on a carved knob in front of him. He knew he must not look round, though he was anxious to know whether Cocks and Sayler had seated the people properly. His mind was as full of detail as a hive is full of bees. He was tired out, and he had earache, but he hardly noticed it. He had laboured unremittingly at the funeral. It was the last thing he could do for Dick, whom he had once been fond of, whom he had known better than anyone, for whom he had worked so ruefully and faithfully ; who had caused him so many hours of exasperation, and who had failed and frustrated him at every turn in his work for the estate.

He had arranged everything himself, the distant tenants' meals, the putting up of their horses. He had chosen the bearers, and had seen the gloves and hat-bands distributed, and the church hung with black. His mind travelled over all the arrangements, and he did not think anything had been forgotten. And all the time at the back of his mind also was the thought that no will was forthcoming, even while he followed the service.

" Dick might have left Hulver to me. ' We brought nothing into the world and it is certain we can carry nothing out.' Poor old Dick ! I dare say he meant to. But he was too casual, and had a bee in his bonnet. But if he had done nothing else, he ought to have made some provision for Mary Deane and his child. He could not tell Molly would die before him. 1 For a thousand years in Thy sight are but as yesterday.' Seeing Harry is what he is and Janey is to have Noyes, Dick might have remembered me. I shall have to work the estate for Harry now, I suppose. Doesn't seem quite fair, does it ? ' 0 teach us to number our days: that we may apply our hearts unto wisdom.' Never heard Black read the service better. He'll be a bishop some day. And now that Dick has forgotten me, how on earth am I ever to marry ? ' Man that is born of woman hath but a short time to live and is full of misery. 1 That's the truest text of the whole lot."

Roger looked once at Annette, and then fixed his eyes once more on the carved finial of the old oaken bench on which he was sitting, where his uncle had sat before him, and where he could just remember seeing his grandfather sit in a blue frock-coat thirty years ago. He looked for the hundredth time at the ragged staff of the Warwicks carved above the bear, the poor bear which had lost its ears if it ever had any. His hand in its split glove closed convulsively on the

bear's head. How was he going to marry Annette !

Annette's eyes rested on the flower-covered coffin hi front of her, but she did not see it. She was back in the past. She was kneeling by Dick's bed with her cheek against the pillow, while his broken voice whispered, " The wind is coming again, and I am going with it."

The kind wind had taken the poor leaf at last, the drifting shredded leaf.

And then she felt Roger look at her, and other thoughts suddenly surged up. Was it possible— was it possible—that Dick might part her and Roger? Their eyes met for an instant across the coffin.

Already Roger looked remote, as if like Dick he were sinking into the past. She felt a light touch on her hand. The choir had risen for the anthem.

CHAPTER XXXII

" Mon Dieu, mon Dieu, la vie est Ik,

Simple et tranquille. Cette paisible rumeur-la Vient de la ville.

Qu'as-tu fait, O toi que voila

Pleurant sans c^sse, Dis, qu'as-tu fait, toi que voila

De ta jeunesse ? "

PAUL VBRLA.INE.

THE sound of the anthem came faint and sweet over the ivied wall into the garden of the Dower House, where Harry was standing alone under the cedar in his black clothes, his hands behind his back, mournfully contemplating the little mud hut which he and Tommy had made for the hedgehog which lived in the garden. His ally Tommy, who was a member of the choir, was absent. So was the hedgehog. It was not sitting in its own house looking out at the door as it ought to have been, and as Tommy had said it would. Harry had shed tears because the hedgehog did not appreciate its house. That prickly recluse had shown such unwillingness to intrude, to force his society on the other possible inmates, indeed, although conscious

of steady pressure from behind, had offered

such determined and ball-like resistance at the front door, that a large crack had appeared in the wall.

Harry heaved a deep sigh, and then slowly got out his marbles. Marbles remain when hedgehogs pass away.

Presently the nurse, who had been watching him from the window, came swiftly from the house, and sat down near him, on the round seat under the cedar.

" Must I stop ? " he said docilely at once, smiling at her.

u No, no," she said, trying to smile back at him. " Go on. But don't make a noise."

He gravely resumed his game, and she gazed at him intently, as if she had never seen him before, looking herself how worn and haggard in the soft September sunshine.

It was one of those gracious days when the world seems steeped in peace, when bitterness and unrest and self-seeking " fold their tents like the Arabs, and as silently steal away." No breath stirred. High in the windless spaces above the elms, the rooks were circling and cawing. The unwhispering trees laid cool, transparent shadows across the lawns. All was still—so still that even the hedgehog, that reluctant householder, came slowly out of a clump of dahlias, and hunched himself on the sun-warmed grass.

The woman on the bench saw him, but she did not point him out to Harry. Why should not the hedgehog also have his hour of peace ? And presently, very pure and clear, came Annette's voice: " They shall hunger no more, neither thirst any more, neither shall the sun light on them, nor any heat."

The Riff Choir knew only two anthems. The nurse leaned her tired head in its speckless little cap against the trunk of the cedar, and the tears welled up into her eyes.

She was tired, oh ! so tired of hungering and thirsting, and the sun and the dust, so tired of the trampling struggle and turmoil of life, of being pushed from pillar to post, from patient to patient. For seventeen grinding years she had earned her bread in the house of strangers, and she was sick to death of it. And she had been handsome once, gay and self-confident once, innocent once. She had been determined that her mother should never know want. And she had never known it—never known either the straits to which her daughter had been reduced to keep that tiny home together. That was all over now. Her mother was dead, and her lover, if so he could be called, had passed out of her life. And as she sat on the bench she told herself for the hundredth time that there was no one to fight for her but herself. She felt old and worn-out and ashamed, and the tears fell. She had not been like this, cunning and self-seeking, to start with. Life had made her so. She shut her eyes, so that she might not see that graceful, pathetic creature, with its beautiful eyes fixed on the marbles, of whom she had dared to make a cat's paw.

But presently she felt a soft cheek pressed to hers, and an arm round her neck.

" Don't cry, Nursie," Harry said gently. ' Brother Dick has gone to heaven," and he kissed her, as a child might kiss its mother. She winced at his touch, and then pushed back her hair, still thick and wavy, with the grey just beginning to show in it, and returned his kiss.

And as he stood before her she took his hands and held them tightly, her miserable eyes fixed on him.

A silent sob shook her, and then she said—

" You know where God lives, Harry? "

Harry disengaged one hand and pointed to the sky above him. He was not often sure of giving the right answer, but he had a happy confidence that this was correct.

' Yes," she went on, " God lives in the sky and looks down on us. He is looking at us now."

Harry glanced politely up at the heavens and then back at his companion.

" He is looking at us now. He hears what I say. I'm not one that believes much in promises. Nobody's ever kept any to me. But I call Him to witness that what I have taken upon myself I will perform, that I will do my duty by you, and I will be good to you always and be your best friend, whatever may happen —so help me God."

CHAPTER XXXIII

"But I wait in a horror of strangeness—

A tool on His workshop floor, Worn to the butt, and banished His hand for evermore."

W. E. HENLEY.

IN the sick-room all was still.

Lady Louisa lay with her eyes open, fixed. Blended with the cawing of the rooks came the tolling of the bell for her son's funeral. Janey had told her of Dick's death, had repeated it gently several times, had recounted every detail of the funeral arrangements and how her sister Lady Jane was not well enough to come to England for it. How the service was taking place this afternoon and she must go to it, but she should not be away long : Nurse would sit with her while she was away. How Harry was not to be present, as he had been frightened at the sight of the plumed horses. It was more than doubtful whether her mother understood anything at all of what she told her, whether she even heard a voice speaking. But Janey mercifully told her everything on the chance, big things and small : Dick's death, and the loss of Harry's bantam cock, the Harvest Thanksgiving vegetable marrow, and the engagement of the

Miss Blinketts' niece to a rising surgeon, and their disappointment that instead of giving her a ring his only present to her had been a snapshot of himself performing an operation. Scores of little things she gleaned together and told her. So that if by any hundredth part of a chance she could indeed still hear and understand she might not feel entirely cut off from the land of the living.

Her mother heard and understood everything. But to her it was as if her prison was at such an immense distance that communication was impossible. Janey's voice, tender and patient, reached down to her as in some deep grave. She could hear and understand and remember. But she could make no sign.

Ah! How much she remembered, as the bell tolled for Dick's last home-coming I Her thoughts went back to that grey morning three-and-thirty years ago when she had seen his face for the first time, the little pink puckered face which had had no hint in it of all the misery he was to cause her. And she recalled it as she had seen it last, nearly a year ago, hardly human, already dead save for a fluctuating animal life. And she remembered her strenuous search for a will, and how Dick's valet had told her that his master had been impressed by the narrowness of his escape when he injured his head, and had actually gone out on purpose to make his will the day he went to Fontaine-bleau, but had been waylaid by some woman.

She had found the name and address of his man of business, and had been to see him, but could extract nothing from him except that Mr. Le Geyt had not called on him on the day in question, had not made any will as far as his knowledge went, and that he had ceased to employ him owing to a quarrel. Dick's business relations with every one except Roger always ended in a quarrel sooner or later—generally sooner. She had made up her mind that Dick must die without leaving a will. It was necessary for the sake of others. But she had not told herself what she should do with a will of his if she could get hold of it. But she had not been able to discover one. The whole situation rose before her, and she, the only person who had an inkling of it, the only person who could deal with it, was powerless.

She had accumulated proofs, doctor's evidence, that Harry's was only a case of arrested development, that he was quite capable of taking his part in life. She had read all these papers to the nurse when first she came to Riff, and had shown herself sympathetic about Harry, which Janey had never been. Janey had always, like her father, thought that if Dick died childless Hulver ought to go to Roger, had not been dislodged from that position even by her mother's thrust that she said that because she was in love with him. Nurse in those first days of her ministry had warmly and without arri&re pens&e encouraged Lady Louisa in her contention

that Harry was only backward, and had proved that she was partly right by the great progress he made under her authority. She had been indefatigable in training him, drawing out his atrophied faculties.

The papers which Lady Louisa had so laboriously collected were in the drawer of the secretaire, near the fire. The key was on her watch-chain, and her watch and chain were on the dressing-table. Nurse had got them out and put them back at her request several times. She knew where they were.

And now that Dick was dead, Nurse would certainly use them on Harry's behalf, exactly as she herself had intended to use them.

Unscrupulous, wanton woman !

A paroxysm of rage momentarily blinded her. But after a time the familiar room came creeping stealthily back out of the darkness, to close in on her once more.

She had schemed and plotted, she had made use of the shrewd, capable woman at her bedside. But the shrewd, capable woman had schemed and plotted too, and had made use of her son, her poor half-witted Harry. For now, at last, now that power had been wrested out of her own safe hands into the clutch of this designing woman, Lady Louisa owned to herself that Harry was half-witted. She had intended him, her favourite child, to have everything, and Janey and Roger to be his protective satellites She had perfect confidence in Roger.

But now this accursed, self-seeking woman, who had made a cat's paw of Harry, had ruined everything. She, not Roger, would now have control of the property. She would be supreme. Harry would be wax in her hands. Her word would be law. She could turn her out of the Dower House if she wished it. Everything— even the Manvers diamonds in the safe downstairs which she had worn all her life—belonged to her now. Everything except in name was hers already—if Dick had died intestate. And no doubt he had so died. How she had hoped and prayed he would do as he had done! How could she have guessed that his doing so would prove the worst, immeasurably the worst calamity of all? Lady Louisa was appalled. She felt sick unto death.

She had laboured for her children's welfare to the last, and now she had been struck down as on a battlefield, and the feet of the enemy were trampling her in the dust.

The door opened, and the adversary came in. She and her patient eyed each other steadily. Then the nurse went to the dressing-table and took the watch with its chain and pendant key, and opened the drawer in the secretaire. Lady Louisa watched her take out a bundle of papers and put them in her pocket. Then she locked the drawer and replaced the watch, and returned to the bedside. She wiped away the beads of sweat which stood on Lady Louisa's forehead, touched her brow and nostrils with

eau-de-Cologne, and sat down in her accustomed place. Lady Louisa saw that her eyes were red.

" If looks could kill, yours would kill me, milady," she said. " It's been hard on you to have me to tend you. But that's all over now. Don't you fret about it any more. I shall go away to-morrow, and I don't suppose you'll ever be troubled by the sight of me in this world again."

Presently Janey came in, and the nurse at once withdrew. She took off her gloves, and put back her heavy veil.

" It is all over," she said, with the familiar gesture of stroking her mother's hand. " Such a sunny, quiet day for Dick's home-coming. We ought all to be thankful that his long imprisonment is over, that his release has come."

The other prisoner heard from the depths of her forlorn cell.

" And I ought to tell you, mother, that there is no will. Aunt Jane and Roger have looked everywhere, and made inquiries. I am afraid there is no longer any doubt that Dick has died without making one. So you will have your wish." The gentle voice had a tinge of bitterness. " Everything will go to Harry."

When Janey came downstairs again she found Roger sitting in the library with a hand on each knee. He looked worn out.

She made fresh tea for him, and he drank
it in silence, while she mended his split glove.

" Well, it's over," he said at last.

" All the arrangements were so carefully made," she said softly, putting her little thumb into the big thumb of his glove, and finding where the mischief had started. He watched her without seeing her.

" I think everything went right," he said. " I hope it did, and Black did his part. I never heard him read so well."

11 I thought the same."

Roger was so accustomed to hear this expression from Janey whenever he made a statement that he had long since ceased to listen to it.

"I'm thankful there was no hitch. I could not sleep last night, earache or something, and I had an uneasy feeling—very silly of me, but I could not get it out of my head—that one of those women would turn up and make a scene."

" From what you've told me, Mary Deane would never have done a thing like that."

"No. She was too proud, but there was the other one, the Fontainebleau one. I had a sort of idea she might have been in the church. Queer things happen now and then. I didn't like to look round. Mustn't be looking about at a funeral. I suppose you didn't see anyone that might have been her?"

Janey laid down the glove.

" I didn't look round either," she said.

CHAPTER XXXIV

" Others besides Moses have struggled up the mountain only to be shown the promised land, and to hear the words : Thou shalt see it with thine eyes, but shalt not pass over."

THE following morning saw Janey and Roger sitting opposite each other once more, but this time in his office-room, staring blankly at each other. In spite of her invariably quiet demeanour, she was trembling a little.

" I am afraid you must believe it, Roger,"

" Good Lord ! " was all Roger could say, evidently not for the first time.

There was a long silence.

" When did she tell you ? "

" This morning, after breakfast. She and Harry came in together when I was writing letters, hand in hand, as if they were in a novel, and she said they had been married three months."

11 Three months ! "

11 Yes."

" Why, they must have been married in June."

" Yes."

11 Good Lord ! "

Janey told him how they had been married at Ipswich at a Registry Office. " Her brother,
who is a solicitor, was one of the witnesses. She showed me a copy of the certificate. She seems to have been very—methodical/' " It won't hold. Poor Harry is a loony." " I hinted that, but she only smiled. I think she must have gone thoroughly into that before she took any step. And then she looked at him, and he said like a parrot that it was time he took his proper place in the

world and managed his own affairs."

" I never in my life heard such cheek." " After a bit I sent away Harry. He looked at her first before he obeyed, and she signed to him to go. She has got absolute control over him. And I tried to talk to her. She was very hard and bitter at first, and twitted me with having to put up with her as a sister-in-law. But I could not help being sorry for her. She was ashamed, I'm sure, of what she'd done, though she tried to carry it off with a high hand. She's not altogether a bad woman."

" Isn't she ? Well, she's near enough to satisfy me. I don't know what you call bad if kidnapping that poor softy isn't. But the marriage can't hold. It's ridiculous."

" She says it will, and I think she'll prove to be right. She is a shrewd woman, and after all Harry is twenty-three. Besides, mother's always stuck to it that he was only backward, and she got together medical evidence to attest her view. Mother has always wanted to guard against Harry being passed over."

" Dick could leave the property to anyone he liked. It wasn't entailed. He was perfectly free to leave it to Jones, if he wanted to. Poor Jones I He's down with gout at the Lion. He won't get a shilling."

" Yes. But mother foresaw that Dick might never get a will made. He never could get anything done. And I am afraid, Roger, that if he had made a will, mother would have got hold of it if she could."

" Janey ! " said Roger, deeply shocked. " You don't know what you're saying."

" Oh yes, I do. I feel sure, if poor Dick had made a will, Aunt Jane and mother between them would have "

" Would have what ? "

" Would have destroyed it."

" You simply don't know what you're saying. No one destroys a will. It's a very serious crime, punishable by law. And you are accusing your own mother of it."

" Mother has done some strange things in her time," said Janey firmly. " It's no good talking about it or thinking about it, but Jones told me that when she went to Paris last autumn she looked through all Dick's papers, and went to see his lawyer."

" I went to see him too, and he told me she had been, and had been very insistent that Dick had made a will and left it in his charge, and said that he wanted to make some altera-^ tion in it."

" Last autumn ! But Dick was not capable then of wishing anything."

" Last autumn, I tell you, since his illness."

They both looked at each other.

11 Well, it's no use thinking of that at this moment," said Janey. " The question is, what is to be done about Nurse? "

11 Pay her up, and pack her off at once." ' She's gone already. She said it was best that she should go. I've telegraphed for another. But she'll come back as Harry's legal wife, Roger, I do believe."

" This medical evidence in Harry's favour— where does Aunt Louisa keep it ? "

" In her secretaire. She made me get it out, and read it to her since her last visit to Paris. I could not bear to look at it. It was all so false. And I know she showed it Nurse. It was after that Nurse worked so hard to make Harry more amenable, more like other people. She slaved with him. I believe she was quite disinterested at first."

" She has certainly done him a lot of good."

" And he's fond of her. He's frightened of her, but he likes her better than anyone, much better than me. Before she left she told every servant in the house, and the men in the garden. At least, she took Harry round with her and made him say to each one of them, ' This is my wife.' The whole village knows by now. And she has taken the medical evidence about him. She made no secret of it. She said she sent it yesterday to her brother."

" She stole it, in fact."

" She said that as his wife she thought she ought to put it in safe keeping. I told her she need not have been afraid that we should destroy it. She said she knew that, but that those who deceived others never could trust anyone else. Roger, she has done a very wicked and shameless thing, for the sake of a livelihood, but I think she is suffering for it. And I believe, in spite of herself, she had a kind of devotion for mother. She had done so much for her. She never spared herself. She felt leaving her."

" Did she ask about the will ? "

" No. I think there was a general feeling of surprise that the will was not read after the funeral."

" Well, my good girl, how could we, when we couldn't find one?"

" I know, I know. But what I mean is, it must soon be known that no will is forthcoming."

" Of course it is bound to come out before long."

11 Have you asked Pike and Ditton, Dick's London men ? "

" Yes. I wrote to them days ago. They know of nothing. There is no will, Janey. We have got to make up our minds to it. Pritchard is coming over this morning about the probate, and I shall have to tell him. "

Something fierce crept into Janey's gentle face.

" Oh, Roger, it is such a shame ! " she stammered. "If ever any man deserved Hulver it is you."

11 Dick once said so," said Roger. " Last time he was here, two years ago, that time he never came to the Dower House though I begged him to, and I went round the park with him, and showed him where I had cut down the oak avenue in the old drive. It went to my heart to do it, but he had left me no choice, insisted on it. And when he saw the old trees all down he was quite taken aback, and he said, 1 Roger, it is you who ought to have had Hulver. You'd have kept it together, while I'm just pulling it to pieces stick by stick. I must reform, and come and settle down here, and marry Mary. By God I must.' That was the last time he was here, just before he sold the Liverpool property."

" Everything seems to be taken from you, Roger," said Janey passionately. " And to think that this unscrupulous woman will have absolute power over everything 1"

" She will be able to turn me off," said Roger. " She will get in another agent—put in her brother, I should think. I always disliked her, and she knew it. Now she will be able to pay off old scores."

Roger looked out of the window, and his patient, stubborn face quivered ever so slightly.

It would have been a comfort to Janey to think that she should one day inherit Noyes, if there had been any question of his sharing it with her. But the long-cherished hope that they might some day share a home together had died. It had died hard, it had taken a grievous time to die, but it was dead at last. And Janey had buried it, delved a deep grave for it in the live rock of her heart.

" I don't see how I am ever to marry now/ 1 he said hoarsely. " I can't count on the two hundred a year from the agency and this cottage. Even that may go to-morrow. It wasn't much. It wasn't enough to set up house on, but even that is as good as gone."

" I have thought lately that you had it in your mind to marry."

A small tear suddenly jumped out of Roger's eye, and got held up in his rough cheek.

" I want to marry Annette," he said.

" Yes, my dear, I guessed it."

" Dreadfully. You don't know, Janey. Dreadfully."

" I know, my poor boy," she said,—" I know all about it." And she came and stood by him and patted his hand.

For a moment Roger sobbed violently and silently against her shoulder.

Then he drew himself away, and rummaged for his pocket-handkerchief.

" You are a brick, Janey," he said gruffly.

CHAPTER XXXV

" The thing on the blind side of the heart,

On the wrong side of the door ; The green plant groweth, menacing Almighty lovers in the spring; There is always a forgotten thing, And love is not secure."

G. K. CHESTERTON.

THE news of Harry's marriage, which was convulsing Riff, had actually failed to reach Red Riff Farm by tea-time. The Miss Blinketts, on the contrary, less aristocratically remote than the Miss Nevills, had heard it at midday, when the Dower House gardener went past The Hermitage to his dinner. And they were aware by two o'clock that Janey had had a consultation with Roger in his office, and that the bride had left Riff by the midday express from Riebenbridge.

It was the general opinion in Riff that " she'd repent every hair of her head for enticing Mr. Harry."

In total ignorance of this stupendous event, Aunt Harriet was discussing the probable condition of the soul after death over her afternoon tea, in spite of several attempts on the part of Annette to change the subject.

" Personally, I feel sure I shall not even lose consciousness," she said, with dignity. " With some of us the partition between this world and the next is hardly more than a veil, but we must not shut our eyes to the fact that a person like Mr. Le Geyt is almost certainly suffering for his culpability in impoverishing the estate ; and if what I reluctantly hear is true as to other matters still more reprehensible "

" We know very little about purgatory, after all," interrupted Aunt Maria wearily.

" Some of us who suffer have our purgatory here," said her sister, helping herself to an apricot. " I hardly think, when we cross the river, that "

The door opened, and Roger was announced. He had screwed himself up to walk over and ask for Annette, and it was a shock to him to find her exactly as he might have guessed she would be found, sitting at tea with her aunts. He had counted on seeing her alone.

He looked haggard and aged, and his black clothes became him ill. He accepted tea from Annette without looking at her. He was daunted by the little family party, and made short replies to the polite inquiries of the Miss Nevills as to the health of Janey and Lady Louisa. He was wondering how he could obtain an interview with Annette, and half angry with her beforehand for fear she should not come to his assistance. He was very sore. Life was going ill with him, and he was learning what sleeplessness means, he who had never lain awake in his life.

The door opened again, and contrary to all precedent the Miss Blinketts were announced.

The Miss Blinketts never came to tea except when invited, and it is sad to have to record the fact that the Miss Nevills hardly ever invited them. They felt, however, on this occasion that they were the bearers of such important tidings that their advent could not fail to be welcome, if not to the celebrated authoress, at any rate to Miss Harriet, who was not absorbed in ethical problems like her gifted sister, and whose mind was, so she often said, " at leisure from itself, to soothe and sympathize."

But the Miss Blinketts were quite taken aback by the sight of Roger, in whose presence the burning topic could not be mentioned, and who had no doubt come to recount the disaster himself—a course which they could not have foreseen, as he was much too busy to pay calls as a rule. They were momentarily nonplussed, and they received no assistance in regaining their equanimity from the lofty remoteness of the Miss Nevills' reception. A paralysing ten minutes followed, which Annette, who usually came to the rescue, made no attempt to alleviate. She busied herself with the tea almost in silence.

Roger got up stiffly to go.

" I wonder, Mr. Manvers, as you are here,"

said Aunt Maria, rising as he did," whether you would kindly look at the dairy roof. The rain comes in still, in spite of the new tiling. Annette will show it you." And without further demur she left the room, followed by Annette and Roger.

' I am afraid," said the authoress archly, with her hand on the door of her study, " that I had recourse to a subterfuge in order to escape. Those amiable ladies who find time hang so heavily on their hands have no idea how much I value mine, nor how short I find the day for all I have to do in it. My sister will enjoy entertaining them. Annette, I must get back to my proofs. I will let you, my dear, show Mr Manvers the dairy."

Roger followed Annette down the long bricked passage to the laiterie. They entered it, and his professional eye turned to the whitewashed ceiling and marked almost unconsciously the stain of damp upon it.

" A cracked tile," he said mechanically. 1 Two. I'll see to it."

And then, across the bowls of milk and a leg of mutton sitting in a little wire house, his eyes looked in a dumb agony at Annette.

" What is it ? What is it ? " she gasped, and as she said the words the cook entered slowly, bearing a yellow mould and some stewed fruit upon a tray.

Roger repeated the words " cracked tiles," and presently they were in the hall again.

11 I must speak to you alone," he said desperately ; " I came on purpose."

She considered a moment. She had no refuge of her own except her bedroom, that agreeable attic with the extended view which had been apportioned to Aunt Catherine, and which she had inhabited for so short a time. The little hall where they were standing was the passage-room of the house. She took up a garden hat, and they went into the garden to the round seat under the apple tree, now ruddy with little contorted red apples. The gardener was scything the grass between the trees, whistling softly to himself.

Roger looked at him vindictively.

' I will walk part of the way home with you," said Annette, her voice shaking a little in spite of herself, " if you are going through the park."

11 Yes, I have the keys."

" He has found out about Dick and me," she said to herself, " and is going to ask me if it is true."

They walked in silence across the empty cornfield, and Roger unlocked the little door in the high park wall.

Once there had been a broad drive to the house where that door stood, and you could still see where it had lain between an avenue of old oaks. But the oaks had all been swept away. The ranks of gigantic boles showed the glory that had been.

" Uncle John was so fond of the oak avenue/

said Roger. " He used to walk in it every day. There wasn't its equal in Lowshire. Anne de la Pole planted it. I never thought Dick would have touched it."

And in the devastated avenue, the scene of Dick's recklessness, Roger told Annette of the catastrophe of Harry's marriage with the nurse, and how he had already seen a lawyer about it, and the lawyer was of opinion that it would almost certainly be legal.

" That means," said Roger, standing still in the mossy track, " that now Dick's gone, Harry, or rather his wife, for he is entirely under her thumb, will have possession of everything, Welmesley and Swale and Bulchamp, not that Bulchamp is worth much now that Dick has put a second mortgage on it, and Scorby—and Hulver."

He pointed with his stick at the old house with its twisted chimneys, partly visible through the trees, the only home that he had ever known, and his set mouth trembled a little.

11 And that woman can turn me out tomorrow," he said. " And she will. She's always disliked me. I shan't even have the agency. It was a bare living, but I shan't even have that. I shall only have Noyes. I've always done Noyes for eighty pounds a year, because Aunt Louisa wouldn't give more, and she can't now even if she was willing. And I'm not one of your new-fangled agents, been through Cirencester, or anything like that,

educated up to it, scientific and all that sort of thing. Uncle John was his own agent, and I picked it up from him. When I lose this I don't suppose I shall get another job."

With a sinking heart, and yet with a sense of relief, Annette realized that Roger had heard nothing against her, and that she was reprieved for the moment. It was about all she did realize.

He saw the bewilderment in her face, and stuck his stick into the ground. He must speak more plainly.

11 This all means," he said, becoming first darkly red and then ashen colour, ' that I am not in a position to marry, Annette. I ought not to have said anything about it. I can't think how I could have forgotten as I did. But— but "

He could say no more.

" I am glad you love me," said Annette faintly. " I am glad you said — something about it."

" But we can't marry," said Roger harshly. " What's the good if we can't be married?"

He made several attempts to speak, and then went on : "I suppose the truth is I counted on Dick doing something for me. He always said he would, and he was very generous. He's often said I'd done a lot for him. Perhaps I have, and perhaps I haven't. Perhaps I did it for the sake of the people and the place. Hulver's more to me than most things. But he

told me over and over again he wouldn't forget me. Poor old Dick! After all, he couldn't tell he was going to fall on his head! There is no will, Annette. That's the long and the short of it. And so, of course, nearly everything goes to Harry."

" No will ! " said Annette, drawing in a deep breath.

" Dick hasn't left a will," said Roger, and there was a subdued bitterness in his voice. " He has forgotten everybody who had a claim on him : a woman whom he ought to have provided for before every one else in the world, and Jones, Jones who stuck to him through thick and thin and nursed him so faithfully, and—and me. It doesn't do to depend on people like Dick, who won't take any trouble about anything."

The words seemed to sink into the silence of the September evening. A dim river mist, faintly flushed by the low sun, was creeping among the farther trees.

" But he did take trouble. There is a will," she said.

Her voice was so low that he did not hear what she said.

" Dick made a will," she said again. This time he heard.

He had been looking steadfastly at the old house among the trees, and there were tears in his eyes as he slowly turned to blink through them at her.

" How can you tell ? " he said apathetically.

And as he looked dully at her the colour ebbed away from her face, leaving it whiter than he had ever seen a living face.

" Because I was in the room when he made it— at Fontainebleau."

Roger's face became overcast, perplexed.

" When he was ill there ? "

" Yes."

Dead silence.

11 How did you come to be with Dick ? "

It was plain that though he was perplexed the sinister presumption implied by her presence there had not yet struck him.

" Roger, I was staying with Dick at Fontainebleau. I nursed him—Mrs. Stoddart and I together. She made me promise never to speak of it to anyone."

" Mrs. Stoddart made you promise ! What was the sense of that ? You were travelling with her, I suppose? "

" No. I had never seen her till the morning I called her in, when Dick fell ill."

" Then that Mrs. Stoddart I met at Noyes was the older woman whom Lady Jane found looking after him when she and Jones came down ? "•

11 Yes."

Silence again. He frowned, and looked apprehensively at her, as if he were warding something off.

" And I was the younger woman," said Annette, " who left before Lady Jane arrived."

The colour rushed to his face.

" No," he said, with sudden violence, " not you. I always knew there was another woman, a young one, but—but—it wasn't you, Annette. 11

She was silent.

" It couldn't be you 1"—with a groan.

" It was me."

His brown hands trembled as he leaned heavily upon his stick.

" I was not Dick's mistress, Roger."

" Were you his wife, then ? "

" No."

" Then how did you come to ? But I

don't want to hear. I have no right to ask. I have heard enough."

He made as if to go.

Annette turned upon him in the dusk with a fierce white face, and gripped his shoulder with a hand of steel.

" You have not heard enough till you have heard everything," she said.

And holding him forcibly, she told him of her life in Paris with her father, and of her disastrous love affair, and her determination to drown herself, and her meeting with Dick, and her reckless, apathetic despair. Did he understand ? He made no sign.

After a time, her hand fell from his shoulder. He made no attempt to move. The merciful mist enclosed them, and dimmed them from each other. Low in the east, entangled in a clump of hawthorn, a thin moon hung blurred as if seen through tears.

" I did not care what I did," she said brokenly. " I did not care for Dick, and I did not care for myself. I cared for nothing. I was desperate. Dick did not try to trap me, or be wicked to me. He asked me to go with him, and I went of my own accord. But he was sorry afterwards, Roger. He said so when he was ill. He wanted to keep me from the river. He could not bear the thought of my drowning myself. Often, often when he was delirious, he spoke of it, and tried to hold me back. And you said he wouldn't take any trouble. But he did. He did, Roger. He made his will at the last, when it was all he could do, and he remembered about Hulver—I know he said you ought to have it— and that he must provide for Mary and the child. His last strength went in making his will, Roger. His last thought was for you, and that poor Mary and the child."

Already she had forgotten herself, and was pleading earnestly for the man who had brought her to this pass.

Roger stood silent, save for his hard breathing. Did he understand ? We all know that " To endure and to pardon is the wisdom of life." But if we are called on to pardon just at the moment we are called on to endure ! What then? Have we ever the strength to do both at the same moment? He did not speak. The twilight deepened. The moon drew clear of the hawthorn.

" You must go to Fontainebleau," she went on, " and find the doctor. I don't know his name, but it will be easy to find him. And he will remember. He was so interested in poor Dick. And he brought the notary. He will tell you who has the will. I remember now I was one of the witnesses."

" You witnessed it ! " said Roger, astounded. His stick fell from his hands. He looked at it on the ground, but made no motion to pick it up. 11 Yes, I witnessed it. Dick asked me to. Everything will come right now. He wanted dreadfully to make it right. But you must forget about me, Roger. I've been here under false pretences. I shall go away. I ought never to have come, but I didn't know you and Janey were Dick's people. He was always called Dick Le Geyt. And when I came to be friends with you both, I often wished to tell you, even before I knew you were his relations. But I had promised Mrs. Stoddart not to speak of it to anyone except "

" Except who ? " said Roger. " Except the man I was to marry. That was the mistake. I ought never to have promised to keep silence. But I did, because she made a point of it, and she had been so kind to me when I was ill. But I ought not to have agreed to it. One ought never to try to cover up anything one has done wrong. And I had a chance of telling you, and I didn't take it, that afternoon we drove to Halywater. Mrs. Stoddart had given me back my promise, and oh ! Roger, I meant to tell you. But you were so nice I forgot everything else. And then, later on, when we were in the deserted garden and I saw the little lambs and the fishes, I was so dreadfully sorry that everything else went out of my head. I feel I have deceived you and Janey, and it has often weighed upon me. But I never meant to deceive you. And I'm glad you know now. And I should like her to know too."

Her tremulous voice ceased.

She stood looking at him with a great wistful-ness, but he made no sign. She waited, but he did not speak. Then she went swiftly from him in the dusk, and the mist wrapped her in its grey folds.

Roger stood motionless and rigid where she had left him. After a moment, he made a mechanical movement as if to walk on. Then he flung himself down upon his face on the whitening grass.

And the merciful mist wrapped him also in its grey folds.

Low in the east the thin moon climbed blurred and dim, as if seen through tears.

CHAPTER XXXVI

" The paths of love are rougher Than thoroughfares of stones."

THOMAS HARDY.

ROGER lay on his face, with his mouth on the back of his hand.

Years and years ago, twenty long years ago, he had once lain on his face as he was doing now. He and Dick had been out shooting with the old keeper, and Dick had shot Roger's dog by mistake. He had taken the catastrophe with a stolid stoicism and a bitten lip. But later in the day he had crept away, and had sobbed for hours, lying on his face under a tree. The remembrance came back to him now. Never since then, never in all those twenty years, had he felt again that same paroxysm of despair. And now again Dick had inadvertently wounded him ; Dick, who never meant any harm, had pierced his heart. The wound bled, and Roger bit his hand. Time passed.

He did not want to get up any more. If he could have died at that moment he would have died. He did not want to have anything more to do with this monstrous cheat called life. He

did not want ever to see anyone again. He

felt broken. The thought that he should presently get to his feet and stump home through the dusk to his empty rooms, as he had done a hundred times, filled him with a nausea and rage unspeakable. The mere notion of the passage and the clothes-peg and the umbrella-stand annihilated him. He had reached a place in life where he felt he could not go on.

Far in the distance, carried to his ear by the ground, came the muffled thud and beat of a train passing beyond the village, on the other side of the Rieben. He wished dully that he could have put his head on the rails.

And the voice to which from a little lad he had never shut his ears, the humdrum, prosaic voice which had bidden him take thought for Mary Deane and her child, and Janey, and Betty Hesketh, and all who were " desolate and oppressed," that same small voice, never ignored, never silenced, spoke in Roger's aching, unimaginative heart. The train passed, and as the sound throbbed away into silence Roger longed again with passion that it had taken his life with it. And the still small voice said, 1 That is how Annette felt a year ago."

He got up and pushed back the damp hair from his forehead. That was how Annette had felt a year ago. Poor, unwise, cruelly treated Annette 1 Even now, though he had heard her

story from her own lips, he could not believe it, could not believe that her life had ever had in it any incident beyond tending her old aunts, and watering her flowers, and singing in the choir. That was how he had always imagined her, with perhaps a tame canary thrown in, which ate sugar from her lips. If he had watched her with such a small pet he would have felt it singularly appropriate, a sort of top-knot to his ideal of her. If he had seen her alarmed by a squirrel, he would have felt indulgent; if fond of children, tender ; if jealous of other women, he should not have been surprised. He had made up a little insipid picture of Annette picking flowers by day, and wrapped in maiden slumber in a white room at night. The picture was exactly as he wished her to be, and as her beautiful exterior had assured him she was. For

Annette's sweet face told half the men she met that she was their ideal. In nearly every case so far that ideal had been a masterpiece of commonplace; though if prizes had been offered for them Roger would have won easily. Her mind, her character, her individuality had no place in that ideal. That she should have been pushed close up against vice; that she, Annette, who sang " Sun of my soul " so beautifully, should have wandered alone in the wicked streets of Paris in the dawn, after escaping out of a home wickeder still; that she should have known treachery, despair ; that she should have been stared at as the chance mistress of a disreputable man ! Annette ! It was incredible.

And he had been so careful, at the expense of his love of truth, when they took refuge in Mary Deane's house, that Annette should believe Mary Deane was a married woman and her child born in wedlock. And she, whose ears must not even hear that Mary had been Dick's mistress, she, Annette, had been Dick's mistress too, if not in reality, at any rate in appearance.

Roger's brain reeled. He had forgotten the will. His mind could grasp nothing except the ghastly discrepancy between the smug picture of Annette which he had gradually evolved, and this tragic figure, sinned against, passionate, desperate, dragging its betrayal from one man to another. Had she been Dick's mistress ? Was it really possible that she had not ? Who could touch pitch and not be defiled ? Women always denied their shame. How hotly Mary Deane had denied hers only a few months before the birth of her child 1

Roger reddened at the thought that he was classing Annette, his beautiful lady, with Mary. Oh ! where was the real truth ? Who could tell it him ? Whom could he trust ?

" Janey."

He said the word aloud with a cry. And Janey's small brown face rose before him as he had known it all his life, since they had been children together, she the little adoring girl, and he the big condescending schoolboy. Janey's crystal truthfulness, her faithfulness, her lifelong devotion to him, became evident to him. He had always taken them for granted, known where to put his hand on them, used them without seeing them, like his old waterproof which he could lay hold of on its peg in the dark. She had always been in the background of his life, like the Rieben and the low hill behind it against the grey sky, which he did not notice when they were there, but from which he could not long absent himself without a sense of loss. And Janey had no past. He knew everything about her. He must go to her now, at once. He did not know exactly what he wanted to say to her. But he groped for his stick, found it, noticed that the dew was heavy and that there would be no rain after all, and set off down the invisible track in the direction of the village, winking its low lights among the trees.

CHAPTER XXXVII

" Happiness is inextricably interwoven with loyalty, love, unselfishness, the charity that never fails. In early life we believe that it is just these qualities in those we love that make our happiness, just the lack of them that entail our misery. But later on we find that it is not so. Later on we find that it is our own loyalty, our own love and charity in which our happiness abides, as the soul abides in the body. So we discover at last that happiness is within the reach of all of us, the inalienable birthright of all of us, and that if by misadventure we have mislaid it in our youth we know where to seek it in after years. For happiness is mislaid, but never lost."—M. N.

JANEY had the doubtful advantage over other women that men (by men I mean Roger) always knew where to find her. She was as immovable as the church or the Rieben. It was absolutely certain that unless Lady Louisa was worse, Janey would come down to the library at nine o'clock, and work there beside the lamp for an hour before going to bed. The element of surprise or uncertainty did not exist as far as Janey was concerned. And perhaps those who are always accessible, tranquil, disengaged, ready to lend a patient and sympathetic ear, know instinctively that they will be sought out in sorrow and anxiety rather than in joy. We do not engage a trained nurse for picnic

parties, or ask her to grace the box seat when

we are driving our four-in-hands. Annette is singled out at once as appropriate to these festive occasions. If anyone thought of Janey in connection with them, it was only to remark that she would not care about them. How many innocent pleasures she had silently wished for in her time which she had been informed by her mother, by Dick, even by Roger, were not in her line.

To-night, Janey deviated by a hairbreadth from her usual routine. She came down, seated herself, and instead of her work took up a book with the marker half-way through it, and was at once absorbed in it. She was reading The Magnet for the second time.

Since her conversation with Mr. Stirling in the Hulver garden, Janey had read The Magnet, and her indifference had been replaced by a riveted attention. She saw now what other people saw in his work, and it seemed to her, as indeed it seemed to all Mr. Stirling's readers, that his books were addressed to her and her alone. It did not occur to her that he had lived for several years in her neighbourhood without her detecting or even attempting to discern what he was. It did not occur to her that he might have been a great asset in her narrow life. She was quite content with being slightly acquainted with every one except Roger, and her new friend Annette. She tacitly distrusted intimacy, as did Roger, and though circumstances had brought about a certain intimacy with

Annette, the only girl within five miles, she had always mental reservations even with her, boundaries which were not to be passed. Janey had been inclined to take shelter behind these mental reservations, to raise still higher the boundary walls between them, since she had known what she called " the truth about Annette." She had shrunk from further intercourse with her, but Annette had sought her out, deliberately, persistently, with an unshaken confidence in Janey's affection which the latter had not the heart to repel. And in the end Janey had reached a kind of forlorn gratitude towards Annette. Her life had become absolutely empty : the future stretched in front of her like some flat dusty high road, along which she must toil with aching feet till she dropped. She instinctively turned to Annette, and then shrank from her. She would have shrunk from her altogether if she had known that it was by Roger's suggestion that Annette made so many little opportunities of meeting. Annette had been to see her the day before she went to Noyes, and had found her reading The Magnet, and they had had a long conversation about it.

And now in Janey's second reading, not skipping one word, and going over the more difficult passages twice, she came again upon the sentence which they had discussed. She read it slowly.

" The publican and the harlot will go into the Kingdom before us, because it is easier for them

to flee with loathing from the sins of the flesh, and to press through the strait gate of humility, than it is for us to loathe and flee the sins of the spirit, egotism, pride, resentment, cruelty, insincerity ."

Janey laid down the book. When Annette had read that sentence aloud to her, Janey had said, " I don't understand that. I think he's wrong. Pride and the other things and insincerity aren't nearly as bad as—as immorality."

" He doesn't say one is worse than the others," Annette had replied, and her quiet eyes had met Janey's bent searchingly upon her. " He only says egotism and the other things make it harder to squeeze through the little gate. You see, they make it impossible for us even to see it—the strait gate."

"He writes as if egotism were worse than immorality, as if immorality doesn't matter," said Janey stubbornly. How could Annette speak so coolly, so impersonally, as if she had never deviated from the rigid code of morals in which Janey had been brought up! She felt impelled to show her that she at any rate held sterner views.

Annette cogitated.

"Perhaps, Janey; he has learnt that nothing makes getting near the gate so difficult as egotism. He says somewhere else that egotism makes false, mean, dreadful things ready to pounce on us. He's right in the order he puts them in, isn't he? Selfishness first, and then pride. Our pride gets wounded, and then resentment follows. And resentment always wants to inflict pain. That is why he puts cruelty next."

"How do you know all this?" said Janey incredulously.

"I know about pride and resentment," said Annette, "because I gave way to them once. I think I never shall again."

"I don't see why he puts insincerity last."

"Perhaps he thinks that is the worst thing that can happen to us."

"To be insincere?" said Janey, amazed.

"Yes. I certainly never have met a selfish person who was sincere, have you? They have to be giving noble reasons for their selfish actions, so as to keep their self-respect and make us think well of them. I knew a man once— he was a great musician—who was like that. He wanted admiration dreadfully, he craved for it, and yet he didn't want to take any trouble to be the things that make one admire people. It ended in "

"What did it end in?"

'Where insincere people always do end, I think, in a kind of treachery. Perhaps that is why Mr. Stirling puts insincerity last, because insincere people do such dreadful things without knowing they are dreadful. Now, the harlots and the publicans do know. They have the pull of us there."

Janey's clear, retentive mind recalled every word of that conversation, the last she had had with Annette, which had left an impression on her mind that Annette had belittled the frailties of the flesh. Why had she done that? Because she had not been guiltless of them herself.

In such manner do some of us reason, and find confirmation of that which we suspect. Not that Janey suspected her of stepping aside. She was convinced that she had done so. The evidence had been conclusive. At least, she did not doubt it when Annette was absent When she was present with her she knew not how to believe it. It was incredible. Yet it was so She always came back to that.

But why did she and Mr. Stirling both put insincerity as the worst of the spiritual sins? Janey was an inexorable reader, now that she had begun. She ruminated with her small hands folded on the open page.

And her honest mind showed her that once —not long ago — she had nearly been insincere herself: when she had told herself with vehemence that it was her bounden duty to Roger to warn him against Annette. What an ugly act of treachery she had almost committed, would have committed if Mr. Stirling had not come to her aid. She shuddered. Yes, he was right. Insincerity was the place where all meannesses and disloyalties and treacheries lurked and had their dens like evil beasts, ready to pounce out and destroy the wayfaring spirit wandering on forbidden ground.

And she thought of Nurse's treachery for the sake of a livelihood with a new compassion. It was less culpable than what she had nearly been guilty of herself. And she thought yet again of Annette. She might have done wrong, but you could not look at her and think she could be mean, take refuge in subterfuge or deceit. " She would never lie about it, to herself or others/' Janey said to herself. And she who had lied to herself, though only for a moment, was humbled.

She was half expecting Roger, in spite of their conference of this morning, for she knew that he was to see the lawyer about probate that afternoon, and the lawyer might have given an opinion as to the legality of Harry's marriage.

Presently she heard his step in the hall, and he came in. She had known Roger all her life, but his whole aspect was unfamiliar to her. As she looked at him bewildered, she realized that she had never seen him strongly moved before, never in all these years until now. There is something almost terrifying in the emotion of unemotional people. The momentary confidence of the morning, the one tear wrung out of him by perceiving his hope of marriage suddenly wiped out, was as nothing to this.

He sat down opposite to her with chalk-white face and reddened, unseeing eyes, and without any preamble recounted to her the story that Annette had told him a few hours before. " She wished you to know it," he said.

An immense thankfulness flooded Janey's heart as she listened. It was as if some tense nerve in her brain relaxed. He did know at last, and she, Janey, had not told him. He had heard no word from her. Annette had confessed to him herself, as Mr. Stirling had said she would. She had done what was right— right but how difficult. A secret grudge against Annette, which had long lurked at the back of Janey's mind, was exorcised, and she gave a sigh of relief.

At last he was silent.

" I have known for a long time that Annette was the woman who was with Dick at Fontaine-bleau," she said, her hands still folded on the open book.

" You might have told me, Janey."

" I thought it ought to come from her." ' You might have told me when you saw— Janey, you must have seen for some time past —how it was with me."

" I did see, but I hoped against hope that she would tell you herself, as she has done."

11 And if she hadn't, would you have let me marry her, not knowing ? "

Janey reflected.

" I am not sure," she said composedly, " what I should have done. But, you see, it did not happen so. She has told you. I am thankful she has, Roger, though it must have been hard for her. It is the only thing I've ever kept back from you. It is a great weight off my mind that

you know. Only I'm ashamed now that I ever doubted her. I did doubt her. I had begun to think she would never say."

" She's the last person in the world, the very last, that I should have thought possible "

He could not finish his sentence, and Janey and he looked fixedly at each other.

" Yes," she said slowly, " she is. I never get any nearer understanding how anyone like Annette could have done it."

Roger in his haste with his story had omitted the evil prologue which had led to the disaster.

" She wished you to know everything," he said, and he told her of Annette's treacherous lover, and her father's infamy, and her flight from his house in the dawn.

" She was driven to desperation," said Janey. " When she met Dick she was in despair. I see it all now. She did not know what she was doing, Roger. Annette has been sinned against."

" I should like to wring that man's neck who bought her, and her father's who sold her," said Roger, his haggard eyes smouldering.

There was a long silence.

" But I don't feel that I can marry her," he said, with a groan. " Dick and her I—it sticks in my throat, — the very thought seems to choke me. I don't feel that I could marry her, even if she would still have me. She said I must forget her, and put her out of my life. She feels everything is over between us. It's

all very well/' savagely, " to talk of forgetting anyone — like Annette," and he beat his foot against the floor.

Janey looked at him in a great compassion. 11 He will come back to me," she said to herself, " not for a long time, but he will come back. Broken and disillusioned and aged, and with only a bit of a heart to give me. He will never care much about me, but I shall be all he has left in the world. And I will take him, whatever he is."

She put out her hand for her work and busied herself with it, knowing instinctively that the occupation of her hands and eyes upon it would fret him less than if she sat idle and looked at him. She had nothing to learn about how to deal with Roger.

She worked for some time in silence, and hope dead and buried rose out of his deep grave in her heart, and came towards her once more. Was it indeed hope that stirred in its grave, this pallid figure with the shroud still enfolding it, or was it but its ghost ? She knew not.

At last Roger raised a tortured face out of his hands.

11 Of course, she says she is innocent," he said, looking hopelessly at Janey.

Janey started violently. Her work fell from her hands.

" Annette—says—she—is—innocent," she repeated after him, a flame of colour rushing to her face.

" Yes. Mary Deane said the same. They always say it."

Janey shook as in an ague.

She saw suddenly in front of her a gulf of infamy unspeakable, ready to swallow her if she agreed with him—she who always agreed with him. He would implicitly believe her. The little gleam of hope which had fallen on her aching, mutilated life went out. She was alone in the dark. For a moment she could neither see nor hear.

" If Annette says she is innocent, it's true," she said hoarsely, putting her hand to her throat.

The room and the lamp became visible again, and Roger's eyes fixed on her, like the eyes of a drowning man, wide, dilated, seen through deep water.

" If Annette says so, it's true," she repeated. " She may have done wrong. She says she has. But she does not tell lies. You know that."

" She says Dick did not try to entrap her, that she went with him of her own accord."

" But don't you see that Dick did take advantage of her, all the same, a mean advantage, when she was stunned by despair? I don't suppose you have ever known what it is to feel despair, Roger. But I know what it is. I know what Annette felt when her lover failed her."

" She told me she meant to drown herself. She said she did not care what became of her."

' You don't know what it means to feel like that."

Roger heard again the thud and beat of the distant train in the sod against his ear.

" Yes, I do," he said, looking at her under his heavy brows.

" I don't believe you. If you had, you would understand Annette's momentary madness. She need not have told you that. She need not have blackened herself in your eyes, but she did. Can't you see, Roger, will you never, never understand that you have had the whole truth from Annette ?—the most difficult truth in the world to tell. And why do you need me to hammer it into you that she was speaking the truth to you? Can't you see for yourself that Annette is upright, as upright as yourself ? What is the good of you, if you can't even see that ? What is the good of loving her—if you do love her—if you can't see that she doesn't tell lies? I'm not in love with her,—there have been times when I've come very near to hating her, and I had reason to believe she had done a wicked action,—but I knew one thing, and that was that she would never lie about it. She is not that kind. And if she told you that in a moment of despair she had agreed to do it, but that she had not done it, then she spoke the truth, the whole truth, and nothing but the truth."

Roger could only stare at Janey, dumfounded. She who in his long experience of her had always listened, had spoken so little beyond comment or agreement, now thrust at him with a sword of determined, sharp-edged speech. The only two women he thought he knew were becoming absolute strangers to him.

" If I had been in Annette's place, I would have died sooner than own that I agreed to do wrong. I should have put the blame on Dick. But Annette is humbler than I am, more loyal than I am, more compassionate. She took the blame herself which belongs to Dick. She would not speak ill of him. If I had been in her place, I should have hesitated a long time before I told you about the will. It will ruin her good name. I should have thought of that. But she didn't. She thought only of you, only of getting your inheritance for you. Just as when Dick was ill, she only thought of helping him. Go and get your inheritance, Roger. It's yours, and I'm glad it is. You deserve it. But there's one thing you don't deserve, and that is to marry Annette. You're not good enough for her."

Janey had risen to her feet. She stood before him, a small terrible creature with blazing eyes. Then she passed him and left the room, the astounded Roger gaping after her.

He waited a long time for her to return, but she did not come back.

CHAPTER XXXVIII

" Les seuls défauts vraiment terribles sont ceux qu'on prend pour des qualités."—H. RABUSSON.

" WHEREVER we go," said Aunt Harriet complacently from her sofa that evening, " weddings are sure to follow. I've noticed it again and again. Do you remember, Maria, how when we spent the summer at Nairn our landlady's son at those nice lodgings married the innkeeper's daughter ? And it was very soon after our visit to River View that Mary Grey was engaged to the curate. Which reminds me that I am afraid they are very badly off, for I heard from him not long ago that he had resigned his curacy, and that as his entire trust was in the Almighty the smallest contribution would be most acceptable ; but I did not send anything, because I always thought Mary ought not to have married him. And now we have been here barely fifteen months and here is Harry Manvers marrying the nurse. The Miss Blinketts tell me that she is at least fifteen years older than him. Not that that matters at all if there is spiritual affinity, but in this case Really, Annette, I think your wits must be woolgathering. You have put sugar in my coffee, and you know as well as possible that I only have a tiny lump not in the cup, but in the spoon."

Annette expressed her contrition, and poured out another cup.

" Did Roger Manvers say anything to you about Harry's marriage, Annette ?" said Aunt Maria. " I thought possibly he had come to consult us about it, but of course he could say nothing before the Miss Blinketts. They drove him away. I shall tell Hodgkins we are not at home to them in future.' 1

" He just mentioned the marriage, and that he had been seeing a lawyer about it."

" If every one was as laconic as you are, my love," said Aunt Harriet, with some asperity, " conversation would cease to exist; and as to saying ' Not at home ' to the Miss Blinketts in future, Maria, you will of course do exactly as you please, but I must own that I think it is a mistake to cut ourselves entirely adrift from the life of the neighbourhood at a — a crisis like this. Will the marriage be recognized ? Ought we to send a present ? Shall we be expected to call on her? We shall have to arrive at some decision on these subjects, I presume, and how we are to do so if we close our ears to all sources of information I'm sure I don't know."

" Mayn't we have another chapter of The Silver Cross ? " said Annette in the somewhat strained silence that followed. Aunt Maria was correct-

ing her proof sheets, and was in the habit of reading them aloud in the evenings.

" Yes, do read, Maria," said Aunt Harriet, who, however trying her other characteristics might be, possessed a perennial fund of enthusiastic admiration for her sister's novels. " I could hardly sleep last night for thinking of Blanche's estrangement from Frederic, and of her folly in allowing herself to be drawn into Lord Sprofligate's supper party by that foolish Lady Bonner. Frederic would be sure to hear of it."

" I am afraid," said Aunt Maria, with conscious pride, " that the next chapter is hardly one for Annette. It deals, not without a touch of realism, with subjects which as a delineator of life I cannot ignore, but which, thank God, have no place in a young girl's existence."

11 Oh, Maria, how I disagree with you I " interposed Aunt Harriet before Annette could speak. " If only I had been warned when I was a young, innocent, high-spirited creature, if only I had been aware of the pitfalls, the snares, spread like nets round the feet of the young and the attractive, I should have been spared some terrible disillusionments. I am afraid I am far too modern to wish to keep girls in the total ignorance in which our dear mother brought us up. We must march with the times. There is nothing that you, being what you are, Maria, nothing that you with your high ideals could write which, however painful, it could harm

Annette to hear." (This was perhaps even truer than the enunciator was aware.) " She must some time learn that evil exists, that sin and suffering are all part of life."

Annette looked from the excited figure on the sofa to the dignified personage in the armchair, and her heart was wrung for them both. Oh I Poor dears ! poor dears ! Living in this shadowy world of their own in which reality never set foot, this tiny world of which Aunt Harriet spoke so glibly, which Aunt Maria described with such touching confidence. Was she going to shatter it for them ?—she whom they were doing their best to guide into it, to make like themselves.

" I am rather tired," she said, folding up her work. " I think I will go to bed, and then you can read the chapter together, and decide whether I can hear it later on."

" It is very carefully treated, very lightly, I may say skilfully touched," said Aunt Maria urbanely, whose previous remark had been entirely conventional, and who had no intention of losing half her audience. " I think, on the whole, I will risk it. Sit down again, Annette. Let me see, how old are you ? "

" Twenty-three."

" Many women at that age are wives and mothers. I agree with you, Harriet. The danger we elders fall into is the want of realization that the younger generation are grown up. We must not make this mistake with you, Annette, or treat you as a child any longer, but

as—ahem I—one of ourselves. It is better that you should be made aware of the existence of the seamy side of life, so that later on, if you come in contact with it, your mind may be prepared. Chapter one hundred and twenty-five. The False Position."

CHAPTER XXXIX

" All other joy of life he strove to warm, And magnify, and catch them to his lip : But they had suffered shipwreck with the ship, And gazed upon him sallow from the storm."

GEORGE MEREDITH.

/

ROGER went to Fontainebleau. He looked at the oaks as they came close up on both sides of the line, and thought that they needed thinning, and made a mental note of the inefficiency of French forestry. And he put up at an old-fashioned inn, with a prim garden in front, with tiny pebbled walks, and a fountain, and four stunted clipped acacia trees. And he found the doctor in the course of the next morning ; and the doctor, who had not realized Dick's death under another name, gave him the notary's address ; and the notary explained by means of an interpreter that Monsieur Le Geyt had warned him emphatically not to give up the will to his mother, if she came for it, or sent for it after his death. Only to Monsieur Roger Manvers his cousin, or Mademoiselle Manvers his sister.

And when Roger had presented his card, and the credentials with which his English lawyer had supplied him, the will was produced. The

notary opened it, and showed him Dick's signature, almost illegible but still Dick's, and below it the doctor's and his own; and at the bottom of the sheet the two words, Annette Georges, in Annette's large childish handwriting. Roger's heart contracted, and for a moment he could see nothing but those two words. And the notary explained that the lady's signature had not been necessary, but she had witnessed it to pacify the dying man. Then Roger sat down, with a loudly hammering heart, and read the will slowly—translated to him sentence by sentence. It gave him everything : Hulver and Welmesley, and Swale and Scorby, and the Yorkshire and Scotch properties, and the street in the heart of Liverpool, and the New River Share. There was an annuity of five hundred a year out of the estate and the house at Aldeburgh to Harry, and the same sum to Mary Deane for life and then in trust to her daughter, together with a farm in Devonshire. But except for these bequests, everything was left to Roger. Dick had forgotten Jones his faithful servant, and he had forgotten also that he had parted with his New River Share the year before to meet his colossal losses on the day, still talked of in racing circles, when Flamingo ran out of the course. And the street in Liverpool, that gold mine, was mortgaged up to the hilt. But still in spite of all it was a fine inheritance. Roger's heart beat. He had been a penniless man all his life ; and all his life he

had served another's will, another's caprice, another's heedlessness. Now at last he was his own master. And Hulver, his old home, Hulver which he loved with passion as his uncle and his grandfather had loved it before him, Hulver was his.

Mechanically he turned the page and looked at the last words of the will upon it, and poor Dick's scrawl, and the signature of the witnesses. And all the joy ebbed out of his heart as quickly as it had rushed in as he saw again the two words, Annette Georges.

He did not sleep that night. He lay in a bed which held no rest for him, and a nameless oppression fell upon him. He was over-tired, and he had suffered severely mentally during the past week. And it seemed as if the room itself exercised some sinister influence over him. Surely the mustard-coloured roses of the wallpaper knew too much. Surely the tall gilt mirror had reflected and then wiped from its surface scenes of anguish and despair. Roger sat up in bed, and saw himself a dim figure with a shock head reflected in it. The moonlight lay in a narrow band upon the floor. The blind tapped against the window ledge. Was that a woman's white figure crouching near the window, with bent head against the pane I It was only the moonlight upon the curtain, together with the shadow of the tree outside. Roger got up and fastened the blind so that

the tapping ceased, and then went back to bed again. But sleep would not come.

He had read over the translation of the will several times. It, and the will itself, were locked into the little bag under his pillow. His hand touched it from time to time.

And as the moonlight travelled across the floor, Roger's thoughts travelled also. His slow, honest mind never could be hurried, as those who did business with him were well aware. It never rushed, even to an obvious conclusion. It walked. If urged forward, it at once stood stock-still. But if it moved slowly of its own accord, it also evaded nothing.

Then Dick must have distrusted his mother just as Janey had done. Roger had been shocked by Janey's lack of filial piety, but he at once concluded that Dick must have " had grounds " for his distrust. It did not strike him that Janey and Dick might have had the same grounds—that some sinister incident locked away in their childish memories had perhaps warned them of the possibility of a great treachery.

No doubt Janey was not mentioned in Dick's will because it had always been understood that Noyes would go to her. Lady Louisa had given out that she had so left it years before.

" That was what was in the old woman's mind, no doubt," Roger said to himself, " to let Janey have Noyes, and get Hulver and the rest for Harry if possible, even if she had to destroy Dick's

will in my favour. She never took into her calculation, poor thing, that by the time Dick died she might be as incapable of making another will as he was himself. Seems as if paralysis was in the family. If she knew I had got Hulver after all, she'd cut Janey out of Noyes like a shot if she could, and leave it to Harry. But she can't. And Harry'11 do very nicely in that little house at Aldeburgh with five hundred a year. Play on the beach. Make a collection of shells, and an aquarium. Sea anemones, and shrimps. And his wife can take charge of him. Relieve poor Janey. I shall put in a new bathroom at Sea View, and I shall furnish it for him. Some of the things Mary Deane had would do. He would like those great gilt mirrors and the sporting prints, and she'd like the walnut suite. That marriage may not be such a bad thing after all. Hope poor Aunt Louisa won't understand anything about it, or my coming in for Hulver. It would make her perfectly mad. Might kill her. But perhaps that wouldn't be such a very bad thing either. Silver lining to cloud, perhaps, and give Janey a chance of a little peace/ 1

Roger's mind travelled slowly over his inheritance, and verified piece by piece that it was a very good one. In spite of Dick's recklessness, much still remained. The New River Share was gone. Dick had got over a hundred thousand for it, but it had been worth more. And the house in Eaton Square was gone, and Princess

Street was as good as gone. He should probably be wise to let the mortgagors foreclose on it. But Hulver remained intact, save for the loss of the Raeburn and the oak avenue. How cracked of Dick to have sold the Raeburn and cut down the oak avenue when, if he had only consulted him, Roger could have raised the money by a mortgage on Welmesley. But he ought not to be blaming Dick after what he had done for him. On the contrary, he ought to put up a good monument to him in Riff Church ; and he certainly would do so. Hulver was his—Hulver was his. Now, at last, he had a free hand. Now, at last, he could do his duty by the property, unhampered by constant refusals to be allowed to spend money where it ought to be spent. He should be able to meet all his farmers on a better footing now. No need to put off their demands from year to year, and lose the best among them because he could not meet even their most reasonable claims. He could put an entire new roof on Scorby Farm now, instead of tinkering at it, and he would pull down those wretched Ferry Cottages and rebuild them on higher ground. He knew exactly where he should put them. It was a crying shame that it had not been done years ago. And he would drain Menham marsh, and then the Menham people would not have agues and goitres. And he should make a high paved way across the water meadows to Welysham, so that the children could get to school dry-shod.

He could hardly believe that at last he was his own master. No more inditing of those painfully constructed letters which his sense of duty had made incumbent on him, letters which it had taken him so long to write, and which were probably never read. Dick had never attended to business. If people could not attend to business, Roger wondered what they could attend to. And he would make it right about Jones. Jones need never know his master had forgotten him. Roger would give him an annuity of a hundred a year, and tell him it was by Dick's wish. Dick certainly would have wished it if he had thought of it. Roger gave a sigh of relief at the thought of Jones. And he should pension off old Toby and Hesketh and Nokes. They had worked on the estate for over forty years. Roger settled quantities of detail in numberless little mental pigeonholes as the moonlight travelled across the floor.

All through the day and the long evening, whenever he had thought of Annette, his mind had stood stock-still and refused to move. And now at last, as if it had waited till this silent hour, the thought of Annette came to him again, and this time would not be denied. Once more his resisting mind winced and stood still. And Roger, who had connived at its resistance, forced it slowly, reluctantly, to do his bidding.

He could marry Annette now. Strange how little joy that thought evoked ! He would have given everything he possessed two days ago— not that he possessed anything—to have been able to make her his wife. If two days ago he had been told that he would inherit Hulver and be able to marry her, his cup would have been full. Well, now he could have her, if she would take him. He was ashamed, but not as much as he ought to have been, of his momentary doubt of her. Fortunately, only Janey knew of that doubt. Annette would never know that he had hesitated. Now that he came to think of it, she had gone away from him so quickly that he had not had time to say a word.

Roger sighed heavily.

He knew in his heart that he had not quite trusted Annette when he ought to have done. But he did absolutely trust Janey. And Janey had said Annette was innocent. He need not cudgel his brains as to whether he would still have wanted to marry her if she had been Dick's mistress, because she never had been. That was settled. Annette was as pure as Janey herself, and he ought to have known it without Janey having to tell him.

Roger turned uneasily on his bed, and then took the goad which only honest men possess, and applied it to his mind. It winced and shrank back, and then, seeing no help for it, made a step forward.

Annette had given him his inheritance. He faced that at last. She had got the will made. But for her, Dick would have died intestate.

And but for her it was doubtful whether the will would ever have come to light. Neither the notary nor the doctor had at first connected the death of Mr. Manvers with that of Dick Le Geyt, even when Roger showed them the notice in the papers which he had brought with him. Annette had done everything for him. Well, he would do everything for her. He would marry her, and be good to her all his life.

Yes, but would she care to marry a man who could only arrive at his inheritance by smirching her good name ? The will could not be proved without doing that. What wicked folly of Dick to have asked her, poor child, to witness it I And how exasperatingly like him 1 He never considered the result of any action. The slur on Annette's reputation would be publicly known. The doctor and the notary who had told him of Annette's relation to Dick could but confirm it. No denial from them was possible. And sooner or later the ugly scandal would be known by every creature at Riff.

Roger choked. Now he realized that, was he still willing to marry her ? He was willing. He was more than willing, he was absolutely determined. He wanted her as he had never wanted anything in his life. He would marry her, and together they would face the scandal and live it down. Janey would stick to them. He loathed the thought of the whispering tongues destroying his wife's good name. He sickened at it, but it was inevitable.

But would Annette on her side be willing to marry him, and bear the obloquy that must fall upon her ? Would she not prefer to leave Riff and him for ever ? That was what he must ask her. In his heart he believed she would still take him. " She would bear it for my sake," he said to himself. " Annette is very brave, and she thinks nothing of herself."

A faint glimmer of her character was beginning to dawn in her lover's shaken mind. The " Sun-of-my-soul," tame-canary, fancy portrait of his own composition, on which he had often fondly dwelt, did not prove much of a mainstay at this crisis, perhaps because it lacked life. Who can lean upon a wooden heart ! It is sad that some of us never perceive the nobility of those we love until we need it. Roger had urgent need of Annette's generosity and unselfishness, urgent need of her humility. He unconsciously wanted all the greatest qualities of heart and mind from her, he who had been drawn towards her, as Janey well knew, only by little things—by her sweet face, and her violet eyes, and the curl on her white neck.

After all, would it be best for her that they should part?

Something in Roger cried out in such mortal terror of its life that that thought was dismissed as unendurable.

" We can't part," said Roger to himself. " The truth is, I can't live without her, and I won't We'll face it together."

But there was anguish in the thought. His beautiful lady who loved him ! That he who held her so dear, who only asked to protect her from pain and ill, that he should be the one to cast a slur upon her 1 But there was no way out of it.

He sobbed against his pillow.

And in the silence came the stammered, half-choked words, " Annette, Annette 1 "

But only the room heard them, which had heard the same appeal on a September night just a year ago.

CHAPTER XL

" Twice I have stood a beggar Before the door of God."
EMILY DICKENSON.

"I DON'T find either of you very helpful," said Aunt Harriet plaintively.

Her couch had been wheeled out under the apple tree, and her sister and niece were sitting with her under its shade after luncheon. During the meal Aunt Harriet had at considerable length expounded one of the many problems that agitated her, the solution of which would have robbed her of her principal happiness in life.

Her mind, what little there was of it, was spasmodically and intermittently employed in what she called " threshing out things." The real problems of life never got within shouting distance of Aunt Harriet, but she would argue for days together whether it was right—not for others but for her—to repeat as if she assented to them the somewhat unsympathetic utterances of the Athanasian Creed as to the fate in store for those who did not hold all its tenets.

" And I don't believe they will all go to hell fire," she said mournfully. " I'm too wide-minded, and I've lived too much in a highly

cultivated society. The Miss Blinketts may, but I don't. And I know as a fact that Mr. Harvey does not believe it either. . . . Though, of course, I do accept the Athanasian Creed. I was able to assure Canon Wetherby so only yesterday, when I discussed the subject with him. He said it was the corner-stone of the Church, and that in these agnostic days we Church people must all hold firmly together, shoulder to shoulder. I see that, and I don't want to undermine the Church, but "

" Suppose you were to leave out that one response about hell fire," said Annette, " and say all the rest."

" I am afraid my silence might be noticed. It was different in London, but in a place like Riff where we, Maria of course more than I, but still where we both stand as I may say in the forefront, take the lead in the religious life of the place, good example, influential attitude, every eye upon us. It is perplexing. For is it quite, quite truthful to keep silence ? 1 Dare to be true. Nothing can need a lie.' How do you meet that, Annette ? or,' To thine own self be true, and it will follow as the night to day '—I mean as the day to night—' thou canst not then be false to anybody.' What do you say to that, Annette ? "

Annette appeared to have nothing to say, and did not answer. Aunt Maria, slowly turning the leaves of a presentation volume from Mr. Harvey, said nothing either.

" I don't find either of you particularly helpful," said Aunt Harriet again. " You are both very fortunate, I'm sure, not to have any spiritual difficulties. I often wish I had not such an active mind. I think I had better ask Mr. Black to come and see me about it. He is always kind. He tells me people constantly unburden themselves to him."

" That is an excellent idea," said Aunt Maria promptly, with a total lack of consideration for Mr. Black, who perhaps, however, deserved his fate for putting his lips to his own trumpet. " He has studied these subjects more than Annette and I have done. Ask him to luncheon to-morrow."

Aunt Harriet, somewhat mollified, settled herself among her cushions, and withdrew her teeth as a preliminary to her daily siesta. Aunt Maria, who had been bolt upright at her desk since half-past nine, took off her spectacles and closed her eyes.

A carriage was heard to rumble into the courtyard.

" Fly, my dear, fly," said Aunt Harriet, " catch Hodgkins and tell her we are not at home. I'm not equal to seeing anyone till four o'clock. I should have thought all the neighbourhood must have realized that by now. Save me, Annette."

Annette hurried into the house, and then through a side window suddenly caught sight of Mrs. Stoddart's long grim face under a parasol, and ran out to her and dragged her out of the carriage.

" I thought you had gone," she said, holding her tightly by her mantilla, as if Mrs. Stoddart might elude her even now. The elder woman looked at Annette's drawn face and thrust out her under lip. She had feared there would be trouble when Annette told Roger of her past, and had asked Mr. Stirling to let her stay on at Noyes a few days longer. As she sat by Annette in the parlour at Red Riff she saw that trouble had indeed come.

" You have told your Roger," she said laconically, looking at the girl with anger and respect. " I don't need to ask how he has taken it."

Annette recounted what had happened, and once again Mrs. Stoddart experienced a shock. She had come prepared to hear that Roger had withdrawn the light of his countenance from Annette, and to offer stern consolation. But the complication caused by Annette having informed Roger of the existence of the will, and the fact that she had witnessed it, overwhelmed her.

A swift spasm passed over her face.

" This is the first I've heard of you witnessing it," she said, sitting very bolt upright on the sofa.

Annette owned she had entirely forgotten that she had done so until Roger had told her no will was forthcoming.

" Then it all came back to me," she said.

" It's not to be wondered at that you did not remember, considering you became unconscious with brain fever a few hours later," said Mrs. Stoddart in a perfectly level voice. And then, without any warning, she began to cry.

Annette gazed at her thunderstruck. She had never seen her cry before. What that able woman did, she did thoroughly.

" I thought I had seen to everything," she said presently, her voice shaking with anger, " taken every precaution, stopped up every hole where discovery could leak out, and fortune favoured you. My only fear was that Dick's valet, who was at the funeral, might recognize you. But he didn't."

" I told you he did not see me at the station that day I went with Dick."

" I know you did, but I thought he might have seen you, all the same. But he evidently didn't, or he would have mentioned it to the family at once. And now—now all my trouble and cleverness and planning for you are thrown away, are made absolutely useless by yourself, Annette : because of your suicidal simpleness in witnessing that accursed will. It's enough to make a saint swear."

Mrs. Stoddart wiped her eyes, and shook her fist in the air.

" Providence never does play fair," she said. ' I've been outwitted, beaten, but it wasn't cricket. I keep my self-respect. The question remains, What is to be done ? "

" I shall wait till Roger comes back before I do anything."

" I take for granted that Roger Manvers and his cousin Janey will never say a word against you ?— that they will never ' tell,' as the children say."

" I am sure they never will."

" And much good that will do you when your signature is fixed to Dick's will! That fact must become known, and your position at Fontainebleau is bound to leak out. Roger can't prove the will without giving you away. Do you understand that ? "

" I had not thought of it."

" Then every man, woman, and child at Riff, including your aunts, will know about you."

"Yes,"—a very faint "Yes," through white lips.

" And they will all, with one consent, especially your aunts, believe the worst."

" I am afraid they will."

There was a long silence.

" You can't remain here, Annette."

" You said before at Fontainebleau that I could not remain, but I did."

Mrs. Stoddart recognized, not for the first time, behind Annette's mildness an obstinacy before which she was powerless.

As usual, she tried another tack.

" For the sake of your aunts you ought to leave at once, and you ought to persuade them to go with you, before the first breath of scandal reaches Riff."

' Yes, we must all go. Of course we can't go on living here, but I would rather see Roger first. Roger is good, and he is so kind. He will understand about the aunts, and give me a few days to make it as easy to them as it can be made, poor dears."

' You ought to prepare their minds for leaving Riff. I should not think that would be difficult, for they lamented to me that they were buried here, and only remained on your account."

" Yes, they always say that. I will tell them I don't like it, and as they don't like it either, it would be best if we went away."

" You are wishing that nothing had been kept from them in the first instance?" said Mrs. Stoddart, deeply wounded, though she kept an inflexible face.

" Yes," said Annette; "and yet I have always been thankful in a way they did not know. I have felt the last few days as if the only thing I really could not bear was telling the aunts. But this will be even worse—I mean that you say everybody will know. It will wound them in their pride, and upset them dreadfully. And they are fond of me now, which will make it worse for them if it is publicly known. They might have got over it if only Roger and Janey knew. But they will never forgive me putting them to public shame."

" Come and live with me," said Mrs. Stoddart fiercely. " I love you, Annette." And in her heart she thought that if her precious only son, her adored Mark, did fall in love with Annette he could not do better. " Come and live with me."

" I will gladly come and live with you for a time later on."

" Come now."

" Not yet."

" It's no use stopping," she said, taking the girl by the shoulders. " What's the good ? Your Roger won't marry you, my poor child."

" No," said Annette firmly, though her lips had blanched. " I know he will not. But— I ran away before when some one would not marry me, and it did not make things any better— only much, much worse. My mind is made up. I will stay this time."

CHAPTER XLI

" Il ne suffit pas d'etre logique en ce monde ; il faut savoir vivre avec ceux qui ne le sont pas."— VALTOUR.

IN later years Annette remembered little of the days that passed while Roger was in France. They ought to have been terrible days, days of suspense and foreboding, but they were not. Her mind was at rest. It had long oppressed her that her two best friends, Roger and Janey, were in ignorance of certain facts about her which their friendship for her and their trust in her gave them a right to know. With a sinking of the heart, she said to herself, "They know now." But that was easier to bear than "They ought to know."

If she had hoped for a letter from Roger none came, but I hardly think she was so foolish as to hope it.

Janey had been to see her, had climbed up to her little attic, and had stretched out her arms to her. And Annette and she had held each other closely, and looked into each other's eyes, and kissed each other in silence. No word passed between them, and then Janey had gone away again. The remembrance of that wordless embrace lay heavy on Janey's sore heart. Annette, pallid and worn, had blamed no one, had made no excuse for herself. How she had misjudged Annette !—she, her friend.

But if Annette felt relief about Roger and Janey, the thought of the aunts brought a pang with it, especially since Mrs. Stoddart's visit. They had reached the state of nerves when the sweeps are an event, a broken window-cord an occasion for fortitude, a patch of damp on the ceiling a disaster. They would be wounded to the quick in their pride and in their affection if any scandal attached to her name ; for they had become fond of her since she had devoted herself to them. While she had been as a young girl a claim on their time and attention they had not cared much about her, but now she was indispensable to them, and she who formerly could do nothing right could now hardly do anything wrong. Oh ! why had she concealed anything from them in the first instance ? Why had she allowed kind, clever Mrs. Stoddart to judge for her what was right when she ought to have followed her own instinct of telling them, before they had come to lean upon her? " Mrs. Stoddart only thought of me," Annette said to herself. " She never considered the aunts at all," which was about the truth.

Their whole happiness would be destroyed, the even tenor of their lives broken up. Aunt Maria often talked as if she had plumbed the greatest depths to which human nature can sink. Aunt Harriet had more than hinted that many dark and even improper problems had been unravelled in tears beside her couch. But Annette knew very well that these utterances were purely academic and had no connection with anything real, indicating only the anxious desire of middle age, half conscious that it is in a backwater, to impress on itself and others that— to use its own pathetic phrase—it is "keeping in touch with life."

The aunts must leave Riff, and quickly. Mrs. Stoddart was right. Annette realized that their lives could be reconstructed like other mechanisms : taken down like an iron building and put up elsewhere. They had struck no root in Riff as she herself had done. Aunt Harriet had always had a leaning towards Bournemouth. No doubt they could easily form there another little circle where they would be admired and appreciated. There must be the equivalent of Canon Wetherby wherever one went. Yes, they must leave Riff. Fortunately, both aunts had only consented, much against the grain, to live in the country on account of their sister's health; both lamented that they were cut off from congenial literary society ; both frequently regretted the move. She would have no difficulty in persuading them to leave Riff, for already she had had to exercise a certain amount of persuasion to induce them to remain. She must prepare their minds without delay. For once, Fortune favoured her.

Aunt Harriet did not come down to breakfast, and the meal was, in consequence, one of the pleasantest of the day, in spite of the fact that Aunt Maria was generally oppressed with the thought of the morning's work which was hanging over her. She was unhappy and irritable if she did not work, and pessimistic as to the quality of what she had written if she did work. But Aunt Harriet had a knack of occasionally trailing in untoileted in her dressing-gown, without her toupee, during breakfast, ostensibly in order to impart interesting items of news culled from her morning letters, but in reality to glean up any small scraps of information in the voluminous correspondence of her sister. She did so the morning after Mrs. Stoddart's visit, carrying in one hand her air-cushion, and with the other holding out a card to Aunt Maria, sitting bolt upright, neatly groomed, self-respecting, behind her silver teapot.

" Oh, Maria! See what we miss by living in the country."

Aunt Maria adjusted her pince-nez and inspected the card.

" Mission to the women of the Zambesi! H'm! H'm!"

" The Bishop will speak himself," almost wailed Aunt Harriet. " Don't you see it, Maria? 'Will address the meeting.' Our own dear Bishop !"

" If you are alluding to the Bishop of Booley-24

woggah, you never went to the previous meetings of the Society when we were in London."

" Could I help that ? " said Aunt Harriet, much wounded. " Really, you sometimes speak, Maria, as if I had not a weak spine, and could move about as I liked. No one was more active than I was before I was struck down, and I suppost it is only natural that I should miss the va et vient, the movement, the clash of wits of London. I never have complained,—I never do complain,—but I'm completely buried here, and that's the truth."

" We came here on Catherine's account," said Aunt Maria. " No one regretted the move more than I did. Except Mr. Stirling, there is no one I really care to associate with down here." " Why remain, then," said Annette, " if none of us like it?"

Both the aunts stared at her aghast. " Leave Red Riff ! " said Aunt Maria, as if it had been suggested that she should leave this planet altogether.

" Why, Annette," said Aunt Harriet, with dignity, " of course we should not think of doing such a selfish thing, now we have you to think of—at least, I speak for myself. You love the country. It suits you. You are not intellectual, not like us passionately absorbed in the problems of the day. You have your little milieu, and your little innocent local interests— the choir, the Sunday school, your friends the Miss Blinketts, the Manvers, the Blacks. It

would be too cruel to uproot you now, and I for one should never consent to it."

11 Aren't you happy here, Annette, that you wish to move ? " said Aunt Maria dryly.

It slid through Annette's mind that she understood why Aunt Maria complained that few of her friends had remained loyal to her. She looked straight in front of her. There was a perceptible pause before she spoke again.

" I have been happy here, but I should not like Red Riff as a permanency."

" Oh! my dear love," said Aunt Harriet, suddenly lurching from her chair and kneeling down beside Annette, while the little air-cushion ran with unusual vigour into the middle of the room, and then subsided with equal suddenness on the floor. " I feared this. I have seen it coming. Men are like that, even the clergy—I may say more especially the clergy. They know not what they do, or what a fragile thing a young girl's heart is. But are you not giving way to despair too early in the day ? Don't you agree with me, Maria ? This may be only the night of sorrow. Joy may come in the morning."

Annette could not help smiling. She raised her aunt, retrieved the air-cushion, replaced her upon it, and said—

" You are making a mistake. I am not—interested in Mr. Black."

" I never thought for a moment you were," said Aunt Maria bluntly. "Mr. Black is all very well—a most estimable person, I have no doubt.

But I don't see why you are in such a hurry to leave Riff."

" You both want to go, and so do I. As we all three wish to go, why stay ? "

" Personally, I am in no hurry to go till I have finished The Silver Cross," said Aunt Maria. " No one misses the stimulus of cultivated society more than I do, but I always feel London life, with its large demands upon one, somewhat of a strain when I am composing. And the seclusion of the country is certainly conducive to work."

" And as for myself," said Aunt Harriet, with dignity, " I would not willingly place a great distance between myself and dear Cathie's grave." Aunt Maria and Annette winced. " And I'm sure I don't know who is wanting to leave Riff if it isn't you, Maria. Haven't I just said that I never do complain ? Have I ever complained ? And there is no doubt, delicate as I am, I am the better for the country air." Aunt Harriet was subsiding into tears and a handkerchief. " Sea only nine miles off—crow flies—fresh cream, new-laid eggs, more colour—Canon Wetherby noticed it. He said,' Some one's looking well. 1 And nearly a pound gained since last weighed. And now all this talk about leaving, and putting it on me as if it was my suggestion."

" It was mine," said Annette cheerfully, with the dreadful knowledge which is mercifully only the outcome of affection. " I retract it. After all, why should you both leave Riff if you like living here ? Let us each go on our way, and do what suits us best. You must both stay, and I will go."

There was a dead silence. The two aunts looked aghast at Annette, and she saw, almost with shame, how entirely she had the whip hand. Their dependence on her was too complete.

" I don't understand this sudden change on your part," said Aunt Maria at last. " Is it only a preamble to the fact that you intend to leave us a second time ? "

" Not if you live in London," said Annette firmly, " or—Bournemouth ; but I don't care for the country all the year round, and I would prefer to move before the winter. I'm rather afraid of the effect the snow might have on me." Aunt Harriet looked terrified. " I believe it lies very deep, feet deep, all over Lowshire. Mrs. Stoddart has asked me to winter with her in London, so perhaps I had better write and tell her I will do so. And now I must go and order dinner."

She got up and left the room, leaving her two aunts staring as blankly at each other as after their sister's funeral.

" Maria," said Aunt Harriet in a hollow voice, " we have no knowledge of the effect of wide areas of snow upon my constitution."

" And so that was what Mrs. Stoddart came over about yesterday ? " said Aunt Maria. " She wants to get Annette away from us, and make her act as unpaid companion to her. I must say it is fairly barefaced. Annette's place is with us until she marries, and if it is necessary I shall inform Mrs. Stoddart of that fact. At the same time, I have had it in my mind for some time past that it might be advisable to shut up this house for the winter months and take one in London. 11

CHAPTER XLII

" There are seasons in human affairs when qualities, fit enough to conduct the common business of life, are feeble and useless, when men must trust to emotion for that safety which reason at such times can never give."— SYDNEY SMITH.

ANNETTE had been waked early by two young swallows which had flown into her room, and had circled swiftly round it with sharp, ecstatic cries, and then had sped out again into the dawn.

She dressed, and went noiselessly into the garden, and then wandered into the long meadows that stretched in front of the house. The low slanting sunshine was piercing the mist which moved slowly along the ground, and curled up into the windless air like smoke. The dew was on everything. She wondered thef blades of grass could each bear such a burden of it. Every spider's web in the hedgerow, and what numbers there seemed, all of a sudden had become a glistening silver-beaded pocket. Surely no fly, however heedless, would fly therein. And everywhere the yellow tips of the groundsel had expanded into tiny white fluffy balls of down, strewing the empty fields,

floating with the floating mist.

But though it was early, the little world of Riff was astir. In the distance she could hear the throb of the mill, and close at hand across the lane two great yellow horses were solemnly pacing an empty clover-field, accompanied by much jingling of machinery and a boyish whistle. Men with long rakes were drawing the weeds into heaps, and wreaths of smoke mingled with the mist. The thin fires leaped and crackled, the pale flames hardly wavering in the still, sunny air.

Instinctively Annette's steps turned towards the sound of the mill. She crossed the ford by the white stepping-stones, dislodging a colony of ducks preening themselves upon the biggest stone, and followed the willow-edged stream to the mill.

There had been rain in the night, and the little Rieben chafed and girded against the mill-race.

She watched it, as a year ago she had watched the Seine chafe against its great stone bastions. The past rose before her at the sight and sound of the water, and the crinkling and circling of the eddies of yellow foam.

How unendurable her life had seemed to her on that day! And now to-day life was valueless. Once again it had been shattered like glass. She had been cast forth then. Now she was cast forth once more. She had made herself a little niche, crept into a crevice where she had thought no angel with a flaming sword would

find her and drive her out. But she was being driven out once more into the wilderness. She had no abiding city anywhere.

From where she stood she looked past the mill to the released and pacified water circling round the village, and then stretching away, silver band beyond silver band, in the direction of Riebenbridge. The sun had vanquished the mist, and lay warmly on the clustered cottages and the grey church tower, and on the old red and blue façade of Hulver among its hollies. And very high up above it all stretched a sky of tiny shredded clouds like a flock of a thousand thousand sheep.

How tranquil it all was, and how closely akin to her, how fraught with mysterious meaning !— as the kind meadows and trees ever do seem fraught where we have met Love, even the Love that is unequal, and presently passes away.

She must leave it all, and she must part with Roger. She had thought of him as her husband. She had thought of the children she should bear him. She looked at the water with eyes as tearless as a year ago, and saw her happiness pass like a bubble on its surface, break like the iridescent bubble that it is on life's rough river. But the water held no temptation for her to-day. She had passed the place where we are intolerant of burdens. She saw that they are the common lot. Roger and Janey had borne theirs in patience and in silence and

without self-pity for years. They were her ideal, and she must try to be like them. She did not need her solemn promise to Dick to keep her from the water's edge, though her sense of desolation was greater to-day than it had been a year ago. For there had been pride and resentment in her heart then, and it is not a wounded devotion but a wounded self-love which arouses resentment in our hearts.

She felt no anger to-day, no bitter sense of humiliation, but her heart ached for Roger. Something in her needed him, needed him. There was no romance now as she had once known it, no field of lilies under a new moon. Her love for Roger had gone deeper, where all love must go, if it is to survive its rainbow youth. She had thought she had found an abiding city in Roger's heart. But he had let her leave him without a word after her confession. He had not called her back. He had not written to her since.

" I am not good enough for him," said Annette to herself. " That is the truth. He and Janey are too far above me."

She longed for a moment that the position might have been reversed, that it might have been she who was too good for Roger—only it was unthinkable. But if he had been under some cloud, then she knew that they would not have had to part.

She had reached the stile where the water meadows begin, and instinctively she stood still and looked at her little world once more, and thankfulness flooded her heart. After all, Roger had come in for his inheritance, for this place which he loved so stubbornly. She was not what he thought, but if she had been, if she had never had her mad moment, if she had never gone to Fontainebleau, it was almost certain Dick would never have made his will. She had at any rate done that for Roger. Out of evil good had come —if not to her, to him. She crossed the stile, where the river bent away from the path, and then came back to it, slow and peaceful once more, whispering amid its reeds, the flurry of the mill-race all forgotten. Would she one day—when she was very old— would she also forget ?

Across the empty field thin smoke wreaths came drifting. Here too they had been burning the weeds. At her feet, at the water's edge, blue eyes of forget-me-not peered suddenly at her. It had no right to be in flower now. She stooped over the low bank, holding by a twisted willow branch, and reached it and put it in her bosom. And as she looked at it, it seemed to Annette that in some forgotten past she had wandered in a great peace by a stream such as this, a kind understanding stream, and she had gathered a spray of forget-me-not such as this, and had put it in her bosom, and she had met beside the stream one that loved her : and all had been well, exceeding well.

A great peace enfolded her, as a mother enfolds
her new-born babe. She was wrapt away from pain.

Along the narrow path by the water's edge Roger was coming : now dimly seen through the curling smoke, now visible in the sunshine. Annette felt no surprise at seeing him. She had not heard of his return, but she knew now that she had been waiting for him.

He came up to her and then stopped. Neither held out a hand, as they looked gravely at each other. Then he explained something about having missed the last train from Ipswich, and how he had slept there, and had come out to Riebenbridge by the first train this morning.

" I have the will," he said, and touched his breast. And his eyes passed beyond her to the familiar picture he knew so well, of Riff beyond the river, and the low church tower, and the old house among the trees. He looked long at it all, and Annette saw that his inheritance was his first thought. It seemed to her natural. There were many, many women in the world, but only one Hulver.

His honest, tired face quivered.

" I owe it to you," he said.

She did not answer. She turned with him, and they went a few steps in silence ; and if she had not been wrapt away from all pain, I think she must have been wounded by his choosing that moment to tell her that the notary had pronounced Hulver " Heevair," and that those French lawyers were a very ignorant lot. But he was in reality only getting ready to say something, and it was his habit to say something else while doing so. He had no fear of being banal. It was a word he had never heard. He informed her which hotel he had put up at in Ipswich, and how he had had a couple of poached eggs on arrival. Then he stopped.

" Annette," he said, " of course you understood about my not writing to you, because I ought to have written/'

Annette said faintly, as all women must say, that she had understood. No doubt she had, but not in the sense which he imagined.

" I owe it all to you," he said again, " but I shouldn't have any happiness in it unless I had you too. Annette, will you marry me ? "

She shook her head. But there would be no marriages at all if men took any notice of such bagatelles as that. Roger pressed stolidly forward.

" I had not time to say anything the other day," he said, hurrying over what even he realized was thin ice. " You were gone all in a flash. But—but, Annette, nothing you said then makes any change in my feeling for you. I wanted to marry you before, and I want to marry you now."

11 Didn't they—the doctor and the notary— didn't they tell you when you saw my signature that I was—guilty ? "

" Yes," said Roger firmly, " they did. The doctor spoke of you with great respect, but he did think so. But you have told me you were not. That is enough for me. Will you marry me, Annette? "

1 You are good, Roger," she said, looking at him with a great tenderness,—" good all through. That is why you think I am good too. But the will remains. My signature to it remains. That must be known when the will is proved. Mrs. Stoddart says so. She said my good name must suffer. I am afraid if I married you that you and Janey would be the only two people in Riff who would believe that I was innocent."

" And is not my belief enough ? "

She looked at him with love unspeakable.

" It is enough for me," she said, " but not for you. You would not be happy, or only for a little bit, not for long, with a wife whom every one, every one from the Bishop to the cowman, believed to be Dick's cast-off mistress."

Roger set his teeth, and became his usual plum colour.

" We would live it down."

" No," she said. " That is the kind of thing that is never lived down—at least, not in places like this. I know enough to know that."

He knew it too. He knew it better than she did.

He got the will slowly out of his pocket and opened it. They looked together at her signature. Roger saw it through tears of rage, and crushed the paper together again into his pocket.

" Oh ! Annette," he said, with a groan. " Why did you sign it ? "

" I did it to please Dick," she said.

Across the water the church bell called to an early service. Roger looked once more at his little world, grown shadowy and indistinct in a veil of smoke. It seemed as if his happiness were fading and eddying away into thin air with the eddies of blue smoke.

" We must part," said Annette. " I am sure you see that."

The forget-me-not fell from her bosom, and she let it lie. He looked back at her. He had become very pale.

" I see one thing," he said fiercely, " and that is that I can't live without you, and what is more, I don't mean to. If you will marry me, I'll stand the racket about the scandal. Hulver is no good to me without you. My life is no good to me without you. If you won't marry me, I'll marry no one, so help me God. If you won't take me, I shall never have any happiness at all. So now you know !—with your talk of parting."

She did not answer. She stooped and picked up the forget-me-not again, and put it back in her bosom. Perhaps she thought that was an answer.

" Annette," he said slowly, " do you care for me enough to marry me and live here with me ? You as my wife and Hulver as my home are the two things I want. But that is all very well for me. The scandal will fall worst on you. If I can stand it, can you ? "

" Yes."

" It will come very hard on you, Annette."

11 I don't mind."

" I shan't be able to shield you from evil tongues. There is not a soul in the village that won't end by knowing, sooner or later. And they think all the world of you now. Can you bear all this—for my sake ? "

" Yes."

" And yet you're crying, Annette."

" I was thinking about the aunts. They will feel it so dreadfully, and so will Mrs. Nicholls. I'm very fond of Mrs. Nicholls."

He caught her to him and kissed her passionately.

" Do you never think of yourself? " he stammered. " You chucked your name away to please poor Dick. And you're ready to marry me and brave it out—to please me."

" You are enough for me, Roger." She clung to him.

He trembled exceedingly, and wrenched himself away from her.

11 Am I ? Am I enough ? A man who would put you through such a thing, even if you're willing, Annette. You stick at nothing. You're willing. But—by God—I'm not."

She looked dumbly at him, with anguish in her violet eyes. She thought he was going to discard her after all.

11 I thought I wanted Hulver more than anything in the world," he said wildly, tearing the will out of his pocket, " but the price is too high. My wife's good name. I won't pay it. Annette, I will not pay it."

And he strode to the nearest bonfire and flung the will into it.

The smoke eddied, and blew suddenly towards them. The fire hesitated a moment, and then, as Annette gazed stupefied, a little flame curled busily along the open sheet.

Before he knew she had moved, she had rushed past him, and had thrust her hands into the fire and torn out the burning paper. The flame ran nimbly up her arm, devouring her thin sleeve, and he had only just time to beat it out with his hands before it reached her hair.

He drew her out of the smoke and held her forcibly. She panted hard, sobbing a little. The will gripped tight in her hand was pressed against her breast and his.

" Annette ! " he said hoarsely, over and over again. Still holding the will fast, she drew away from him, and opened it with trembling, bleeding fingers, staining the sheet.

" It is safe," she said. " It's safe. It's only

scorched. You can see the writing quite clear through the brown. Look, Roger, but you mustn't touch it. I can't trust you to touch it. It is safe. Only the bottom of the sheet is burnt where there wasn't anything written. Look ! Dick's name is there, and the doctor's, and the notary's. Only mine is gone. . . . Oh, Roger ! Now my name is gone, the will is— just about right, isn't it ? "

Roger drew in his breath, and looked at the blood-smeared, smoke-stained page.

" It is all right now," he said in a strangled voice. And then he suddenly fell on his knees and hid his convulsed face in her gown.

" You mustn't cry, Roger. And you mustn't kiss the hem of my gown. Indeed, you mustn't. It makes me ashamed. Nor my hands : they're quite black. Oh ! how my poor Roger cries ! "

THE END

Printed in Great Britain
by Amazon